A WAVE OF
THE WINGS

J. D. BENSON

Sunhigh Press
Thurmont, Maryland

A Wave of the Wings
J. D. Benson
© 2012

Sunhigh Press
P. O. Box 64
Thurmont, MD 21788
Sunhigh@rescuedrecords.com

ISBN 978-0615596761

Printed in the United States of America

"Since You've Been Gone"
Words and music by Aretha Franklin and Ted White
©1968 Fourteenth Hour Music Inc., and Cotillion Music, Inc.

"When You Wish Upon a Star"
Lyrics by Ned Washington, Music by Leigh Harline
©1940 Bourne Company, New York, NY

8th Man theme song
Written by Winston Sharples for the Paramount U.S. release, 1965

Predictability: Does the Flap of a Butterfly's Wings in Brazil Set Off a Tornado in Texas?
by Edward N. Lorenz
Presented before the American Association for the Advancement of Science
December 29, 1972

The Empty Fortress: Infantile Autism and the Birth of the Self
by Bruno Bettelheim
©1967 by Bruno Bettelheim

Autism and Clostridium tetani: a hypothesis
By E. R. Bolte
Medical Hypotheses 1998 Aug;51(2):133-44

Back cover photo by Patricia Benson

Pencil illustrations
sketched by the author.

These stories are dedicated to all the butterflies,
and to those who know the joy of loving them.

Especially Patty.

BOOK ONE: JACK

Whatever you do may seem insignificant,
but it is very important that you do it.
--Gandhi

CHAPTER ONE

H E CAME home in the fall. It wasn't like fall in Florida; Salem Street was ornamented with brown and orange leaves, once neatly raked into piles, now slowly scattering in the light breeze. The Maryland sky was gray and the trees were mostly bare. It seemed cold, though some children riding bikes nearby didn't wear jackets. Maybe he'd grown used to the warmer weather. Maybe he'd just gotten older. He looked at his hands: they seemed smaller and smoother, and the tiny brown spots were gone. Maybe he'd just gotten younger?

Jack Oliver had already been walking for a while, but didn't really connect with his surroundings until he began to recognize specific things, and one by one, little buried memories were exhumed before his eyes. The first was Dick West's birch green Volkswagen Beetle. For the two years Dick served in Vietnam, the tiny car didn't move from that spot in front of his parents' house.

Just past the future veteran's VW stood a familiar stop sign. It actually read *Stop Nixon* thanks to the spray can of an anonymous artist, and though it was rumored that Gary Miller had added the 'Nixon' part, no one ever actually admitted to the deed.

Wayne Beatty's house sat just across the street from the dubiously-decorated sign. When Jack and his friends played baseball in that intersection, the street corners were bases and Wayne's house was a perfect marker in "center field." (Gary Miller once joked that any ball hit through the Beatty's picture window should be a ground rule double!)

Jack visually explored the memories that covered his old street, but it was a memorable *scent* that nudged him at last into the reality of where he was. The sweet, pungent aroma of burning leaves came from a column of smoke in Leo Bolden's back yard. The gray vapor scattered in the wind like the unburned leaves on the street, and the air filled with a familiar wispy haze. There was no doubt: Jack was back.

Looking up toward the smoke, he spied another old friend: the utility pole he used as a target when hitting Wiffle balls. His eyes were drawn to the attached electric line, following its path across the street to the eaves of a little brick rambler...

...and there was Jack's old house, every bit as unimpressive as he remembered. The windows were dark and the driveway was empty, and he noticed his old Schwinn three-speed lying in the yard as he cautiously approached the front door. It felt eerie being there again, under the bare frame of an awning that had once covered the concrete porch. A hailstorm ruined the canvas, and it was almost a year before his parents could afford to replace it.

Hey-- that was a clue! It was probably 1970. Jack had an isolated memory of a particular date that year, April 13, when he heard the distressing news about Apollo 13 and looked up at the sky from that porch: something he couldn't have done with the canvas there. He cataloged a lot of his own life's events based on their proximity to news stories, so yes; this *had* to be fall of 1970, and he had to be twelve years old. Now Jack realized he'd have to make many other deductions like that one, and he was just beginning to grasp the enormity of what he was doing.

Surprisingly the front door was unlocked, and when it swung open, a large tomcat thumped against Jack's legs as it bolted outside. Tigger! Or was it Pounce? If this was indeed 1970, it could only be Pounce. Jack would need to keep track of those things as well. He stepped across the threshold and gently closed the door behind him.

The only light inside was the gray afternoon sun that filtered through the half-closed white metal blinds, and though the house was just a cracker-box, Jack still felt dwarfed by the environment. The last time he'd stood in this spot he was in his twenties, and nearly six feet tall; now he was twelve, and maybe five-foot-two, and the ceiling seemed higher and the walls farther apart. The air was stuffy: he recalled that the furnace only ran when people were home, to save electricity. Jack moved hesitantly, feeling rather like a burglar; what if someone outside saw him and called the police?

He reassured himself that it was okay to be in his own house, and taking a deep, stuffy breath, he looked around for a light source.

"I remember this," he said out loud as he located a familiar old lamp. "Hey!" he repeated, "I remember this!" he laughed, surprised by the high-pitched little boy's voice that emerged from his throat. He played with his "new" instrument for a moment, singing "A-B-C-D-E-F-G..." and "Billie Jean is not my lover..." suddenly realizing that "Billie Jean" wouldn't be written for several years. Jack mused that maybe now *he* could be the one to write it, although he couldn't really understand most of the words. So maybe instead he should write "Stairway to Heaven" or "New York, New York." But it would be tough to sell himself as an overnight musical prodigy, especially since at this age he had yet to take any music lessons. And besides, that wasn't why he was here. Well, probably not.

With a light now burning, he could get a better look at everything. He recognized all the furniture, and in fact much of it still occupied his mother's house in 2010. Here, it was forty years newer, but somehow that just made it seem older.

Jack began a walk-through, collecting details as he went. The light switch in the dining room made a loud click as he flipped it on.

Oh yeah-- they used to do that, didn't they?

He opened the door to a "closet" and found himself looking down the basement stairs.

Did these really used to be here?

In the kitchen was an old white Norge refrigerator, the kind with a chrome door-handle that latched securely from the outside.

Don't they know how dangerous these are?

And though the kitchen was tiny, there was still room for a small Formica table. This was where the four of them sat down each night and confirmed that they really were a family. The sight was calming. It was indeed Jack's house, and he was supposed to be here; though he didn't know exactly why. The extraordinary encounter he'd had a few minutes earlier left him with more questions than answers...

CR♦♦ℰ

"Is this a dream?" Jack asked, half-blinded by the bright whiteness that came from everywhere. He seemed to be in some sort of room, but there were no distinct boundaries. Something resembling clouds, or maybe closer to cotton candy, was all around him. It was indescribable: he thought that if he could see the wind, or feel a beam of light, it might be like this stuff.

"No, Jackie Boy, it's not a dream," said a voice.

There was no clear point of origin for the utterance, and at first Jack thought it may have come from inside himself. "Am I in Heaven?" he addressed the vague entity.

"Heaven only looks like this in the movies."

The voice, like the surroundings, defied description. Jack thought that if he could touch a sound, this is probably what it would feel like. He now sensed that it was both inside and outside of him as he asked: "Well then, where are we? And who are you?"

"Let's just call this place the 'White Room.' And I'm Francis; I'd say I was pleased to meet you, but I already know you!"

Jack recognized something about this being, but couldn't pinpoint it. "I know you too," he said, "but who are you?"

Francis laughed a very human laugh and said, "That's funny! I see the Irish in you hasn't been diluted too much."

"I'm a quarter Irish," Jack said proudly.

"Well then, you're only three-quarters shy!" Francis chided.

Only now did Jack notice that this voice was speaking with an Irish brogue; he'd been feeling the words rather than hearing them. "You said your name is Francis? Can I see you?" he asked.

"Surely you can. Just look into the mirror," Francis replied.

Jack looked around for a mirror, but saw only the white stuff. He looked at his feet: he was standing on it, but he also felt like he was floating. "There's only this holy... magic cotton candy," he said.

Francis laughed again. "There is plenty of that, isn't there? But try again, Jackie. Remember: look *into* the mirror. You won't see anything if you just look *at* it."

Jack was a little annoyed by the word games, but tried to do as Francis said. Almost immediately he saw it: not really a mirror per-se, but the reflection of his middle-aged, corpulent body, suspended there in mid-air. He made a face and moved his hand; the mirror image did the same. "So this is you, Francis?" he asked his own likeness.

"No, *this* is me!" Suddenly there was another man with a red beard and piercing green eyes standing behind Jack's reflection, slightly to one side.

Jack wheeled around to get a look at the specter behind him, but there was no one there. He slowly turned back to face himself and Francis, who said:

"I'm not behind you. You're looking at me."

Jack could only see Francis' face and one shoulder. The rest of him was hidden behind Jack's own image. "That's a neat trick... c'mon, who are you?"

"O'Docherty's the name," Francis smiled and waited for the inevitable response.

Jack laughed out loud: "Francis O'Docherty! You're my great-grandfather!"

"Why, I'm greater than *that*, boy! I believe I'd be your great-*great*-grandfather."

Francis O'Docherty: he was the first of Jack's Irish ancestors in America. As a child, Jack remembered seeing an old charcoal portrait of the man, looking rather plain and beardless. Jack's mother still had Francis' naturalization papers, dated 1860, in a box of O'Docherty heirlooms.

Jack couldn't help it: he spun around once more to try and get a better look at the 'real' person, but there was no form behind him. "Why can I only see your reflection?" he asked.

"It's not a reflection, it's me." Francis replied. "You're the one that's a reflection."

Jack adjusted his glasses and took a closer look at the surreal picture before him. He noticed that his own likeness seemed two-dimensional, almost like a projected image, while Francis looked more round and real.

"And what I see is my own flat image standing behind you,"
the Irishman added.

Jack was intrigued. "How...?"

"A man can't look upon his own face, so he never sees himself
like others do. *He* only sees his image in the mirror, but *they* see
something much more substantial." Francis looked Jack in the eye:
"So for the time being, Jackie, you're the reflection and I'm the
substance!"

Jack glanced once more over his shoulder, still not convinced
that this strange meeting was for real. "I'm not good at this kind of
thing... can you just tell me what's going on?"

"I'll be glad to tell you as much as you can understand at one
time," Francis began, "let me start by telling you about myself.
Have a seat."

Jack looked around for a chair, quickly realizing there wasn't
one.

"It's okay, just sit," Francis said.

Jack sat tentatively, feeling the "holy magic cotton candy"
filling in the space under his bottom. "This is *too* cool..." he
whispered.

"This is *way* cool!" Francis responded with a grin.

Jack was surprised to hear such a 'modern' phrase coming
from such an old man. But then again, Francis looked to be about
Jack's age. He continued to stand as Jack sat down, and more of
his image was uncovered. Francis wore the clothing Jack would
have expected from a mid-nineteenth century man: a brown three-
piece suit with a visible watch fob.

"So Jack, do you know your Irish history?"

"A little, I guess. In school I learned about Saint Patrick,
Oliver Cromwell, and the potato famine."

"Well, let's skip ahead to the famine. In fact, that's the best
place to start. You see, I lived through it, and left Ireland because
of it..."

"You did?" Jack interrupted. "I thought it was over by 1851.
You came over in 1860."

Francis patiently continued. "You've always been one to
memorize dates, haven't you, Jackie? You got that from me, you

know. And you're right that the potatoes were growing again, but for Irish Catholics the damage was more long-lasting. Most of us had either died or left, so I left too: on a ship to America. And that was 1855, not 1860."

Jack shook his head. "But I've seen the papers...?"

"The papers from 1860 mark my citizenship. By then I'd already lived in America five years."

"Oh sure, that makes sense," Jack said.

"Well," Francis teased, "this next part probably won't. You see, as soon as I arrived, I turned around and took the same ship back to Ireland again."

Jack sensed an imminent conundrum, but gave logic the benefit of the doubt. "So you made *two* trips in 1855?"

"Only sort of," Francis replied. "I really came back in 1865."

Alas, logic had lost.

"How is that possible?" Jack frowned. "The math doesn't work!"

Francis paused. "Like I said, Jackie, I'll be glad to tell you as much as you can understand at one time. For now, what's important is that I came back."

"I've never heard that story before. Aunt May used to talk about the Irish relatives, but she never mentioned you making a second trip."

"That's because she didn't know. In fact, Jack, you're the first person on Earth I've ever told about it."

Jack thought it was probably an honor to be privy to such a confession, but he was mostly just confused. "Okay; but why *me?*"

Francis smiled playfully. "Because my boy, you have the chance to make the same journey!"

"What? You mean to Ireland?"

"No, not to Ireland! Anybody can go there. This is a trip only you can make."

"A trip where, then?" Jack probed.

"That remains to be seen. But if your trip is anything like mine, I think you'll find it full of unexpected things..."

ભ✦✦ઇ

"Jack? Is that you?" said an unexpected voice from the hallway.

Startled, the young boy nearly jumped out of his skin; he thought he was alone in the house! "Yeah..." he answered tentatively, scrambling to recall who this might be.

"Were you singing 'The A-B-C Song' a minute ago?" the decidedly female voice inquired. It was his sister Jeannie.

"Uhh... I was just clearing my throat," Jack answered. He tried to clear his throat for effect, but it only produced a raspy squeak. A few minutes earlier, his throat had been much larger, and he was still adjusting to the change.

"Don't ever take up music," said the slim brown-haired girl, walking into the kitchen from her room across the hall. She still lived at home and got out of school an hour earlier than Jack.

He was surprised by her young appearance and by the fact that she was taller than him. His first inclination was to embrace the sibling he only saw every year or two, but he wisely quashed the desire. Instead, he began to calculate: if he was twelve, then she must be sixteen.

"Why are these lights on?" Jeannie demanded.

"It's dark in here," he replied, "why did *you* have them off?"

"*I* was asleep until you started 'singing.' You're such a 'tard!" she shot back, flouncing off to her room again.

"Gee, that went well," Jack chuckled to himself, as the muffled tones of Jeannie's record player began to sound through the closed door:

"Baby baby sweet baby,

There's something that I just gotta say..."

Aretha Franklin! He remembered that his sister played that record several times a day for months, and everyone in the house grew tired of it. But what was the name of that song? It couldn't just be "Baby Baby Sweet Baby" could it? That would have to be a question for later.

The music became less distinct as Jack moved down the hallway and into his own room with anticipation, preparing for a flood of memories in his private space. He was not disappointed.

His eyes fell first on the colorful array of stickers that were affixed to the headboard of his oak bed: Batman, various baseball players, Cap'n Crunch; it was like a reunion of old buddies, each with their own story. One in particular caught his attention: a little yellow sticker that just said *Launch Pad*. He remembered that it came in a gum pack with instructions to place it on the seat of a chair. Naïve Jack didn't get the joke, and Jeannie had to explain why it was funny.

His mind became a sponge as he looked all around his room, soaking up puddles of memories. The blue ribbed bedspread was new: it had come from Sears. The light green paint on the walls was called "Sea Moss." He'd chosen it himself. His mother made those curtains, his father got the bongo drums in the Bahamas, and Aunt May gave him the Dr. Seuss books for Christmas when he was five...

"...I remember it all!" he said, whirling around enthusiastically to get a look at the rest of the room. But when he saw his dresser, he stopped cold and let out a gasp. It wasn't the piece itself that was so shocking, but rather what he saw in the attached mirror.

"Holy sh--" he began, but his immature voice reminded him that he shouldn't be talking like that. He corrected himself, whispering "...wow," as he examined his own reflection. He was chubbier than he remembered; his skin was pallid and oily, and he was generally unkempt with messy hair and a small stain on his shirt. He looked into his own green eyes and then grinned at himself, revealing a mouthful of yellowish teeth. "Is this really what I used to look like?" he asked in disbelief. "Crap! This is what I *do* look like."

He found his way to the bathroom and grabbed a washcloth, thoroughly scrubbing his face and neck. He also wanted to brush his teeth, but discovered there were four toothbrushes to choose from. Great...! Which one was his? How could he determine something like that without asking Jeannie, and how could he ask without raising eyebrows? He'd have to take a chance. His favorite color was green, and the only green toothbrush looked pretty gnarly. But in light of his own appearance, Jack surmised that this was in fact, probably his brush. He ran the water very hot in an attempt to kill whatever germs might be lurking on those bristles, and brushed more thoroughly than any twelve-year-old normally would.

After the quick cleanup, Jack spent the next twenty minutes wandering around the house inspecting, remembering, and bonding. He stepped into the back yard to greet the trees he climbed as a boy, but was distracted by movement in the yard next door.

It was Wendy! A forgotten, familiar sight, there was the sprightly young girl, practicing her baton twirling as she did every afternoon. Jack did a double-take with adult eyes, observing her curvy young figure and trying to remember why he hadn't ever been interested in her. His friends thought he was lucky to live next door to such a "little fox," but he never shared their enthusiasm. When they were very small, he and Wendy used to play together, but pre-adolescence had put some distance between them. Now he couldn't remember if it was okay for a twelve-year-old to like girls, or when he was first able to admit that he found them rather intriguing. *What would happen if I went over and talked to her right now?* he wondered. Siding with caution, Jack headed back into the house as the young majorette tossed her baton, oblivious to the complicated mess of thoughts that had just centered on her.

As he stepped into the kitchen wondering where his mother might be, Jack noticed something he'd missed before: a note attached to the oven door with a little magnet shaped like an apple.

Jack: heat up cc's and pot's.
Home by 6.
Mom.

"Heat up cc's and pot's? What the hell does that mean?" he exclaimed, covering his mouth as he caught himself "swearing" again. He reasoned that "hell" really wasn't such a bad word, but maybe it was better for a twelve-year-old to assume that it was. Hoping to decipher the note, he opened the old Norge and looked in the tiny freezer compartment up top. It all came back to him when he saw two conspicuously-placed frozen packages: Mrs.

Paul's deviled crab cakes, and some frozen twice-baked potatoes. "…and Mom's not here because she teaches class piano after school. Ha!" he gloated to no one.

"Baby baby sweet baby,
There's something that I just gotta say…"
…once again blared from Jeannie's room, as if to try and cover up the sound of Jack's voice.

He felt a strong sense of déjà vu as the well-worn record resonated through the little kitchen. He laughed at himself: "Jack, you idiot! You're in your own past, of *course* it's déjà vu."

He sang along with the bass line as he perused the frozen cardboard instructions, and considered speeding up the process by defrosting everything in the microwave… that wasn't there. "Jack, you idiot!" he said again.

As the old oven preheated, he re-familiarized himself with the contents of the cabinets and drawers. After setting the table for four and the timer for thirty-five minutes, he decided to explore the extended world with a little help from the television.

"Baby Baby Sweet Baby" started up yet again as he relocated to the living room and plopped down on the sofa, looking for the remote that also wasn't there. In a quirky way, he found he rather liked the sound of "Jack, you idiot!" and after saying it once more, decided it would be his 'phrase of the day.'

He stood up and manually turned on the portable TV. After several seconds the picture came into focus and Jack was pleased to see that it was in color. "At least we've got *that*," he remarked, though the choice of channels was another matter. Out of thirteen spots on the dial, ten of them brought in static, and the remaining three were local news. How could he have had so many happy childhood memories of television when only three channels were functional? "Boy have I gotten spoiled," he said, turning the dial to channel four, where a conservative-looking anchorman spoke:

"President Nixon and Senator Edmund Muskie are expected to present opposing arguments later tonight, giving voters a preview of what will likely be the upcoming presidential contest in 1972. In back-to-back fifteen-minute television spots…"

"Edmund Muskie? It's gonna be George McGovern," Jack said. He switched to channel seven, where a sophisticated female reporter was talking:

"In a report from London, political insiders say Prime Minister Edward Heath will soon end the six-year-old ban on weapons sales to South Africa..."

"And Nelson Mandela is sitting in prison right now," Jack said incredulously, "but I bet nobody would believe me if I told them how it'll turn out."

He stopped paying attention to the television as his mind began to fill with ideas. Imagine all the good he could do with his forty years of future knowledge! Maybe he could stop wars, or sound warnings about natural disasters and terrorist attacks. *Maybe I'm really here for a bigger purpose*, he thought.

Before he had the chance to further explore that philanthropic notion, Jack's thoughts were interrupted by the jingling of keys in the front lock. He anticipated it would probably be one of his parents, and hoped they wouldn't notice anything unusual about him. After all, he was now technically older than they were! But as a mysterious young woman stepped through the door, Jack felt like he was meeting his mother for the first time...

CR◆◆ΒΟ

"...you see," said Francis, "I first met my own great-grandfather (that's just one 'great') in this same White Room, a hundred and forty-five years ago. And yes, that was indeed 1865!"

Jack's eyes grew wider as he listened with interest. He loved having dates and finite periods of time to relate things to, and now there also seemed to be a dynastic element to this conversation, which made it even more intriguing.

"Liam Quinn," Francis continued, "was my mother's mother's father, and he too once made the trip. In fact, a lot of people have done it." By now Jack was enthralled as Francis continued to spin his story: "And just as Liam showed it to me, I'm showing it to you."

"What are you showing me?" Jack asked.

Francis spoke purposefully: "Jackie, you have the chance to change something-- one thing-- about your life."

"Change something?" Jack responded. "Like what?"

"That's up to you," Francis replied, "just like my one change was up to me."

"What did you change?"

"I got on that ship and came to America. And I stayed! And it was as if the first trip never took place."

There was a pregnant pause before Jack spoke. "Wait a minute... you mean..."

Francis stroked his beard. "To put it simply, I didn't really cross the ocean twice. I went back and made the first crossing again."

"...like going back in time?"

"Time is very misunderstood; I'd say it's more like visiting another place in your life. But if you want to relate it to time, that may help you make sense of it."

"This is crazy!" Jack quickly reviewed every bit of information that had been presented to him thus far: the ubiquitous white fluff, the familiar talking ancestor, the impossible idea of time travel and the opportunity to alter the past. "I've gotta be dreaming this," he said.

"No Jack, you're not."

He took a good look at his backwards, two-dimensional self sitting there in front of the red-bearded Irishman. He didn't really like what he saw. He was probably fifty pounds overweight, his clothes didn't fit particularly well and he needed a haircut. His life had become so busy that he seldom found time for personal grooming, and when he did get a free moment, he was usually too exhausted to make it productive. He wondered how he managed to end up this way. "I look like hell," he said.

"That's just your reflection. Don't look at it; look at me. That's why I'm here!"

"You look pretty good, actually," Jack said. "You seem healthy, well dressed, well groomed..."

"Bah! That's all the superficial stuff! Okay; don't look *at* me, look *into* me; just like you did with the mirror."

"Look *into* you? I don't understand," Jack replied.

Francis was quiet for a moment before he spoke again. "No, you're right; of course you don't. You're not there yet."

"Where am I not?"

Francis smiled, "Well, the lessons of life are part of a whole curriculum. Once you understand enough of them you begin to see how they fit together. And you, Jackie, just need to learn a few more."

"What does that have to do with looking into you?"

Francis put a hand on the shoulder of Jack's reflection and said, "I can't explain it. Once you see it on your own, you'll find it's a very good thing."

Jack thought he felt the warmth of an invisible hand on his shoulder as he offered up his questions. "Well... what should I change? Should I have majored in business instead of music?"

"I don't know."

"Is there something about my marriage or the way I raised my kids?"

"I don't know."

"Can I stop my father from getting cancer?"

"I don't know. And he says 'hello' by the way."

Unable to process that last idea, Jack forced himself to press on with the really big looming question: "Francis, why is this happening, and why did they send *you*?"

"It only happens when the moment is right, Jack," he replied, "and 'they' didn't send me; I'm not some Hollywood angel trying to earn his wings!"

"But you *are* from..." Jack was a little embarrassed, "...the afterlife?"

Francis chuckled. "We don't really see it as 'before' and 'after;' it's all just 'life.' But you don't see that yet."

"Then *help* me see it, Francis!"

Francis sighed. "Okay. Look, Jack: suppose we took a caterpillar and dropped him into a room full of butterflies. He wouldn't understand them; in fact he probably wouldn't even see most of them! But the butterflies would understand, because each of them had been a caterpillar once."

A strange feeling welled up in Jack's chest. "I get it. So I'm the caterpillar."

"Just remember," Francis said, "he'll one day be a butterfly too. He just has to spend some time in his cocoon first."

Jack looked around at the White Room. "Is that what this is?"

"Well, this is actually 'holy magic cotton candy,'" Francis answered slyly, "but you can think of it as a big cocoon if you like. This is where you'll grow."

"Grow?"

"That is, if you decide to join the butterflies."

The reality of what was happening had begun to dawn on Jack. He spoke more cautiously: "How do I do that?"

"I can help you get started," Francis said, "but before you do anything you need to realize what a gift you've been given, and also what a responsibility it is!"

Jack could no longer contain the feeling in his chest as his thoughts gave way to emotions. He wept silently; then giggled out loud; then blinked his eyes, in case this was just some foolish figment that could be escaped that easily. His whole body tingled as he considered the unbelievable opportunity, feeling anxious and yet somehow secure about the thought of going back. Briefly indulging his self-doubt, he asked, "What if I totally screw it up?"

"I don't have an answer for that," Francis said calmly.

Jack thought such an ambiguous reply should have been off-putting; but somehow it just made him all the more eager to take a running leap. He just hoped he wasn't throwing himself into an abyss. He took a deep breath and said: "I want to be a butterfly."

"You're sure?" Francis asked.

"I'm sure." Jack replied with reluctant certainty.

Francis smiled and reached somewhere into the midst of the "holy magic cotton candy," producing a single piece of paper. With all the ceremony of a referee at a boxing match he said: "Well then, h-e-e-ere's the rules!"

Jack couldn't help but laugh.

Francis laughed back, and his emerald eyes twinkled as he spoke: "Okay, so remember I'm just repeating what's on here, so don't be trying to kill the messenger if it doesn't make sense, okay?"

Jack smiled and said, "I promise never to kill a butterfly."

"Okay then." Francis cleared his throat and began to read: "You'll be there when you need to." He paused. "I bet you thought there'd be more than that!"

"You mean that's *it?*" Jack scoffed. "That's 'The Rules'?"

Francis furrowed his brow and replied: "I guess that's more like 'The Rule.'"

"But that's so vague," Jack pleaded, "what age-- what year will I go back to? How will I know what I'm supposed to do?"

Francis sighed sympathetically and replied, "If you look too hard you'll miss it, Jackie. It's not about what you think you're *supposed* to do; it's about what you *need* to do..."

☙ ◆ ◆ ❧

"Jack, honey, you need to bring your bike inside," was the first thing his mother said.

Young Jack just stared at the slender brunette. Forty fewer years somehow made more of a difference in Marie than they had in Jeannie. He calculated that his mom was now only forty years old. "My bike... okay," he answered, half-dazed.

"It's getting dark," she said. "I keep forgetting that daylight saving time kicked in last week." She had the remnants of a southern accent, something that had gradually faded altogether in the coming years. It sounded strange but familiar.

"So, how was uh... piano?" Jack asked politely.

Marie set her purse on the desk by the door and half-dropped a tote bag full of music books on the floor. "Piano was fine, thank you for asking. Did you get supper going?"

"Yeah," he said, "it's in the oven now. And I set the table."

As she took off her light coat, Jack was struck by how beautiful his mother was. He'd never really paid attention before.

Marie started toward the kitchen, following the aroma of deviled crabs and baked potatoes. "You set the table? That's Jeannie's job."

"Oh, I guess I forgot," Jack said, following behind her and feeling rather awkward. He tried to recall how he spoke to his mom when he was twelve.

"What did you do in school today?" Marie asked.

Jack stopped short, not having any idea what happened earlier that day. He hoped his mother was just making polite conversation like he was. He swallowed hard and faked an answer: "Oh, all the usual stuff. Math, shop, science..." Uh-oh, had he just blown it? Was he even taking those classes in... whatever grade he was in?

"Do you have any homework?" she asked, obliviously reaching into the cupboard for a can of green beans.

He heaved a silent sigh of relief. "Homework? Umm... I forget. I'll check later."

"Okay, honey. Would you open this for me?" she said, handing him the can.

Jack located the can opener straight away, very glad that he'd just re-learned the kitchen a few minutes earlier.

Marie took the opened can, poured it into a saucepan, and tossed the empty container into the trash.

"Shouldn't that go in the recy--" Jack stopped himself in mid-sentence. He almost slipped up again.

"The what?"

Jack had forgotten that in this era, "recycling" was not yet a household word. "Uh... the right side of the stove," he answered, impressed by his own smooth recovery.

"Oh, no," she responded, "we can use the little burner for a small pan like this." She looked at the table set for four. "I guess you also forgot your dad is out of town."

Again Jack had no idea, but answered, "Oh yeah, that's right." By now he realized his mom was unaware of his cautious behavior.

"Would you tell Jeannie supper's almost ready?" she asked.

"Sure!" He made the very short trip to his sister's bedroom and knocked loudly on the door. Apparently his pounding couldn't compete with the blaring record player, for she didn't respond. Remembering that he was expected to be the impish little brother, he knocked once more, rather quietly, and then just opened the door.

"Jack!! Don't you ever knock?" Jeannie yelled.

"Supper's ready," he said with a Cheshire grin, "and I did knock."

Jeannie turned off the record player saying, "How could supper be ready? I haven't set the table yet."

"I did it for you!" Jack boasted, willingly taking credit for something that was a complete accident.

"You're probably just trying to make me look bad," she said, "or do you want a favor?"

"Nope, nothing like that," Jack answered, "it's just my altruistic side."

"Your *what* side?" Jeannie responded blankly.

Oops, yet another slip. "It's a vocabulary word from school," he said, wondering how he'd ever get through the night. *Talk like a twelve year old*, he reminded himself.

"C'mon, you two, let's eat," Marie called out from the kitchen, and the siblings scrambled to get there.

By 2010, Jack had lived long enough to see the family meal lose its honored place in American society. In that world where *TV Guide* dictated schedules and cell phone texts were the standard form of communication, he'd all but forgotten just how comforting this tradition could be for a child. Even though his father was a missing piece that evening, the remaining three still sat and ate together, and while it was certainly about having a meal, it was even more about *sharing* a meal. It was a time of affirmation. Jack couldn't remember if he'd experienced it this strongly the first time around, but sitting here now eating frozen deviled crabs with the two ladies in his young life, he felt a greater sense of peace than he had in many years.

The trio washed dishes and cleaned up the kitchen as Jack listened to stories about Marie's childhood and Jeannie's friends at school. Pounce the cat came home hungry at 7:30, and at 8:00 Jack took a most welcome shower, changing into a pair of pajamas he remembered once he had them on. At 8:30 he joined Jeannie in front of the TV for *Rowan and Martin's Laugh In*, and afterward continued to dial-surf the three major networks. He now remembered why he had such fond early memories of television, as programs like *Mayberry R.F.D.* and *The Doris Day Show* played on the little color set. He basked in the forgotten treasures of this house, reliving the carefree joy and security of being a kid. By the time Carol Burnett had wrapped up her program at 11:00, Jack was intoxicated with a wonderful drowsiness. He said his goodnights and headed off to bed, wondering how he ever could have forgotten this feeling. "Jack, you idiot," he mumbled, smiling to himself as he settled in under his new blue bedspread. Pounce curled up next to him, and they both immediately fell asleep. He began to dream…

ಢ♦♦໊

"…if you look too hard you'll miss it, Jackie," Francis said. "It's not about what you think you're *supposed* to do; it's about what you *need* to do." Then he grinned. "Read 'The Rule!'"

Jack was silent.

Francis handed over the paper. "Here, just keep it in your pocket."

Jack stood up as he took the page and folded it into quarters. He looked strangely at Francis and asked, "Can't you even give me a hint?"

The Irishman's eyes grew wider, almost as if he were offended. "My journey was my journey," he said, "and all I had to do was get on a boat! But you're a traveler who hasn't even left yet; it'd be foolish of me to try and divine your destination! What happens next is up to you. So are you ready, Jackie Boy?"

Jack stuffed the folded paper into his pants pocket and took a deep breath. "I wish I knew more, but if this is the best I can do, then yes, I guess I'm ready."

Francis flashed a knowing smile. "Oh Jackie, this isn't just the best you can do; this is the best there is! Have a nice trip."

"Francis, will I see you again?" As Jack spoke, he realized that he didn't have control over his movement. He took a few involuntary steps forward, and the White Room evaporated into the wispy haze of burning leaves on Salem Street.

CHAPTER TWO

"JACK?" SAID a woman's voice, gently weaving through the silky, smoky clouds of sleep. "Jackie!" she repeated more firmly.

"Violet," Jack replied groggily, "hmm… is it morning already?" Jack sprung awake, startled simultaneously by his own high-pitched voice and by the next question his mother asked:

"Who's Violet?"

Jack sat up in bed and looked around the room. He started to reach for his glasses on the nightstand, but they weren't there, and he didn't need them anyway. As he rubbed his eyes, all the memories of the previous day came swirling back into his head, including the encounter with Francis, which he'd just repeated in his dreams. Now he remembered the story: a fifty-two-year-old man being transported back to his boyhood, possessing his twelve-year-old body and infiltrating 1970 society, just like all the 'time travel' movies he'd seen. And there was his young mother, waking him in the morning.

"Who's Violet?" she repeated.

Jack cranked out a dull response: "Hm--? Oh, Violet, um… I must've been having a dream." Not one of his better efforts, but it worked, and that was all that mattered. His mother didn't need to know she'd just been mistaken for Jack's wife.

"I'm going over to the school now," Marie said.

School! Jack began to quietly panic as he remembered the horrible truth: he went to school! He thought he was probably in the seventh grade, but he didn't remember what classes he was taking, any of his teachers' names, or when to go to which rooms! He doubted he'd recognize any of his friends either, and very quickly began to feel like a pressure cooker. Why, oh why didn't he think of any of this yesterday?

"Jack, did you hear me?" Marie said, unaware that the little boy before her was actually a pot of boiling water.

"School-- oh, I don't feel real good Mom," he moaned, realizing how lame that must have sounded.

"Too bad, I hate to see you sick on your day off." Marie said.

"Day off?"

"Election Day, remember? Schools are closed and I'm working the polls this morning."

"Day off!" The lid flew off the pressure cooker. "Right, closed schools... schools closed," he laughed with relief.

Marie looked at her son strangely: "I don't want to be late. Jeannie's already off with Sandy, and I left an Instant Breakfast for you. Bye, honey." She turned and hurried down the hall.

Jack let out a huge sigh of relief. "Thanks Francis, I owe you one!" He didn't know if Francis could actually hear him, but it was comforting to think of him as a sort of guardian angel.

This was apparently a perfect time to have been sent back. He didn't recall his mother ever having been a poll worker, and he wasn't quite sure who Sandy was, but none of it mattered. He had room to breathe now, and some alone-time to be a little detective. He hopped out of bed and shuffled to the front window just in time to see Marie pull out of the driveway and speed off in a white 1963 Buick. "I forgot about that car." He then went to Jeannie's room, thinking about maybe trying to find her diary, but he decided he was too hungry. Off to the kitchen to find food.

There on the table was a red packet of Carnation Instant Breakfast, just like his mom had said. Next to it was a glass and a spoon. "Now that's service." He got the carton of milk out of the fridge and whipped up a quick morning meal, delighting in the clinking and tinkling of the spoon against the glass while he mixed. As he took his first sip, he happened to glance at the kitchen clock and almost snorted the chocolate goodness out through his nose: "Is it really eleven o'clock?" Jack couldn't believe he'd slept for twelve hours! "No time to waste," he said, and quickly downed the meal-in-a-glass.

He burped proudly, celebrating the fact that he was twelve, and ran back to his room to get dressed. He rifled through his dresser drawers, quickly locating a pair of "tighty-whities" and some fresh socks. In his closet he found a random T-shirt to wear

with the same pants he'd worn the day before. He didn't care if
they matched. His pajamas ended up in a ball on his unmade bed.
"That looks 'twelve,'" he said, setting out for the living room once
more.

In his mind he prioritized his schedule for the day. First, find
out anything about school; second, figure out what to change. Jack
scanned the room, knowing there must be some place where
important documents were kept. There weren't all that many places
to look, and he quickly focused on the desk. There was one drawer
that held file folders: would his mother perhaps have tucked away
his school schedule in there? Jack sat cross-legged on the floor and
pulled the drawer out. The hanging folders were neatly labeled:
Taxes, Bills, Birth certificates...

"...school!" Jack shouted, pulling out that folder. Inside was a
stack of papers, mostly his old report cards from Forest Wood
Elementary School and Jeannie's "progress reports," as they called
them, from junior high. But these were all older documents, and
Jack had to find out where to go *tomorrow*. He replaced the folder
and closed the drawer. He politely ransacked the rest of the desk
drawers, finding nothing of interest, anticipating the panic he'd feel
the next morning if he couldn't locate a schedule.

Jack began pacing through the house proclaiming, "Francis, I
know I already owe you one, but can we make it *two*?" No sooner
were the words out of his mouth than he saw the schedule,
attached to the side of the refrigerator with a little magnet that
looked like a bunch of grapes. He recalled having given that set of
fruit magnets to his mother for Christmas one year. Jack retrieved
the document and began to read silently:

Twin Springs Junior High School
Schedule of classes for: Oliver, John B.
Grade 7
Fall, 1970
H 8:45 - 9:00: Homeroom / / Anderson / / 114
1. 9:10 - 10:00: Science I / / Kefauver / / 223
2. 10:05 - 10:55: Industrial Arts / / Holliday / / 128B...

...and the list went on.

"Perfect!" Jack said, as he scanned the page from top to bottom. He found a pencil on the kitchen counter and searched for a sheet of paper so he could copy the schedule. He couldn't recall where he kept his school supplies, or if he even had any with him the previous day. "Crap!" he yelled. "Is it going to be this much of a struggle to remember *everything*?" Quickly looking for anything else to write on, he reached into the pocket where he kept his house key and discovered what seemed like a large piece of paper, so large in fact that he had some difficulty getting it out. After extracting the sheet which was folded into quarters, he opened it up and realized what it was. In typewritten characters along the top of the page were the words:

You'll be there when you need to.

Jack hadn't looked at the page when Francis gave it to him; he just folded it and stashed it away. Seeing it now, he was surprised that the characters were so plain and unobtrusive. They weren't even well-centered on the page. Shouldn't such an 'ethereal' document be written in fancy gold calligraphy or something of that sort? Even with its plainness, Jack wondered if it would be insulting to Francis if he wrote on it.

Sitting at the little kitchen table, he decided to take a chance, and neatly copied his schedule in number two pencil, just underneath the typing. "There," he said, refolding the sheet and attempting to slip it into his pocket. He now realized that it was in fact rather large, and remembered that his pants had also been larger when he first put the paper into them. He folded the document one extra time and stashed it back with his house key. He knew he'd need it.

Jack decided to look for his schoolbooks later; right now he wanted to take advantage of the opportunity to re-familiarize himself with his life as a pre-adolescent. He returned to the living room and noticed an unread newspaper on the ottoman. "Gold mine," he said, picking it up to read. Again, Jack had to address the concept of relative size; the newspaper seemed huge as he unfolded it in front of him. "I'm more than a foot shorter," he reminded himself, as he scanned the front page:

Tuesday, November 3, 1970
Voters head to polls
Today's weather: mid '60s, chance of a shower
Local man charged with arson
Boys Club to hold raffle

"This isn't as useful as I'd hoped," Jack said as he began to turn pages:

Any Volkswagen muffler $19.95 installed
Chevrolet '67 Belair low miles $1,295.00
Vote Republican for the three E's: Efficiency, Economy, Experience
Canned corn 3 for 42 cents
The very finest of homes, $37,950
Mutt and Jeff

He stopped: "*Mutt and Jeff!* I love *Mutt and Jeff!*" He read the funnies, temporarily getting lost in their quaint innocence. He even started mentally working the crossword puzzle before realizing he was wasting precious time. His efforts to find out about the world around him were turning out to be difficult. The local newspaper seemed to focus more on advertising than on information, and television only offered limited coverage as well. It was clear that he'd become spoiled by having the world at his fingertips, and he yearned for CNN and the Internet. Jack posed a question to himself: "How did we research things before the web?" He also answered himself: "Apparently, we didn't!"

Rather than waste his day lamenting the primitive technology of the time, he resolved to press on with a modified agenda. Retrieving Francis' paper from his pocket again, Jack sat at the desk and found another pencil. He decided to make a list of things that he might be able to change with his knowledge of the coming forty years. "Wow, I really *could* change the course of history! Francis was right; this is a gift and a responsibility." Coming up with random ideas, he began to write in small neat letters:

1. Warn government about World Trade Center attacks
2. Warn Nixon about Watergate
3. Warn John Lennon about assassination
4. Warn about "Black Monday" stock market crash
5. Warn NASA about Challenger disaster
6. Warn Haiti about earthquake
7. Warn about BP Gulf of Mexico spill
8. Warn England about the death of Princess Diana
9. Warn New Orleans about Hurricane Katrina
10. Warn everybody about global warming

Jack stopped and took a look at this lofty list, which was written right beside his seventh grade school schedule. "Who am I kidding?" he said. One by one he considered his own suggestions:

1. *The World Trade Center.* Who would believe a seventh-grader's prediction of something happening thirty-one years in the future? In fact, were those towers even built yet? Jack didn't know.

2. *Warn Nixon about Watergate.* It could certainly open a can of worms if some kid wrote a letter containing knowledge of the president's plan to plant bugs in the next election. And why should he help Nixon anyway? Bad idea.

3. *Warn John Lennon.* Sure, how about this: *Dear Mr. Lennon, in ten years you will be shot by a mentally unstable fan.* Not a good letter.

Jack continued to unravel his own plans:

4. He couldn't remember the year, much less the day, that "Black Monday" had occurred. (Would occur?)

5. No one would even know what a Space Shuttle was in 1970.

6. He also couldn't remember the date of that big Haitian earthquake.

And it went on like that. "I thought I was supposed to be *good* at remembering dates," he said.

Jack realized this was a list of impossibilities. The world was apparently not his to warn, and he couldn't look up the dates of events that hadn't happened yet. One by one he put a line through the items on his list. "Hmm..." he muttered, "if I can't stop bad things, maybe I can start good ones." He began another list:

1. Personal computers
2. Internet
3. Compact discs
4. Cell phones...

Jack didn't get very far before realizing how silly this list also was. Despite his interest in engineering, he had no ability to actually develop any of these things, and any suggestions of the sort coming from of a twelve-year-old boy would be viewed as comic book fantasy. Jack imagined himself standing before the CEO of a big technology company...

...interesting suggestions, young man. I especially like the wireless hand-held telephone that can receive calls, information and television broadcasts from anywhere in the world, and sells for under a hundred dollars! Please help yourself to a lollipop on the way out.

"I guess this is my line-item veto," he said with disgust, crossing out those four suggestions as well. Maybe he was thinking about it wrong. There were other good things he could develop: more important things than inventions. What about stopping genocide in Third World countries, or stopping racism in South Africa... or the U.S.A.? Or maybe instead of stopping something, he could start something-- like a foundation for research into autism or AIDS. Wait, there was no AIDS yet. Maybe that should have been on his first list, in place of John Lennon or Princess Diana.

Again Jack paused, feeling a little silly for indulging himself this way. *I'm just a random guy with my own thoughts. I can't expect to convince the world of anything.* He remembered being a naïve young man who once said, "If only everyone could see things my way, we'd all be fine!" Realizing that he was now that young man again, Jack began to see his life as a series of contradictions, as he viewed his past, which was also his future, in retrospect.

There was the little kid who was unknowingly shielded by the adults around him. He had no knowledge of world affairs, nor did he want any. His main priority was how to come up with a nickel for another pack of Batman cards. He was innocent and ignorant, and blissfully so.

Then came the 'teenager-on-a-mission,' suddenly aware of the world, and desperate to participate in it. With no practical life-experience, he ended up just parroting other people's opinions. A particular schoolteacher was concerned about pollution, so that also became Jack's issue. His friend's mother was a civil rights advocate, so Jack followed suit, randomly repeating whatever parts of her mantra he could remember. His parents attended a traditional Methodist congregation, so it was only natural for Jack to speak out against the "liberalism" that crept its way into the church. It was years before he realized that this was the same liberalism that stood behind the ideologies of his other causes: the ecology and civil rights movements. At the time though, Jack was too inwardly-focused to see that contradiction. Being a teenager was largely an exercise in self-validation, and he would do what was needed in order to make himself feel relevant.

As an adult, he became more selfish, looking for a quick way to get his piece of the pie. After his parents put him through college, he moved from job to job during a time when jobs were plentiful. Jack always felt sure that 'the next one' would be his jackpot career. At age twenty-three he married his nineteen-year-old girlfriend Kate; both of them were too young, and within five years they divorced. Thinking he'd learned from the experience, and going against the advice of his friends, Jack married again just a year later.

His second marriage would last fifteen years and produce two children: a daughter, and a son with autism. The cathartic experience of becoming a parent made Jack revisit his goals and ambitions, and suddenly his pie didn't matter so much anymore. His new instinct was to provide, no matter how hard he had to work to do it. But his second wife Gail turned out to be an ineffectual partner, especially when it came to dealing with their son's handicap. Jack felt like a single parent caring for three children, and believed any opportunity for his own happiness had passed. That is, until he met Violet.

First a friend, then a confidant, and eventually an affair, Violet gave Jack a reason to love life again. She was his best friend, his adoring lover, and his devil's advocate when he needed one. She was also the one other person who understood Jack Junior's disability. It was a messy undertaking and a bit of a local scandal, but they each got divorced and married one another. Violet had two children of her own, and the Oliver house became a very fertile place for the blended family of six.

As the children approached adulthood, it became more expensive to give them what they needed, and Jack had to confront the importance of following a career path, saving for college, and all the other responsible things that he'd never done. He and Violet worked multiple jobs to make ends meet, and though their relationship was pure joy, their life was filled with uncertainties. Maybe *that* was why Jack was here.

"I can't save the world," he said to himself, "and I'm not supposed to." He reread the top line of the paper in front of him and heard Francis' voice echoing in his mind: *you have the chance to change something-- one thing-- about your life.*

"My life," Jack said with resolve, "not Lennon's or Nixon's or the guys' on Wall Street. It needs to be *my* life." He sighed and took one more look at the pencil-cluttered page before folding it up and returning it to his pocket. Just as he did so, he glanced out the living room window and saw someone coming up the front walk.

"Hey, it's Tim!" Jack said with surprise. "This should be interesting!"

Tim Edwards was an old elementary school chum. Going by "Timmy" until the fifth grade, he looked a little taller and darker than Jack remembered. The doorbell rang and Jack jumped up to greet his old friend. It was time to be twelve again.

"Tim! Buddy!" he shouted, throwing the door open.

Tim looked a little uncomfortable with the enthusiasm. "What's your problem, Jack O'Lantern?"

Jack had to quickly adjust his behavior to match his age. "No problem, man. Just glad to, um… be off school."

Tim walked inside and handed Jack a backpack. "I just found this. It's all your stuff, man!"

Jack quickly rifled through the contents: schoolbooks for math, geography and science, a paperback novel called *The Cay*, and all the other supplies he'd been worried about. "You found all this outside?" he asked.

"Yup," Tim replied, "on the corner of Lark and Tenbrook. How could you forget all that junk?"

"I think I was just stupid yesterday. I'd be in some deep doo-doo if I lost this! Thanks!"

"Don't mention it," Tim said. "Hey, have you seen Wendy this morning?"

"No, I haven't been outside yet."

"Since when do you have to go outside? We can watch her from your room!" Well, that answered *one* question: apparently it was okay for a twelve-year-old to like girls.

Now Jack remembered: Wendy always practiced her baton twirling in her back yard, and couldn't be seen from the street; but his bedroom window offered a perfect, unobstructed view of the little pixie. Though he'd never really been interested in her, his friends were, and together they'd sometimes peek through his blinds while she practiced. Jack decided to take the hint, and humored his friend: "You think she's there now?"

"We could go check!" Tim said, already halfway down the hall to Jack's room.

When the two pre-teen boys got together, neither one cared if the bed wasn't made, or if there were dirty clothes balled up on it. Tim knelt on the mattress facing the window, and peeked between two of the metal slats. "She's there," he said, "and she's in *shorts!*"

"Wow, let me see!" Jack replied, joining his buddy at the window. Yes, there was Wendy, looking kind of cute and maybe a little bit curvy, but also very much like a child. Jack was less impressed with her form than he'd been the day before. Yesterday was colder, and Wendy's outfit included jeans, which left more to the imagination. Consequently, Jack had recollected the young lady as she would look later on. But today's short set revealed the spindly legs of a little girl. Jack felt strange for looking, and had to revisit reality. Yes, he was twelve again, but he was also fifty-two. His daughters had once been Wendy's age, and it was his job to protect them from boys like himself, so this was a paradox of sorts.

Meanwhile, Tim seemed to be thoroughly enjoying this bit of prepubescent voyeurism, and Jack let him simmer for a while.

"I hoped she'd wear shorts," Tim said, "that girl's got *legs!*"

Stifling a snicker, Jack tried to take Tim's mental age into account. *I was twelve once,* he thought, *and fortunately, I'm not anymore!*

"She just dropped the baton!" Tim shrieked. "Whoa, bend over, baby!"

It was no use; Jack couldn't help but burst into laughter.

Tim seemed cautiously offended. "What's so funny? She's a fox!"

Jack composed himself and said, "Sorry, Timmy. It's just funny, that's all."

"Well if you think Wendy's funny, you have a *lot* to learn about girls! Why are you acting so weird today, Jack-off?"

"Don't call me that!"

"Jack-off! You're so weird," Tim taunted.

"I'm not weird, you're weird!"

"No, you're weird!"

They began lightly punching each other in the shoulder. At age twelve, it was never about the argument; it was always about the bonding, and Jack re-embraced the childhood precept with ease. They both quickly forgot about Wendy's shorts and began to wrestle.

Very soon, Jack felt a sharp pain: something had poked him. "Ow! What's that?" he yelled.

Both boys stopped.

"Oh, check this out," Tim said, pulling an object from his back pocket. It was a strange little transparent device about four inches long, shaped sort of like an 'S'. "It's made of Plexiglas," he added.

"What do you do with it?" Jack was intrigued, though he thought he may have remembered seeing these devices before.

"You got a belt?"

"Umm... the one I'm wearing."

"Let's use that, then."

Jack took off his belt and gave it to Tim, who proceeded to hang it from the little Plexiglas hook, which he then balanced on the tip of his finger. It looked like it should have fallen off, and the effect was kind of like defying gravity.

Jack the adult understood the physics behind this feat: it was basically an optical illusion. But rather than try and explain it, he just played along. "Wow! Where did you get it?"

"We made 'em in Industrial Farts," Tim replied. "Mr. Holliday had these sheets of Plexiglas and we used coping saws to cut 'em out. I'm gonna make another one for my brother for Christmas."

Jack didn't remember ever making anything so cool in "Industrial Farts," as Tim had so eloquently named it. He did once make a crest-shaped pine plaque with a picture of Snoopy wood-burned into it. The edges were supposed to be perfect right angles, but his were rough and uneven, so he received a 'C' for the project. Wow! He was surprised he remembered all that! "What period do you have Holliday?" he asked.

"Fifth. You know that," Tim said.

"Oh yeah, I forgot. I wish he'd let us make those."

"Didn't your class pick what they wanted to make?"

"Huh? I guess," Jack fumbled.

"Ours did, it was either Plexiglas stuff or those stupid wood plaques, but everybody had to make the same thing so Holliday could have the right tools ready for class."

Well, that explained it. Jack came from the class that made stupid decisions. *I bet that's where I learned it*, he laughed to himself.

Tim returned the little device to his pocket and gave Jack his belt back.

Jack just tossed it on the bed atop his balled-up pajamas. "My mom went to work at the polls," he said, trying to keep the conversation going.

"My parents say there's no point in voting when it's not for President," Tim replied.

Jack was incensed! "Just because it's a mid-term election doesn't mean it's not important," he said. "Remember, today's governors and senators are tomorrow's presidents! You should vote whenever you have the chance!"

Tim began to look out the window again. "What's your problem today, Jack? Shoot. Wendy went inside."

Jack realized that he'd wandered far beyond the normal conversational boundaries of the seventh grade. "I just watched a show on politics, so I'm pumped up. That's all." He felt embarrassed for trying to come up with excuses that way.

Tim wasn't even listening. "Wait, she's coming back…"

It would take some getting-used-to for Jack to settle into this life again. He was still in the tail end of the 'innocent ignorant' stage, and he would need to play the part. It was hard not to speak out for his passionate causes, but his inner crusader would have to lie low for now.

Tim stayed for another couple of hours and they talked about school, girls and sports. Jack faked his way through the conversations: he didn't recall much about school, he knew too much about girls, and he mostly didn't care about sports. Still, he felt he did a formidable job.

They tried to watch some television, but the only shows on at that time of day were soap operas, game shows and the new children's program *Sesame Street*, which Tim said was stupid and would never last. Even so, he remarked how nice it was that Jack's family had a color set.

Looking for something to do, the boys went outside with a Wiffle ball and a hollow plastic bat; probably Jack's one redeeming sports interest. They took turns pitching to each other in the front yard, with the batter aiming for the utility pole in front of Leo Bolden's house. If the ball ever did happen to hit it, they'd count to five before picking up the ball, in case any electricity remained in it. (Jack knew that was ridiculous, but it was their tradition.)

Tim was gone by 2:00, and Jeannie arrived home at 2:30 with Sandy, who Jack recognized as soon as he saw her face. The two girls retreated to Jeannie's room and immediately started playing records. The muffled strains of "Baby Baby Sweet Baby" carried through the house for the um-teenth time since Jack had been home, and he just sighed and flopped down on the sofa, clamping throw-pillows over his ears. He dozed off and began to dream.

CHAPTER THREE

"**T**HE AUTISM," Jack began, "is just going to affect us more and more as JJ gets older."

"M-hm. Hey, there's some things in this catalog I'd like us to order. Janet-- you know, Janet at work? She got these too: they're really pretty kitchen canisters…" Gail smiled and held out an open mail order book which Jack took from her, closed gently, and laid on the kitchen counter.

"Gail, are you even listening to me? I'm talking about something very serious!"

The mousy brown-haired mother of two looked annoyed. "Now I'll have to find that page again! Okay, I'm listening."

"Subject: autism!" he said, placing his open palms on either side of her head and looking her squarely in the eye. "Jack Junior is autistic. It's something we'll have to deal with and plan for and work on… pretty much forever."

Gail looked a little confused as Jack released her from his gentle grip. "I know that," she said. "I know… he is. But I don't see why you had to lose my page. And you just messed up my hair!"

Normally Jack would have been inclined to avoid eye contact, but this seemed important enough that he forced himself to look directly at his wife. The extra effort made no difference; she was obviously still thinking about kitchen canisters. Or her hair.

"Why can't I get any *input* from you on this?" he moaned. "You never hop on board when the subject is autism."

"I have input," she answered indignantly. "I'm his mother."

Jack pressed on: "When we have meetings at school, why is it *me* who does all the talking? You always just *sit* there! When it's time to do any research or reading, I feel like I'm the only one in this house who even cares!"

Gail began to get impatient. "You know I don't have time to read, babe."

"You always have time for those mail order catalogs!" he shot back. He hated it when she called him "babe." It seemed so artificial; and yet in nine years he'd never said so. Now he wondered why.

"Catalogs are different, she said very defensively. "They help me relax."

"Well Gail, some *real* reading wouldn't hurt you any!" Jack replied.

Gail just rolled her eyes. "Hey, *you* asked *me* to marry you! I didn't go to college like you. This is just the way I am."

Early on, Jack had come to realize that his wife placed little value on education, and had no apparent interest in self-improvement. It was something he was able to work around when they first got together. In fact, in a very naïve way, he'd even admired Gail for being so steadfast in her own view of who she was. But he discovered this was a misjudgment once the entity of autism moved into their house, and everything suddenly changed. Everything except for Gail.

"Unhh!! Unhghhh!!" The floor shook lightly as Jack Junior jumped up and down in the adjacent room.

"JJ, not so loud," Gail said, too quietly for him to hear.

And it wouldn't have mattered if he did hear: Jack Junior's autism was so severe that he didn't respond to verbal interaction. "Unhhgghhh!!" He repeated the guttural non-word that supplanted any real speech he maybe could have had.

Exasperated, Jack turned and marched into the living room. "JJ! Knock it off!" he half-shouted at the bouncing five-year-old.

The little boy was standing in front of a large floor-model television. The VCR that sat atop the dark wood case had been used so much that the characters were worn off of the rewind and fast-forward buttons. If he was allowed, Jack Junior would stand in that spot for hours at a time, rewinding little scraps of videos and jumping ecstatically in place as the clips played over and over. The other family members had grown so accustomed to this that they simply tuned it out. A few bars of a children's song or a few lines of a Disney cartoon might be repeated hundreds of times within a single hour. The current programming was an excerpt from *Pinocchio*:

"...when you wish up-- when you wish up-- when you wish up--" repeated endlessly as the diaper-clad elf hopped up and down, grinning from ear to ear, making his growly noise. The air was stinky, and his diaper bulged.

"He needs to be changed," Jack said, reaching for the disposable diapers (the largest size available) and a cylindrical carton of baby wipes. The Olivers always kept those provisions close at hand, since their son needed refreshing many times a day. "JJ! Let's change your diaper."

As always, Jack Junior ignored his father's request.

"...when you wish up-- when you wish up--" was accompanied by more jumping and blissful growling.

Jack Senior finally had to physically pick up his son and move him a few feet away from the set to perform the "oil change" as he called it. The screech that followed would have had the neighbors of any normal child calling the police. But this was JJ; they were all used to it. The builders of these tiny row-houses had done very little to contain sound, and the various tenants were pretty much anaesthetized to each other's disturbances. In one unit, the offending noise might be children running loudly up and down the stairs, shaking the walls next door. In another it could be a teenager blaring Death Metal on his bedroom stereo. So the frequent shrieking that emanated from the Olivers' little place became an accepted part of everyone's everyday life.

"--on a star, your dreams come true." The line was allowed to finish for the first time in more than an hour, and the continuation of the song was now accompanied by the wild wailing of Jack Junior. Meanwhile Jack Senior didn't even flinch; but numbly cleaned his screaming son's bottom with a pop-up wipe. JJ's voice continued to blare while the new dry diaper was fastened in place, and his dad set him back down in front of the television. Only then did the little boy quiet down.

"There you go, Sonny Boy," Jack said quite automatically.

Jack Junior instantly went for the rewind button, relocating 'his spot' with scary precision, and "...when you wish up-- when you wish up--" commenced once more.

Gail had never even left the kitchen. When Jack returned, his wife still stood at the counter flipping through the catalog to relocate *her* spot, though with less accuracy than her autistic son.

"Found it!" she said sharply. "Now don't close this again!" The open book remained on the counter while Gail grabbed a Post-it note and attached the little pink paper square to the page with the really pretty kitchen canisters.

From the next room "...when you wish up-- when you wish up-- when you wish up--" repeated continuously: an endless dirge being played for the dreams of a father.

Even as an infant Jack Junior had behaved strangely, often sitting in front of the Olivers' roll-top desk and flipping the hinged drawer-pulls up and down with his tiny hand. As with the later sport of video rewinding, drawer-pull flipping was something Jack Junior would have done for hours at a time if the sound of the metal clinking hadn't been so annoying. To relieve the din, one or the other parent would move him to the opposite side of the room, but he would always pull himself awkwardly back across the floor and start over again.

By the time JJ was two and still not using any words, his dad had begun to suspect that he might in fact be autistic. He seemed to relate to people the same as he did to toys or furniture. There was no delineation. Living things and inanimate objects were of equal importance, or perhaps equal unimportance, in JJ's world. He thought he could look them all in the eye. And that was why no doctor would diagnose him...

⊱♦♦ॐ

"I appreciate your concern for your son, Mr. Oliver, but we don't believe it's appropriate to call this 'autism.'" The platinum blond physician sat in the examining room with a clipboard, trying to look sympathetic. Her body language revealed that she'd rather have been somewhere else. She was considered one of the area's finest developmental specialists, and the Olivers had waited seven months for this appointment.

"Dr. Shuster," Jack began, "there are services out there that could really help JJ, but it takes a diagnosis of autism even just to get on the waiting lists. We're also interested in an ABA program, which should start by age two, and he's already four!" So there. He'd made his case to yet another doctor, in yet another hospital, while Gail just sat wordlessly with JJ on her lap.

"Again, Mr. Oliver," the doctor said rather abrasively, "we have certain guidelines we have to follow for any diagnosis. Your son makes too much eye contact!"

Jack had heard this before, and had shown up armed for battle with a mentally-rehearsed speech: "I've read the new DSM-IV criteria, and yes, JJ will make some eye contact. Other than that, he fits *eleven* of the *twelve* listed criteria for autism; and I believe he only needs *six* for a diagnosis. Isn't that right?"

The doctor obviously didn't like having her authority questioned. She smiled daggers and replied: "Mr. Oliver, the DSM-IV isn't like a Chinese menu where you just pick things from different columns! It should only be interpreted by professionals. Autism is a condition with a *lot* of stigma attached, and we just don't like to *label* children that way!"

Jack had also heard this before. He realized there was now nothing to lose, so he went ahead and threw the flaming dart: "So *that's* what this is all about? Political correctness? It doesn't matter what the condition *is*; it only matters what it's *called*!"

The doctor stood up slowly. "You are very cynical," she said, just before turning her back and walking out.

A couple of years later, Jack would read an article possibly explaining what had just happened: in the 1990's, doctors were concerned that 'too many' new cases of autism were being diagnosed, and the implications weren't favorable to certain parts of the medical industry. So many physicians simply wouldn't make the diagnosis at all.

JJ was five-and-a-half before the Olivers finally found a pediatrician brave enough to say the 'A-word,' and at long last, appropriate treatment could be pursued. But that had not yet happened on the day of Jack's unpleasant epiphany...

ଔ✦✦ଶ

"Babe, do you think we should get the matching cookie jar too? I'd hate for it to be discontinued if we wanted one later on," Gail said, still poring over the page with the pink sticky note.

"Can you please put that down for a minute, Gail? It really *isn't* important right now!"

The corners of her mouth drew tight, and Jack instantly recognized the onset of the wordless, passive-aggressive rage that so often reared its ugly head in this house. Gail did *not* like for her planning to be interrupted. Ever.

"Come on," he said gently, putting a hand on her shoulder.

She froze, as if his touch was some terrible obscenity.

Jack was in no mood to be the conciliatory enabler his wife had come to expect. He realized that he'd been doing a disservice not just to himself, but also to Gail, and in fact to his whole family, by maintaining his laissez-faire attitude. But he also knew it was pointless to try and talk it over right then, so he withdrew to the living room once more, to watch Jack Junior "play."

"...when you wish up-- when you wish up--" continued ad infinitum as father and son shared the same space in two different worlds, and Jack took a look around the room that represented his life. The worn beige carpet was filthy. The upholstery on the beige sectional sofa needed cleaning. The paint on the neutral beige walls was grimy with handprints. In addition to the large cardboard boxes of video tapes, several plastic bins of toys also lined the perimeter of the room. One housed twenty or more Barbie dolls and another was stuffed full of clothes and accessories for them all. Still others contained filled-up coloring books, Beanie Babies that couldn't be played with in order to preserve the tags, and various older toys that nobody even wanted to play with anymore. But Gail would never get rid of any of it. And Jack had always let that slide. And as he looked at the bouncing five-year-old infant obsessing on a two-second clip from one of his hundreds of videos, Jack realized that JJ's quality of life was in his hands alone. Then he glanced again at the box of Barbies-- and was reminded that he had an equal responsibility to the little girl who also lived there.

JJ's sister Haley was a few months from age seven, and probably had the most positive attitude of anyone in Jack's life. Right now the little blond sprite was outside playing with neighborhood kids, which was a far better place to be than inside this stuffy beige cage. Haley was so easy; never complaining that her brother got an excessive amount of attention. She seemed to have an adult's understanding of why it had to be that way, and was always perfectly accepting of the situation. Her dad was so proud of her; and yet he understood that she needed more of a childhood than she was getting.

He walked to the front window and looked out at the grassy area in front of the row houses, where Haley and five or six other kids played ghost tag as the sun began to go down. If only it could always be like this for her! Jack recalled the previous Christmas, when little Haley had been the object of such dreadful scorn, and her mother literally screamed at her; simply for losing one of Barbie's little plastic shoes in the grass outside. Merry Christmas.

As the television still played *"...when you wish up-- when you wish up--"* Jack finally faced the realization that things would never change unless he forced them to. The big question was, had he waited too long? Had the enabling been so deeply ingrained as to be irreversible? Or for that matter, was change ever really even possible to begin with? He went back into the kitchen to find out.

"We need to talk *now*, Gail!"

His wife had moved to the kitchen table, and sat wordlessly studying the mail order catalog. He thought she might have been waiting for an apology.

"Put that thing away, damn it!" Jack shouted. "You can't spend your whole life ignoring things you can't control!"

"You don't need to swear," she replied quietly. "It's just the way I am."

"Well maybe 'the way you are' isn't a good way to be; have you ever thought about *that*?"

His wife just concentrated harder on the book in front of her, and the muscles in her neck tightened.

Jack finally let loose. "You know what? We *really* need to see a marriage counselor!"

Gail hit the table with one hand as she closed the catalog with the other. She sprung up and glared wild-eyed at her husband. "No! We don't *need* it! There's *not* a problem!!" Her voice cracked as she wailed uncontrollably, darting out of the kitchen and up the front stairs. She slammed the bedroom door loudly.

The walls shook; the neighbors ignored it.

It would have been a perfect moment for Jack to be acutely aware of the deafening silence, but instead he heard "...when you wish up-- when you wish up-- when you wish up--" repeating continuously: an endless dirge being played for the dreams of a husband.

He began to pace back and forth.

"...when you wish up--"

He saw his reflection in an ornamental mirror that hung on the wall.

"...when you wish up--"

He sighed as he spoke to his flat, lifeless image: "I guess this is the first day of the rest of your life, old man."

"...when you wish up--"

He walked outside. Now he just heard crickets, and the faint, laughing voices of the children sharing a game of ghost tag. He sat on his front step in the dark, and watched them play amongst the fireflies.

CHAPTER FOUR

WHEN JACK awoke on the sofa with pillows still covering his head, the light in the room had shifted. The sun was now coming from the direction of the dining room window. He sat up suddenly, trying to chase away that dismal flashback of a dream! He could still see the fireflies flickering around the house as he stood up, but when he took a deep breath of cool air they all disappeared and he was back in 1970.

Jeannie's room was quiet now, and he wondered if she might be asleep too. Teenagers seemed to love sleep. Was Sandy still in the house? Had she left and Jack slept through it? He went to the kitchen to look at the clock. "Three-thirty," he said, "I've been home exactly twenty-three-and-a-half hours." He thought a whole day should have been plenty of time to implement change, and wondered how much longer he needed to stay in this version of his world.

Jack had once read about Edward Lorenz's chaos theory, and *sensitive dependence on initial conditions*. He was intrigued by the implications of his famous quotation: *Does the flap of a butterfly's wings in Brazil set off a tornado in Texas?*

Maybe Jack only needed to change some seemingly insignificant thing in order to make his life better. He saw his empty breakfast glass still sitting on the kitchen table. Maybe if he moved it one inch to the right he might suddenly be spirited away and hear Francis saying, "Congratulations Jackie, you did it!" Or maybe he should move it to the left, but then Francis might say, "Oh no! You blew it, boy!" as the Earth proceeded to explode. Jack just began to giggle at the absurdity of it all.

Looking at the glass made Jack realize he was very hungry. It was now 3:30 and he hadn't had any food since 11:00. Oops-- he also realized he probably should have offered a snack to Tim. "I'm a growing boy," he said, rooting through the pantry. Potato chips, raisins, store-bought gingerbread cookies... nothing really grabbed him, but he was so hungry he grabbed four of the cookies and headed back into the living room.

"Maybe now there's something on television," he said. As it turned out, the afternoon programming before the 5:00 news hour was much more kid-friendly, but Jack was caught completely off-guard when he heard the minor strains of a familiar, forgotten theme song:

"There's a prehistoric monster who came from outer space, Created by the Martians to destroy the human race..."

His jaw dropped and he stared in awe at the black-and-white cartoon playing on his color set. "It's Tobor the Eighth Man!" he said with disbelief. He collapsed cross-legged on the floor right in front of the TV and watched the show from beginning to end. This was an early, cheesy Japanese cartoon dubbed in English, about a super-hero robot. In fact, "Tobor" was "robot" spelled backwards. But the low-quality production and insipid story line made no difference at all. Jack was absorbing his boyhood, remembering feelings rather than thoughts. This was very different than watching *The Carol Burnett Show* the previous night; that kind of programming was for everybody. This cartoon was for *him*. At age twelve he was really too old for a show like *Eighth Man*, but he wasn't watching it for entertainment. He was re-learning what it felt like to be Jack Oliver in 1970, close on the heels of Jack Oliver the little boy.

Equally rejuvenating were the commercials, almost all of which touted toys like the *Close 'n Play Phonograph*, the *Electro-Shot Shooting Gallery*, and a game called *The Last Straw* that featured a collapsing plastic camel.

Before his memory could even catch its breath, Jack got swept into the unyielding current of afternoon programming, and found himself immersed in another Japanese classic, *Speed Racer*. He and his friends had always found it silly that there was actually a cartoon family with the surname of "Racer," but they watched it religiously nonetheless. Adult Jack had grown to shake his head in disbelief at some of the mindless programs that his children would watch, staring open-mouthed at the screen. Now it was all coming back to him: it wasn't about the programs, it was about the security. These were the shows that kids could claim as their own, in their world that existed away from that of their parents. This is what validated them as little people.

Before he was able to get too involved in the plot of *Speed Racer*, his mother walked through the front door and Jack turned off the set. It was time to bond with something besides a television. After dropping her purse on the desk, Marie went straight to the kitchen. Jack stood up and followed behind her as she moved through the house. She attached a little note to the refrigerator door with a magnet shaped like a pear, and for a fleeting moment Jack thought, *Hey-- maybe I could be the one to invent those sticky Post-it notes!* He briskly shook his head, reminding himself of the mental process he'd gone through earlier. *No, that's a bad idea,* he thought.

"Hi Mom, how was the... um, election?" he said.

"We'll find out tomorrow I guess," she answered. She looked tired, and returned to the living room to plant herself in the upholstered armchair. Kicking off her shoes, she sighed and said, "What a day. People are crazy!"

"Crazy is as crazy does," Jack replied, realizing he'd sort of just plagiarized *Forrest Gump*.

Marie looked at him strangely, not sure if she'd just been given a gem of wisdom or a lump of foolishness. "What did you do all day?" she asked.

"Oh, Tim came over, we hit Wiffle balls, and I watched TV for a little bit."

"Any homework you need to finish?"

"Oh! I forgot to check. I'll do that."

"Where's your sister?"

"I'm not sure; I also fell asleep for an hour."

"Did you make yourself some lunch?"

It never occurred to Jack to make himself a meal. Now he remembered seeing cans of Chef Boyardee pasta and various kinds of Campbell's soup in the pantry when he was scouting for snacks. But they required work to prepare, and he didn't even have a microwave at his disposal. It was so much easier just to grab a handful of cookies and go. Thinking like a twelve-year-old, he opted for the easy answer: "Nah, I really didn't get hungry."

There were more questions Marie could have asked, but she didn't want to seem like an interrogator, so she shifted gears. "I told Charlie I'd try to work again tonight from five to seven. Maybe it would be fun for you to come too!"

Jack tried to recall why his mother would be working for someone named Charlie. He faked a reply: "Um... maybe, yeah."

"All we have to do is hand out fliers and be polite," Marie said. "There are a lot of other people there too, all doing what we're doing."

Okay; this must have had something to do with the polls. Jack assumed his mother had been checking registration cards or helping elderly voters use the machines, but now she was talking about handing out fliers. That meant she was campaigning for a candidate. He knew he might be inviting trouble, but he bravely replied, "Sure, why not?"

"Good!" Marie said. "We'll have to leave again in a few minutes, I just came home to check on you and Jeannie and get in a little break."

"I *am* hungry now, can I eat something first?" Jack asked.

Marie answered, "How about some Beefaroni or chicken noodle soup? That's quick."

"How about ravioli?" Jack suggested.

"I'll heat it up if you can try to find your sister and let her know what we're doing. Oh, and tell her there's frozen pizza if she's hungry."

Jack headed for Jeannie's room. The door was open and no one was inside. Had she left while he was asleep? He idled there for a few seconds, trying to think of where to look next. There must have been some memories programmed into his DNA, because his legs instinctively carried him down the basement stairs toward a wood-paneled family room where the Olivers had a second, black-and-white TV set and a nice hi-fi system. The door was closed, and Jack heard the two girls talking. "Aha!" he said to himself as he knocked.

Jeannie answered, peeking through what was little more than a crack. "What is it?" she asked brusquely.

Jack could hear music playing quietly on the stereo in the background. He was surprised that it wasn't "Baby Baby Sweet Baby." He thought the television might also have been on. "I'm going back to the polls with Mom in a couple of minutes. We'll be done at seven. And there's…"

"Okay," Jeannie said, and shut the door.

"…frozen pizza…"

Jack rolled his eyes, bounding back up the stairs into the kitchen just as his mother was tossing the empty Chef Boyardee can into the trash. Pounce had appeared from somewhere and was weaving around her feet in response to the sound of the can opener.

"Your ravioli will be warm in a couple of minutes," Marie said.

"Thanks Mom," Jack answered, taking in the scene and feeling a sense of exhilaration. It was a familiar 'little kid' feeling like the one he used to get waiting for Santa Claus on Christmas Eve, but this time it was just based on the ordinary circumstances of his life. He lived in a house where he was a very important person, yet he had very little responsibility. He had a really cool big sister to torment, and a pretty young mother who was making him his favorite kids' meal before they went out on a little adventure together. There was even a pet cat! It was all so un-extraordinary; and that was precisely what made it so wonderful.

"I should teach you what to say tonight," Marie began.

"What do you mean?" Jack responded, craning his neck to get a look inside the saucepan containing his ravioli.

"When you hand someone a flier, just say: 'Please vote for Charlie Blair for County Council,' and thank them whether they take it or not."

"Charlie Blair? Who's he?"

"I thought I told you about him. He's the guy that will keep the funding in place for our class piano program. Then I'll still have a job next year!"

"Cool," Jack replied, "think he'll win?"

"I hope so, he's been our friend."

The aroma of the ravioli made Jack even hungrier, and he looked into the pan once more. The burner had been inadvertently left on 'high,' and the sauce was beginning to gurgle and spit, as thick liquids sometimes do when they heat too quickly. A bubble of red sauce burst onto the front of Jack's T-shirt. "Yowch!" he exclaimed, feeling tiny hot splatters on his face as well.

His mother was more startled than he was. "Oh!" she squeaked. "Are you alright?"

Jack answered tentatively, "Yeah, I think so. But I've got a big stain on my shirt now!"

Marie hurried to the stove to turn down the burner and stir the pan. "Why don't you go wash your face and change your shirt? I'll have this ready when you get back."

"Okay," Jack said, starting down the hall.

"And this time find a shirt that matches your pants, okay?"

"...okay..."

"We're representing 'Candidate Charlie Blair' after all, and we need to look nice," Marie continued, but by then Jack was already in the bathroom and couldn't hear her.

When he returned to the kitchen washed and dressed, Marie was gone but his steaming bowl of ravioli was waiting on the table, alongside a cold glass of milk. He sat and immediately dug into the feast, savoring the wonderful flavor of the processed, preserved, mass-produced food product. In his forties, Jack had to start keeping track of his sodium, so canned meals like this became 'the enemy.' It was pure bliss to be able to simply eat and enjoy a guilt-free bowl of Chef Boyardee! The flavor somehow seemed so much better than he remembered: had they changed the recipe over time, or did Jack's taste buds perhaps change as he aged? He thought about all the really little kids he'd known who went crazy over meals that he could now barely stand, like cheap boxes of macaroni and powdered cheese, or that noodle soup that came in envelopes with little flavoring packets. Or for that matter, canned pasta!

"For everything, there is a seasoning, turn, turn, turn," he said with a mouthful of ravioli.

Marie hurried back into the kitchen, this time with her coat on. "It's getting colder, so you should wear a jacket. And the polls close at seven o'clock, so we should probably get going as soon as you're done."

Jack knew this translated to "hurry up, slowpoke!" so he wolfed down the remaining ravioli and gulped the milk. It felt so good to eat like a glutton, and surprisingly, tasted even better.

"I'm coming," he said, placing his bowl and glass into the sink. Oops-- should he have done that? Of course it was the thoughtful thing to do, but was it the 'twelve' thing to do? No time to second-guess; he needed to go. He grabbed his jacket and headed outside with his mother.

The 1963 Buick LeSabre was the Olivers' "new" car. Jack vaguely recalled that it had replaced some kind of a long black Plymouth, and was considered a luxurious upgrade. His dad was the champion of car scavengers, and though he never bought an actual *new* car, he managed to find some pretty nice older creampuffs. Jack quickly looked over the mid-sized metallic ox before opening one of the two oversized doors and sliding into the front seat. With the sky now almost dark, he could only see what the little dome light illuminated, but he still got quite an eyeful. Instantly he recognized the interior, with lots of round dials on the dash, a radio with old-style push buttons, and those long bench seats, looking rather like church pews. The plain, padded door panels seemed less familiar, with no built-in stereo speakers and a conspicuous lack of power window, lock and mirror controls. The biggest surprise came when Jack automatically reached for a seat belt, only to find there were none.

"Geez," he remarked quietly.

"What did you say?" his mother asked, setting her purse next to him on the seat.

Uh-oh, was that a no-no? Sometimes "geez" was construed as a derogatory form of "Jesus," but Jack wasn't sure if his parents were among those who would be offended. He recalled once getting in trouble for saying "aw heck" but that may have been more about his tone of voice than about the similarity to "aw hell." He struggled to come up with a safe reply, finally settling on, "Just clearing my throat."

"Oh," Marie said, "I probably made you eat too fast." And it was left at that.

So Jack still didn't know if "geez" was acceptable, but it was undoubtedly best to stay away from it.

The drive to Forest Wood Elementary, Jack's old alma mater and the local polling place, only took a couple of minutes. His body was smaller than the last time he'd been in a car, and with so much less mass, he did a good bit of sliding around as the big Buick swiftly navigated the corners. He quickly came to appreciate the invention of the seat belt. By 1970, every new car had them, but a '63 LeSabre that was probably made in '62, was too old.

Jack looked out the window as his mother drove, seeing his old neighborhood pass by in the dusk. As an adult, he would occasionally revisit the area and look for the houses where his boyhood friends had lived. Though the homes were still there, the trees had grown too big, the yards had grown too small, and the cars parked outside were yuppie SUV's rather than family station wagons. When they finally reached the school, the building loomed before Jack like some huge brick castle in the dark. They parked and got out.

Marie gave Jack several dozen thin paper fliers and said, "Remember, it's: 'Please vote for Charlie Blair for County Council,' and be sure to smile and say thank you. Maybe you should watch me a couple of times."

She moved into a pack of campaigners under a streetlight several yards from the front entrance, as they began to approach a lone woman heading toward the building. It was a little like a pack of wolves all stalking the same prey. Jack watched in awe as his mother somehow managed to reach the unsuspecting voter first with her flier, and made her one-sentence sales pitch sound polite, even as the group of predators gnashed their teeth all around her. After two or three impressive demonstrations, Marie walked back over to Jack and said, "See how it's done? It's all about 'bulling your way through' but staying friendly. Why don't you take the people coming from the other side of the parking lot?"

Jack reluctantly made his way across the sidewalk with his stack of fliers and tried to blend into the pack waiting there, though they made him feel a little claustrophobic. He hated crowds. The first "victim" approaching from Jack's direction was a man in a business suit who looked like he'd just come from work. The campaigners all moved toward him, and Jack tried to keep up but was quickly lost in the fray.

The next voter was a middle-aged blond lady who Jack managed to reach only after several other campaigners had already left their mark. Jack offered her a flier and got as far as "Please vote for..."

...but the woman cut him off with her pitiful appeal: "Oh dear, I have so many fliers already!"

"Maybe this was a bad idea," he said. After a few seconds of re-evaluation he gave himself a quick and quirky mental pep talk: *Remember Jack, you only look twelve. Use your superior intelligence, man!*

Unfortunately, he discovered that this was one job where it was all about physicality. Time after time he was crowded out as voters approached the building, and the bigger, taller wolves got to them first. Jack never cared for sports like soccer and hockey for that very reason: there were too many people all aiming for the same thing, and it was easy to get trampled underfoot. He was usually the one who got the least amount of candy from a piñata, because he couldn't bring himself to push through the swarm of children when it burst. Concert halls and stadiums filled with people were just as bad. He'd once heard the term *demophobia* used to describe the feeling, though he didn't like to think he had an actual 'phobia.'

Jack decided to gear up for one last attempt before raising the white flag, and he spotted a friendly-looking man in jeans and a flannel shirt heading his way. He scrambled to get to him first, but was quickly engulfed by ruthless adults, all with the same goal. Jack ended up helplessly trapped in the pack as it kept pace with the poor victim, and he could see nothing but the coats, legs and shoes of the taller people all around him. The sound was even more unsettling: a cacophonous blend of "please - vote - thank you - Smith - community - Congress - Jones," etc. It may as well have been "fire ants - guitar picks - bean soup and Hail Mary," for all the impact it seemed to have on the voter.

Finally Jack just pushed through the crowd and yelled "Enough!" To his astonishment, the whole group stopped short, and it was just him and the flannel shirt man, all alone on the sidewalk. Stunned, Jack smiled and blurted out: "Please vote for County Blair for Charlie Council!"

The man just glared curiously and asked, "Is he a Democrat or a Republican?"

Jack was embarrassed; even if he had gotten the name right, he still had no idea! He simply held out a flier, which the man took and added to his stack.

Then the man smiled and said, "I don't think you're supposed to be in this close, son!" He pointed to a sign that was planted right where the rest of the pack had stopped:

No Campaigning Beyond This Point.

So much for superior intelligence.

"Oops," Jack said as he crept back into the "safe zone" behind the sign. He heard a few snickers coming from the wolf pack as he made his retreat, and his ears burned with embarrassment. Just when he was about to concede defeat and go wait in the dark shadows of the Buick, he heard his mother calling:

"Jack, can you come over here and help me?"

He blew a sigh of relief and scurried over to Marie, fliers in hand.

"These fliers are hard to carry," she said, "maybe you could hold them for me and replenish the supply as we go."

Twelve-year-old Jack wouldn't have seen what was going on, but the fifty-two-year-old father recognized it right away. This was a clever parenting technique called "loving your kid," and he'd done it many times when his own children were small. Of course his mother wasn't really having trouble carrying her fliers. She saw Jack's awkward situation and was offering him a dignified way out. In fact, Marie was blatantly coddling him, and he'd never been more grateful.

With a certain decorum, he took her fliers and assumed his place as "treasurer," doling out about ten at a time and keeping her supply steady. The method worked well, and for the next ninety minutes the team of Oliver and Oliver campaigned for Candidate Charlie Blair. At 7:00 the polls closed, all the wolves suddenly disappeared, and mother and son returned to their new-used car for the ride home.

"Thanks for saving me," Jack said, as the big white car lumbered down the darkened streets.

"Saving you?" Marie asked. "What do you mean?" She must not have expected Jack to realize what she'd done.

"I'm not the right size for this kind of work!"

"I thought you did just fine."

Jack remembered being twelve the first time around, and how he would have felt if he realized his mother had rescued him. His pre-teen desire for independence would have kicked in, and he would have moped around for the rest of the night, resenting her "interference." Now though, he was coming at it from a parent's perspective, and he realized that the best thing he could do was just let his mother love him. That's how it worked. He also felt that if he pursued it, he might say too much, and he didn't want to endanger his mission.

Jack abruptly changed the subject. "I hope Jeannie got something to eat."

Marie jumped right on board: "You did tell her about the pizza, right?"

"I tried to, but I don't think she heard me."

"Well, she's a big girl. Hopefully she figured it out."

They came through the front door together to find Jeannie watching television. "Hi! *Mod Squad* comes on in fifteen minutes," she said.

"Did you eat?" Marie asked.

"SpaghettiOs," Jeannie answered.

"Oh, you didn't feel like pizza?"

"We had pizza?"

"Didn't Jack tell you?"

"No, he didn't!"

Jack's feathers started to ruffle as he said: "You slammed the door and wouldn't let me finish!"

"You're such a 'tard!" Jeannie snapped.

Marie splayed one hand and held it out to shush them both. "The important thing is that you ate. Tomorrow night I'll cook a real meal again, but right now I'm going to go find some supper for myself." With that, she went off to the kitchen to forage.

Jack and Jeannie looked at each other. There was an unspoken 'oops' as they both realized that their mother had made sure they were fed, though she hadn't eaten herself.

Jack followed Marie into the kitchen, and found her pulling a container of leftover Brussels sprouts from the old Norge. Grabbing a fork from the silverware drawer, she sat down and proceeded to eat them cold.

"Yuck! How can you eat those?" he asked.

"I learned to love them when I was a girl," she answered.

"Cold?"

"Sure, I love cold vegetables! Beets, carrots, tomatoes…"

This was one thing that never made sense to Jack. The temperature of his food was always very important, and some dishes were just supposed to be served warm, including most vegetables. Texture was important, too. Grainy foods like lima beans, liver and hard-boiled egg yolks were hard to swallow, while things like noodles and mashed potatoes were consumed with ease. It was difficult for Jack even to watch someone eat the 'wrong' food. He felt bad that he'd enjoyed such a delicacy as hot canned ravioli, while his mother had cold leftover vegetables. He was never sure whether to believe her when she said she really enjoyed eating that way, partly because he wouldn't have been able to stand it. But beyond that, Jack knew the feeling of giving 'the best' to his kids and taking the leftovers for himself. Whether it was food, clothing or shelter, he never begrudged his provision, and in fact, came to see it as a privilege of parenting. Maybe his mother was also in this place; or maybe she really did like cold vegetables. Or maybe it was both: Marie looked quite content as she finished off the sprouts.

"And now there's no extra plate to wash either," she said, tossing the Tupperware container into the sink.

Jack rejoined Jeannie to watch *Mod Squad*, which he didn't enjoy nearly as much as *Laugh In* the previous night. Throughout the show, he kept thinking about his mother and the natural way that she took care of things. It was just 'what she did,' and she expected no special recognition.

At 8:30 Jeannie was off by herself once more, and Marie suggested a game of Stratego. For Jack, this was an odd recollection: Stratego wasn't the kind of game a boy would ordinarily think of playing with his mother, yet for the Olivers it was quite normal. He hadn't played for decades, and as he re-learned the rules on-the-fly, he uncovered many of the same feelings he'd experienced watching *Eighth Man* earlier in the day. Only this time it wasn't for *him*; it was for *them*. As they shared the board game adventure, Jack realized that during this part of his life, his mom was his best friend. And maybe he was hers.

After Jack emerged victorious (he always wondered if Marie let him win) he found his school backpack and discovered that all he had for homework was to read two chapters of *The Cay* for English. Television offered nothing interesting until 10:00, so Jack made quick work of the reading. Surprisingly, he remembered a lot about this book he hadn't read in forty years.

At 10:00 he and Marie watched *Marcus Welby, M.D.*, and at 11:00 he kissed her on the cheek and headed off to bed. She seemed surprised by the affection. With Pounce accompanying him once more, Jack curled up under the covers and began to dream.

CHAPTER FIVE

"**W**HAT'S DADDY'S name?"
     "Daddis - name - is - Shack - Olifer."
"Good! What's Mommy's name?"
"Mommis - name - is - Gayw - Olifer."
Violet smiled and gave Jack Junior a high-five. "Awesome!" she said with genuine enthusiasm.

He splayed his fingers and grimaced right back at her: his autistic version of a smile.

"Mind if I interrupt?" Jack Senior said, appearing in the doorway. "I have a new 'Top Ten' list!"

"It's time for a breather anyway," Violet answered. "JJ, take a break!"

"Take - a - bwake," the eight-year-old said, very deliberately. He hopped up from the table where he was working with "Miss Violet" and began toe-walking around the room, expelling some of his bundled-up energy.

"Okay, let me see this!" said the pretty, petite brunette, taking the freshly-printed sheet from Jack's hand.

Top Ten Bad (good?)
Names for a New Rock Band

10. Chef Boyardee
9. Without Apologies
8. Fats and Lipids
7. Tuna Platter
6. Frozen Barbies
5. Sputum
4. The Four-loaf Cleavers
3. Re-gifted Fruitcake
2. Bluto

...and the number one bad (good?)
name for a new rock band is...
(drum roll...)

1. Municipal Bladder!

(cymbal crash!)

"Well, it's not David Letterman by any stretch," Violet laughed.

"C'mon, give me a break! I don't have paid writers," Jack responded. "I always judge the name by how it would sound at the end of a set. Like: 'We are Without Apologies and we'll be back in fifteen minutes.'"

"I don't even want to know what a band called 'Sputum' would look like!" Violet mused. "And I notice a lot of these are food-related. Were you hungry when you wrote it?"

"I'm always hungry..."

"And I think I've heard of an actual band called 'Bluto' someplace."

"I don't think anyone will sue me over this list," Jack chuckled.

"Unghhh!!" Jack Junior intoned briefly, splaying his fingers again. The 'autistic behaviors' were not gone by any means, and probably never would be. Nevertheless, the little boy was talking! Even the bursts of guttural sounds seemed like little miracles when heard alongside the real words JJ was now using. And he was also interacting: identifying things, reading and writing words, drawing pictures and playing games. He'd been toilet trained for almost a year. His love affair with the VCR was still hot and heavy, but now at least it could be regulated. The progress was slow but steady, and whenever Jack looked at JJ now compared to JJ when Violet had first started working with him, he was always left speechless. Speechless was good: if Jack wasn't talking, he was listening. And what he heard was a dirge being played backwards-- resurrecting the dreams of a father!

"You're almost done, right?" he asked.

"We're scheduled until one o'clock," Violet replied.

JJ clapped the balls of his hands together, producing a muffled popping noise. He must have liked the sound, because he did it again with a big grimace-smile.

"So, just fifteen minutes? How about if we go to lunch after? I'll treat!" Jack said.

"Hmm..." Violet pretended to mull it over. "Let's see: I can either go back home and open a can of tuna, or go out to lunch with you and JJ. What to do... what to do..."

"I'll take that as a no," Jack jested. "I know how much you love canned tuna. Hey-- 'Canned Tuna!' Maybe that's a better name than 'Tuna Platter.' In fact, maybe *all* the band names should have to do with food. 'Smokey Salmon and the Miracle Whips;' 'Rodent Omelet;' 'The Im-*pastas*...'"

Violet interrupted: "You don't really even need me in order to have a conversation, do you?"

"Oops-- I'm doing it again, aren't I?"

"Oh, a *little*! And-- 'Rodent Omelet'? Ew!!"

"Well then, allow me to rewind and just ask you to lunch again..."

JJ was listening: "We-wind!" He clapped more loudly.

Violet responded to the boy: "No rewinding now, JJ."

"Yikes! I used the 'R'-word," Jack said under his breath. "Sorry..."

"It's okay," she responded lightheartedly, "I think I can get the situation back under control. JJ: time for more lessons!"

"Mow - wessons," the boy mimicked, "and - den - we-wind." He sat immediately back down at the table.

"So, I guess we have a date for one o'clock, then?" Jack queried, making sure Violet knew he was only kidding about the canned tuna. Teasing, even when he was the one doing it, tended to leave behind little seeds of doubt, so Jack always felt better with a literal confirmation.

Violet was just learning this about him. She replied slowly and deliberately: "Yes... Lunch... One o'clock..."

Jack smiled sheepishly; she certainly knew him well.

The ABA program had been in place for two years now, and Violet had been there from the beginning. "Applied Behavior Analysis" is what the initials stood for, referring to the teaching method developed by a Norwegian psychologist. For some kids with autism it helped, for others it did not; so starting an in-home program like JJ's was a gamble for any family. As it turned out though, he took to it like a fish to water, and the result was dramatic. Family and friends alike had trouble believing the changes they saw in him. Many therapists came through the doors of the Oliver house to work with JJ during the course of the program, which would ultimately run for five years. But the one who planned the lessons, organized the data, juggled the schedules and effectively saved JJ's life, was Violet.

The three of them shared a table in the little restaurant that was frequented mostly by locals. They were in there rather a lot, and Jack and Violet were often mistaken for a married couple. Those who knew who they really were would whisper to each other about the "affair" that must have been going on while Gail was at work. But they were wrong. It was really all about Jack Junior, and working together to give him a decent quality of life. And though Jack Senior didn't realize it, for Violet, it was also about *him*, and how she could be a supportive friend to someone she found she truly *liked*!

"I'll have a bowl of chili and a side of cornbread," Jack said to the big, friendly waitress, "and for JJ, how about a grilled cheese sandwich?"

"Gwowled - sheez," JJ parroted as best he could.

"And I'll have the tuna salad," Violet added.

"What?" Jack yapped. "Tuna?? I thought we came here so you could get *away* from tuna!"

"Sorry, but ever since you mentioned it in that list, I've been thinking about tuna."

Jack sighed. "All right... *you* know what you want."

The waitress smiled and rolled her eyes as she walked toward the kitchen, scribbling on her pad. She was used to their antics.

And they talked and laughed and kept JJ involved all through the meal. And then Violet went back to her house and Jack to his;

and they waited for their other children to come home from school. And the sun went down and came back up, and the next day they were even better friends. But that was all, despite what the gossips said.

CR✦✦ಬ

With his rich history of 'career exploration,' Jack had held many different jobs. Currently he was working two, both related to his music degree. Not surprisingly, one of them involved playing piano at a neighborhood restaurant. He'd also gotten a foot in the door at a local college as a part-time music teacher. This dual profession allowed him to be at home with JJ during the days while Gail worked a nine-to-fiver. Once she got home, Jack would leave to go teach a theory class or play the requests people passed to him on cocktail napkins, and Gail would take over the domestic duties. They were like ships passing in the night, and Jack felt slightly guilty for rather liking it that way.

Ever since his grim realization a couple of years earlier, he no longer felt the same affection for Gail. Her mindset still hadn't budged, and her worn-out chant of "…it's just the way I am…" had become a dirge in its own right: not for any of Jack's *dreams*, but for his sense of self. Every morning he would look into the mirror and see a failed, forty-something father brushing his teeth in a cluttered, beige bathroom. And when even his *wife* couldn't-- or wouldn't-- make a single change in herself for the sake of their marriage, he figured he must not be worth changing for. *Who could ever want me?* he'd ask himself, and the only thing that kept him from praying to God to be taken up then and there was the responsibility he felt to Haley and JJ.

Further complicating things was Gail's response to JJ's progress: it was almost as if she resented the fact that he was becoming less dependent on her. Jack thought a psychologist would probably have a name for that, but he didn't have any way of pursuing it. What he did know was that JJ's independence, the very thing that he had fought the hardest for, was met with suspicion and resentment by his wife. But Jack Junior's daily lessons still went on...

CR♦♦ED

"Let's draw Snoopy," Violet said, producing a fresh sheet of paper and a crayon.

"Noopy!" JJ replied, drawing crooked little wax circles that would soon transform into one of his favorite friends.

Jack just watched them through the open door of the little work space he'd cleared out for lessons. He was always delighted to see JJ actually interested in what was being presented. The humanity that had been locked inside the little boy for so long was finally getting to come out and play! Not only was his playmate a miracle worker, but the way she had come to be there was yet another miracle. Jack thought it could only be a divine hand that had scooped up Violet's family on the West Coast and set them down so precisely in the midst of his little neighborhood in Florida. But he'd always largely viewed Violet's instruction as God's gift to JJ. Now he was acknowledging for the first time that her friendship was God's gift to him.

Violet was the first intellectual peer Jack had had in a long time. Able to hold her own in any discussion about Shakespeare or Stephen Hawking, she also appreciated the occasional absurdity, like a "Top Ten" list. She was intuitive and feeling, flawlessly complimenting Jack's more logical personality. So it wasn't all just for JJ's benefit: Jack saw that now. He could see a lot of things now.

The friendship would remain just that for several more years, before some serious issues would eventually cause Violet to call her own marriage into question. The answer turned out to be a decisive no, and the end of a bad relationship became the beginning of a blissful one. And added to the mix were their children: not just Haley and JJ, but also Violet's kids Hope and Will, who would become an indelible part of Jack's life. But as a stepdad, Jack found himself at an impasse: it wasn't that long ago that he'd still been asking: *Who could ever want me?* That question wouldn't go away without a fight, and his tendency was to keep all the children at arm's length emotionally for fear of forcing some interaction that they might not want from him. He hoped they knew how much he loved them by all the other things he did, but he couldn't be sure. So every now and then, Jack found himself doubting his abilities as a father of four…

CR✦✦ℰꝹ

"Maybe *that's* what I can change…" Jack said out loud as he began to emerge from his sleep. The high pitch of his own voice startled him, and he found himself lying in a bed that seemed so big only because his body was so small. For a split-second he struggled to remember where he was, and first thought that November of 1970 was only a part of the dream he'd just had.

"Wow," he said, hearing his immature voice for the second time. Okay, it was no dream. Now he was fully awake. He lay there in the dark, listening to the silence, absorbing the good things he knew about his future. He realized that his life had actually turned out pretty well, and began to wonder if in fact he really needed a change at all. But there was obviously no turning back now. He'd made his decision in the White Room, and right or wrong, it was done.

The clock radio by Jack's bed was one of the early digital ones that had tiny number cards attached to a rotating drum. When Jack had first gotten the unit, he had trouble falling asleep because of the little "click" it made once every minute when a new card flipped over. Within a week or so, he not only grew used to the sound, but found it to be a comfort during the night. It was a subtle reminder that the Earth was still spinning, and that life went on all around him. So when he awoke that shadowy morning at 5:27 a.m., the click was quite welcome. Not only was the world still revolving, but all was right with it. It was so much easier when he knew how the story ended.

He continued to lie quietly as the muffled sound of raindrops on the roof gradually became audible. *Click--* it was 5:28. For the next two hours and two minutes, Jack contentedly listened to the music of the sounds around him: thousands of raindrops and 122 evenly-spaced clicks. He decided if it were actually a piece of music, it might be called *Symphony for Rain and Digital Clock*; with an occasional purring obbligato by Pounce the cat.

CHAPTER SIX

SCHOOL DAYS, school days; dear old golden-rule days...
Jack couldn't get the old tune out of his head as Marie drove him to Twin Springs Junior High School. It was such a gray morning, it seemed almost like night. Car headlights hit the cold steady rain that spilled onto the streets, illuminating showers of tiny wet sparks. The Sun must have overslept that morning: it was a dismal day.

And yet, Jack was giddy with anticipation. He wasn't really sure why, because he had hated junior high school. If anything, he should be nervous and apprehensive, but he wasn't. Perhaps school held the opportunity he was looking for: to make a quick change and get back home to a better life with Violet and the kids.

The windshield wipers on the Buick sloshed back and forth with a muffled thumping sound, and the window defroster whooshed loudly as Jack and his mother drove through the neighborhood. All around them were kids walking to school in hooded rain slickers, looking like little yellow astronauts with back packs. Jack realized he was fortunate to have someone who could drive him when the weather was bad. He'd never thought about it before, but most of these families must have had only one car, or else two parents working day jobs. Why else would so many kids be out in this cold rain? After waiting in line behind a dozen or so cars dropping off the other lucky kids, Marie pulled the Buick into the narrow covered area that protected the front door of the school.

"If it's still raining I'll see you at three-thirty, Jack," she said, as her son slid out of the passenger's seat.

"Okey, dokey!" he answered, with a silliness that matched his mood. He toddled into the building, backpack in tow, raincoat in backpack, and moved slowly down the hallway in front of him. He casually observed the swarms of students passing by every which way. Some were in groups, talking and laughing; others went solo, seemingly oblivious to those around them. Many of them stood at their lockers, juggling books and supplies to prepare for first period. Jack knew that he had a locker too, but he didn't know where it was or what his lock combination might be, so he was prepared to wear his heavy backpack all day if necessary. He took Francis' paper from his pocket and unfolded it.

"Homeroom," he read out loud, "Anderson, room one-fourteen." His voice wasn't even audible with all the noise in the hallway. He looked to his left at the even-numbered classroom doors; *128, 126, 124, 122...* he continued down the hallway, smugly closing in on his destination. *120, 118, 116...* concrete block wall. "Oh, great," he said, "there's no room one-fourteen!"

Quickly he spun around, looking for a sign or a directory. There was nothing. He scoured his memory banks to see if there was any record of the layout of his junior high school building, but that file had long since been erased. Jack doubled back, looking for an intersection or a doorway that might take him to the other side of the offending wall. Logically, that's where the room should be. He saw an exit sign that looked promising, but it led to a staircase, and he knew he didn't need to go to another floor. "Crap!" he shouted. "Crap, crap, crap!"

Jack was dismayed to see the number of students around him thinning out as they all found their respective homerooms, and he knew the late bell would be ringing very soon. He ran all the way back to the front door of the school and looked both ways. To the right was a sign pointing to the cafeteria; to the left was another hallway in which only five or six students still lingered. He began to tire from the weight of his backpack as he clumsily ran down the perpendicular passageway. He could make out the numbers on rooms 101 and 103 to the right, and 127 and 125 to the left. "They're all odd," he said. "Wait a second, they're all *odd!*"

The late bell rang, and various classrooms quickly absorbed the last handfuls of students. Jack bolted back to the now-empty first hallway, this time calling out numbers as he looked to the *right*, something he'd neglected to do earlier. "One-o-two, one-o-four, one-o-six..." he was embarrassed, but more importantly, he was now late. He had assumed the hallways were arranged like city streets. "We all know what happens when you assume," he mumbled, now silently reading the room numbers. *110, 112...*

"...you make an ASS of U and ME!" he said rather loudly, just as he stepped into room 114.

The whole class stared at Jack with wide eyes, as he looked them over. They obviously all heard what he said. One girl giggled. There were three empty seats, and he didn't know which one he was supposed to be sitting in. Did they even have assigned seating? Very quickly he scanned the room to try and identify anyone whose last name he might remember. He sort of recognized the faces, but not well enough to recall names. Wait; there was Vicky! Vicky... something. Never mind. Hey, Andy Norton! Now Jack was getting somewhere. *L, M, N, O...* he recited quickly to himself, as he always had to do when it was time to alphabetize. Even in adulthood it never became automatic. *Norton comes before Oliver,* he thought. There was one seat several desks back from Andy, and taking a chance, Jack sat there. His bulging backpack caused him to lean forward in the seat, and he looked and felt awkward.

"Do we have a problem this morning, Mister Oliver?" the teacher asked. Jack hadn't yet looked toward the front of the room; there stood a tall, thin balding man in a white shirt and brown tie. He must have been "Anderson."

"Sorry," Jack replied, now looking at the floor.

"See me after homeroom," Mr. Anderson said with a glare. He then proceeded to take roll, and Jack discovered that the students were indeed sitting in alphabetical order, and that he had found the correct desk.

"It can only get better from here," he whispered, just as a huge bolt of lightning flashed outside, and thunder shook the windows.

After roll call, morning announcements and the dismissal bell, Jack tentatively approached the teacher, saying, "You wanted to see me?"

"You're not normally tardy, Jack; and if that were the extent of it I'd let this slide. But I can't ignore your language in school, sorry." He handed Jack a yellow slip. "I'm also sending one of these to the principal's office."

Jack looked at the paper.

Tardy Slip
November 4, 1970
from: Anderson
re: John B. Oliver
time in: 8:32 a.m.
unexcused
also engaged in profanity in class

All this just for the word "ass"? he thought to himself. *How times have changed!*

He folded the slip and placed it in his pocket next to Francis' paper, which he realized he needed once again to find his first period class. "Science, Kefauver, room two-twenty-three," he recited from the pencil-marked document. Now that he understood the layout of the even-odd halls, it was easy to find the right class.

As the only student in sight still wearing a backpack, Jack felt like a hunchback as he trudged along. He thought his seventh grade science teacher may have been one *Miss* Kefauver, and this was confirmed when he stepped into room 223. The bright-eyed, freckled redhead looked surprisingly familiar as she sat at her desk, sorting through papers. The room was familiar as well: instead of student desks, there were workstations with black Formica counter tops and scrub sinks; and gas hook-ups for Bunsen burners. Four students could sit at each workstation, and once again Jack had no idea where his correct seat was, so it was a very welcome sound when Paul and Hafeez both called his name and beckoned him over to their station.

"Jackie! Come on in, man!" Paul laughed.

Jack made his way there and sat down with the plump white kid and the skinny Pakistani with Coke bottle glasses. Both of them wore button down shirts, and to Jack, seemed to be 'classic' nerds, just like himself.

"What's with the backpack?" Hafeez asked.

"Um… forgot my locker combination," Jack replied.

"Dummy! Well anyway, it looks like you lose!"

Paul chimed in: "You'll have to pay up today!"

Not only was Jack clueless as to what they were talking about, he could barely remember who they were. Their names popped into his head, but that was all. "Refresh my memory," he began, "pay what?"

"Oh, I see you've developed amnesia!" Paul said.

"Isn't that convenient," Hafeez chided, "but sorry, Pittsburgh kicked their ass!"

Okay, it had something to do with sports. Jack would have to fake his way through. Which Pittsburgh team was this about, who did they beat, and why did Jack have to "pay up" on account of it? And for that matter, why did Hafeez just get away with saying "ass" in class when Jack had gotten in trouble over the same thing five minutes earlier?

"I guess Cincinnati's only golden when it comes to baseball," Paul said.

Now Jack had something to work with. In another very rapid train of thought, he remembered that the Cincinnati Reds had faced the local favorite Baltimore Orioles in the 1970 World Series, hence the "golden" comment. But since Paul had just ruled out baseball, they were probably talking about football. "Pittsburgh" therefore referred to the Steelers, who had likely beaten the Cincinnati Bengals, and since this conversation had waited until Wednesday to happen, the game must have been Monday night. *Damn, I'm good!* he thought to himself. Then he took a bit of a risk and said, "Don't make fun of Cincinnati. Monday nights are tough games to play!" It was a dicey statement, considering he'd only surmised it all. Was there even such a thing as *Monday Night Football* in 1970?

"Twenty-one to ten," Hafeez, replied, "and it was a great game! Too bad for you though, man."

Whew! Apparently, *Monday Night Football* had in fact aired that week, though Jack would never admit he'd been watching *The Carol Burnett Show* instead. Rather, he pressed on: "If only Johnny Bench played football instead of baseball, they would have won!"

The three boys laughed.

Jack was a little concerned about the "pay up" part of this exchange, but before he had a chance to explore it, Miss Kefauver took charge of her class.

"Okay people," she began, "you've all had a day off, now let's get our minds back on science. Remember last time we learned the classifications of living things. Without looking in the book, who can name them?"

Hafeez' hand went up immediately and Miss Kefauver called on him.

"Kingdom, phylum, class, order, family, genus, species," he said without hesitating.

From the other side of the room a smart-alecky-sounding boy remarked: "I think he *is* the genius of the species!"

The class laughed.

"Okay, that's enough!" Miss Kefauver shouted, mostly getting their attention back. "So, what do these classifications mean? For example what is 'kingdom Protista,' anyone?"

A young-looking girl with frizzy black hair raised her hand.

"Yes, Laura?"

"Mushrooms?" Laura responded.

"No, that would be 'kingdom Fungi.' Nice try, though. Come on, 'Protista,' anyone?"

Hafeez raised his hand again.

"Yes, Hafeez?"

"One-celled organisms," he said.

"Correct. So, the four kingdoms again are," she began to write on the blackboard as she listed them, "Protista, Fungi, Plantae and Animalia."

Jack recalled having helped his kids with their science homework, and drilling them on five kingdoms. *Only four kingdoms,* he thought, *and you can't say "ass" either. It's a different world!*

Another boy's hand went up, and Miss Kefauver called on him.

"Yes, Larry?"

"Why isn't a fungus considered a plant?" he asked.

Miss Kefauver's responses were so organized they almost seemed scripted. "In order to be defined as a plant, an organism must perform what process?" she motioned to the entire class.

Half of them simultaneously answered, "Photosynthesis."

"Correct," she said, "and fungi get all of their nourishment from a host, not from the sun. This is why they can grow in dark areas where plants would normally die…"

As Miss Kefauver continued to explain concepts and kingdoms, Jack's wandering eyes fell on Larry, the curly brown-haired, spectacled boy who asked the fungus question. His heart skipped a half-beat when he realized who it was: this was Larry *Berger*. Sometime during this school year, he would be killed in a car accident. Though Larry had only been a casual 'at school' friend, Jack still felt a real sense of grief when he heard about the collision. It was the first time Jack lost someone his own age, and it hammered home the idea that life is finite, even for young boys. By age fifty-two, Jack had seen enough death to have gotten quite used to it. His high school reunions grew smaller as the years went on, and the "lost classmates" list got bigger. But this was only the seventh grade, and for just a moment, Jack entertained the thought of warning Larry. The previous day he'd come up with lots of reasons not to meddle with the future, but they all pertained to things like politics and celebrities and epic disasters. This was different; this was about his schoolmate Larry. Well actually, maybe it wasn't. It was really about what Larry's death represented: Jack's first acknowledgement of his own mortality. When Dick West's father Elmer passed away, he was an old man, and that somehow made it okay. Both of Jack's grandfathers had died when he was too young to remember them, so he never actually experienced their 'loss;' they were just part of the past. But when he heard over the school PA system that fellow student Larry Berger had been killed the previous day, it was impossible not to ask himself: *Why Larry and not me?* And Jack grew up a little bit.

"…so what does it say about the study of taxonomy, that we used to identify only two or three different kingdoms, but now we have four?" Miss Kefauver's voice cut through Jack's morose little daydream and brought him halfway back into the room.

Forgetting the specifics of when and where he was, he absent-mindedly raised a hand and was acknowledged by the freckled teacher.

"Yes, Jack?"

"I think biological classification is an evolutionary process, and with ongoing research, the model is always subject to change. I wouldn't be surprised to see five kingdoms identified in the near future." Before Jack had even finished speaking, he recognized his blunder. *Uh-oh! Way too articulate!* he thought.

The class was silent. Miss Kefauver looked slightly confused, as if she were deciding whether Jack was serious. Even Hafeez, the obvious class egghead, just stared in disbelief.

The brief tension was finally broken by a muffled voice coming from one of the workstations in the back: "Brain fag!"

Most of the class laughed.

Rather than try to identify the profane student, Miss Kefauver seized the moment and chimed in over the trailing laughter with, "Thank you, Jack!" She then huffed a deep breath and said, "So, let's look at how we would classify a human being." She began to write on the board again as she spoke. "Kingdom: Animalia; phylum: Chordata; class: Mammalia; order: Primate..."

...and that was that.

Jack had a curious and interesting time the rest of the morning. "Industrial Farts" proved to be more of a challenge than he had expected. As it turned out, he was in mid-project on his infamous Snoopy plaque, and getting right-angled edges was a real job. All he had to work with was a file, and his undeveloped muscles only allowed a few strokes before he had to stop and rest. It was slow going, and now he remembered why the project had turned out the way it did. After so much filing with very little improvement, young Jack had decided to take the 'C' to save his arms.

He grew restless throughout third period geography, and by the time the bell rang for fourth period lunch he'd worked up an appetite. With his arm muscles still aching, he proceeded to the cafeteria, fingering the coins in his pocket. Sixty cents: in 1970 that would buy a school lunch complete with dessert!

He headed straight for the lunch line, while other kids with brown bags went right to the 'best' tables to save seats for their friends. Getting there first was an obvious advantage of packing a lunch; though with Jack it wouldn't have mattered. He wasn't popular enough to sit at the 'best' tables anyway. Revisiting that reality now, he wondered why it had never mattered to him, and to his credit, he realized that it still didn't.

As he stood in the slow-moving line, enjoying the Chef Boyardee-like aromas wafting from the kitchen, he was startled to feel a warm hand pinching his shoulder. Paul or Hafeez must have been trying to administer the Vulcan death grip.

"Is that all you got?" Jack said snidely as he wheeled around.

He found himself looking into a familiar face that didn't belong to either of them. Instead it was a big kid; probably half a foot taller than Jack, stocky and tow-headed, with a dirty knit shirt. Jack couldn't remember this boy's name, only that he was a bully who tormented him throughout the seventh grade. Now he seemed more like a (very big) little kid than a threat.

"Give me some money," the bigger boy said.

"Screw you!" Jack surprised himself; this is something he would never have said to a bully. But things were different now.

"Give me some money or I'll kill you!" the kid said, his stale breath hitting Jack's face.

"Get off me, or you're in a lot of trouble!" Jack said loudly. A few other kids looked over to see what was going on. Jack felt like the proverbial Chihuahua standing up to a German Shepherd, showing no concern for their difference in size.

The bully looked a little confused, and tried to ramp up his intimidation. He grabbed Jack's arm. "I said give me some money you little pussy!"

"And I said leave me alone or you're in a lot of trouble, you ignorant moron! And I *mean* it!" Jack felt no fear.

"What are you gonna do? Tell the teacher?" The bully feigned a laugh and began to twist Jack's arm.

"Yup," Jack grimaced, "but that's only for starters. Believe me, you'll be in more trouble than I'm worth."

At that moment, the assistant principal, who was also the fourth period "cafeteria Nazi," began walking toward the confrontation.

Jack looked over at him, then back at the bully. "You ready for some *real* trouble?" he challenged.

This bully apparently wasn't used to being bullied; he immediately let go of Jack's arm and awkwardly moved away.

Jack turned back towards the kitchen, shaking his arms and shrugging his shoulders to work out the bully-kinks. His backpack thumped between his shoulder blades.

The assistant principal lost interest when he saw that the episode had apparently ended peacefully.

Jack bought his lunch of Salisbury steak, mashed potatoes and corn, as well as a piece of chocolate cake and a small container of chocolate milk. Carrying a baby-blue molded-melamine lunch tray, he went out in search of a seat, and found himself adrift in a sea of strange faces. *Where to sit? Hmm...* he pondered. Did he have a table of friends where he normally ate lunch?

What a welcome sound it was to hear the chiding voices of Paul and Hafeez: "Over here, Jackie! Time to pay up!"

Were those two ever apart? Even with the threat of an unknown debt due, he was glad to join them.

Jack had no sooner set his tray on the table when Paul confiscated the piece of cake and plopped it down on a napkin.

"What are you doing?" Jack sputtered. He really wanted that cake!

Hafeez took a little plastic knife and cut the cake in half. Then he and Paul each took a portion and "clinked" them together as if they were toasting with champagne.

"To the Pittsburgh Steelers," Paul said.

"Hear, hear!" Hafeez replied.

Jack whined at them both: "Hey, that's my cake! I *need* that sugar!"

"Ask the Bengals for another piece, man," Paul teased with his mouth full, "this is their fault!"

So that was it. Jack had to pay up with his dessert at lunch. *Oh well,* he thought, *it could have been worse.*

The three boys talked and laughed and acted nerdy throughout the period. Jack was able to infer that his two friends didn't have any particular interest in pro sports; it was just a fun fluke that they had bet on this particular game. In fact, it was largely Jack's own doing: since the Ohio baseball team made it to the series, he foolishly assumed that Cincinnati's *football* team would be just as good. The price of his mistake was a piece of chocolate cake with white icing.

When Jack went to return his empty tray he began to recognize more people around him. A few of their names came to mind, but mostly it was just a visual jog of the memory. He once had a thin soft-cover yearbook for seventh grade, and he used it to identify people by finding their pictures. Unfortunately, it was too early in the year for that handy resource, so these would have to remain anonymous familiar faces.

After lunch, he had a very unremarkable English class where Mrs. Lewis randomly handpicked students to read passages from *The Cay*. It was a little embarrassing to hear young, mostly white kids trying to speak in the character Timothy's Caribbean dialect as it was written in the text. Jack knew that in the future society of political correctness, even classic books like *Huckleberry Finn* would be effectively banned from public schools for their allegedly racist portrayals; so he was surprised when one of his kids brought home *The Cay* as a reading assignment. The language must have somehow slipped by the P.C. censors.

The next period was phys. ed.; always the bane of Jack's young life. "Gym" as it was more commonly called, was the one class that was supposed to "separate the men from the boys." If there had actually been any men in the class it might have been different; but in Jack's experience, even the gym teachers were often just overgrown children. He'd once overheard Coach Riddell say "I think Oliver's one of those guys that hates gym," and there was certainly some truth to the allegation. After all, why would any clumsy, flat-footed kid with a generally non-competitive nature, enjoy a class where the bullies were in charge? And when their actions were condoned by the instructor's purposely-turned head, it was a battle that was lost from the beginning. Of course at home Jack enjoyed playing baseball with his friends, but there he got to pick his playmates. At school, kids his size pretty much became punching bags for the bigger, meaner boys who were the "teacher's pets" of the even bigger, even meaner gym coaches. Or at least that's how it had seemed in the seventh grade. Jack hoped he might be able to see things more objectively today.

The class started out problematically; Jack needed to put on his gym uniform, which was in a locker he couldn't identify, sealed with a lock he didn't know the combination to. He decided to take his dilemma right to the top and ask Mr. Riddell for help. Clunking along with his backpack, he approached the tall mesomorph who was standing in the gym, watching some of his pets shoot baskets.

"Mr. Riddell?" Jack was sheepish.

"What's the problem, Oliver?"

"I think I've forgotten which locker is mine, and I can't remember my combination either."

Mr. Riddell looked at Jack in total disbelief. "Jesus H. Christmas! That's an excuse if I ever heard one!"

"No sir," Jack answered, "I really can't remember."

Mr. Riddell scolded back: "You're not one of those guys that hates gym, are you?" Hey, there was that familiar phrase again! Maybe he just liked saying it.

"Don't you have the combinations written down someplace?" Jack asked.

Mr. Riddell looked perturbed, but turned toward his office. "Follow me," he said with some disgust.

Jack had a bit of trouble keeping pace with the much larger man, but made his way into the office where Mr. Riddell was unlocking a file cabinet with one of several keys he wore around his neck along with a metal whistle. He pulled out a file folder and looked inside guardedly, as if Jack might try to get a glimpse of someone else's combination.

Jack chuckled to himself, *Yeah, like I'd want to steal somebody else's dirty gym uniform!*

Mr. Riddell had always seemed so menacing before, but now as Jack watched him make a big deal out of a little situation, he began to feel rather sorry for the man. This was all he had! There was no ring on his hand and no family picture on his desk. The only items on display were his personal high school trophies, dated 1952 and 1953. It was obvious that the most important thing in his life was winning at sports.

He's a sad, pathetic person, Jack thought.

"Okay, Oliver. Your locker is number one-fourteen..."

Oh great, Jack thought, *there's number one-fourteen again!*

"...and your combination is 'thirty-two, twenty, twelve;' sound familiar?"

"I think so," Jack said. He mentally juggled the numbers to help himself remember them: *The first number minus the last number equals the middle number. Wow, that's a great combination!*

"It's gonna take a better excuse than that to get out of *my* class, Oliver," Mr. Riddell said with a condescending wink.

Jack certainly wasn't trying to get out of class, and was a bit insulted by the insinuation. He considered coming back with some eloquent response to put this educational thug in his place, but he thought better of it. If it was so important for him to feel like a big man, who was Jack to deny him that? Also, Mr. Riddell would soon be writing a grade on Jack's report card!

"Thank you sir," Jack said politely, and walked toward the locker room. Once he'd found locker number 114, he retrieved Francis' paper and wrote the combination just underneath the school schedule he'd copied down previously.

The boys in gym would normally have been playing football that day, but because of the heavy rain they stayed inside and organized into haphazard teams for basketball. Jack only got knocked on his behind four or five times, so he considered it a pretty good class. Mr. Riddell was in rare form, throwing out taunts like: "C'mon, men, you gotta be tougher than that! Put a little effort into it!" and other such words of "encouragement." Now Jack remembered why he'd always thought athletics was so pointless: it was all in the presentation.

Seventh period math was a breeze, and when Jack walked out of the school building at 3:30, he was actually happy to see that it was still raining: it meant he had a ride home.

Marie, who didn't teach piano on Wednesdays, picked him up in the Buick and made the triumphant announcement that Charlie Blair had been reelected to his County Council seat, so their work the previous day had not been in vain.

Upon their arrival home, Jack headed straight for the kitchen and grabbed several cookies and a glass of milk, and sat down to watch the last half of *Eighth Man*. His head was spinning from his day at school, and he had a resurrected respect for the tough agenda of the junior high school student. He fell asleep on the couch.

CHAPTER SEVEN

JOSEPH WAS dying. He'd beaten cancer ten years earlier, and often said that every day beyond that was a gift. Now it was back, and he lay half-coherent in a rented hospital bed, with a catheter bag hanging at his side. Jack tried to relax on the king bed that was a familiar fixture in his father's room, but relaxation was difficult, and sleep was out of the question, even at two a.m. The seventy-five-year-old man kept asking to use the toilet, and Jack kept reminding him that he had a bag attached and could just go.

At this point Joseph was really too weak to walk, and it wouldn't have been a good idea to get him up out of bed. The family was taking turns staying with him: Violet had been there the night before and Jack's stepsister was on the schedule as well. Tonight it was Jack's shift. As he lay fully-dressed on top of the bedspread, his mind wandered to many different places, and he thought about the eclectic life his dad had lived.

Joseph had a strict upbringing; his father was an old-line country preacher with five other sons and no daughters. For Joseph with his engineer's mind, it was not the most nurturing of environments: he endured much parental derision for being different. It took many years and the death of both parents before any of the brothers were able to articulate the unspoken tragedy of their early lives: The Church came first, they came last. It seemed backwards somehow; church was supposed to help you live your life, it wasn't supposed to *be* your life. But nevertheless, that's how the cards fell for the Oliver boys. And Joseph felt like the joker in the deck. Though he held his Methodist tradition dear, his life couldn't be all about religion. He saw far beyond the literal borders of the Bible, and wasn't afraid to cross over into those territories. He could easily ask controversial questions and entertain unpopular answers, so long as they were reasonable.

It was effortless for Joseph to accomplish difficult tasks like building, improving and repairing everything in sight. He was a math whiz and a former Marine. He put himself through college and became an engineer and physicist. He worked for NASA designing rockets. He also married Marie and became a father, which was the only hard job he ever had.

"What do engineers use for birth control?" Marie used to tease. The answer: "Their personalities!"

Of course, no joke is funny unless there is some truth in it, and to Jack, that one bordered on hilarious. And tragic. As much as everyone in the family loved one another, it wasn't shown in a typical way. Hugs and kisses were uncomfortable, foreign gestures. The phrase "I love you" was equally awkward, and the balance of parental responsibility was skewed: there was one provider and one nurturer, and their roles didn't intersect.

Once Jeannie and Jack were both married and out of the house, their parents would divorce and set out in different directions. It was surprising to see how quickly Joseph and Marie began to enjoy rich, full lives after splitting up. They both turned out to be strong, independent individuals who, out of necessity, had worked within set parameters during their thirty years together. And now, twenty-five more years had passed, and Joseph's part of the adventure was coming to a close.

"I need to have a bowel movement," Joseph said unabashedly. There was no need for etiquette or modesty during the death process. Jack had once heard the same thing about the birth process from a Lamaze instructor, and was amused by the paradox. Maybe all of life ought to be that way.

"Are you sure you have to go?" he responded. "Last time it was a false alarm."

"Help me to the bathroom," Joseph demanded groggily.

In retrospect, Jack wondered why he ever let his father talk him into it, but he got up to help him into the adjacent bath. The two intertwined men looked like a snail and its shell as they moved ever-so-slowly, but they eventually got Joseph onto the toilet. After a few minutes without success, Jack convinced his disoriented patient to return to bed. He stood Joseph back up, helping to support him with one arm and holding up the catheter bag with the other. That was when Joseph collapsed. All his energy had been sapped getting to the bathroom, and none was left for the return trip. Jack felt his own knees buckling from the weight of his 200-pound father, as they both came down on the cold tile floor. He managed to break Joseph's fall and still keep the bag intact.

Once he got his breath and his bearings back, Jack stood up to assess the situation. There was his dad, the vital, invincible Renaissance man, lying in an exhausted heap. His boxers were rumpled and his T-shirt was stained, and he heaved to catch his breath. Meanwhile, Jack was forty-something, overweight and out of shape. He tried to help Joseph get back up, but it was no use; he was too heavy and too tired to move.

Jack had to go into 'logical mode' and separate himself from the emotion of the situation in order to think it through. This couldn't be his dad lying there; it had to be some generic old man who needed help. Jack had often thought he would be a good emergency worker, pulling injured people out of car wrecks and such. Blood and death didn't bother him, and he could keep a cool head during a crisis. But now there was no blood, no ambulance crew, and the "crisis" was merely a man who was on the floor when he should have been in a bed. Jack was flummoxed by the simplicity of the dilemma. He wasn't strong enough to lift Joseph, and there was no one else around to help. Jack's stepmother was asleep in the next bedroom, but she was nearly eighty, and somewhat frail. She'd already been through so much with this cancer; he didn't want her to lose even more sleep. Jack wasn't used to not having a solution, and even considered calling 911, though that seemed extreme.

"Grab my ankles," Joseph said, in between deep breaths.

"Huh?" Jack responded, surprised to hear his father sounding lucid.

"Get me turned around on my back and pull me by the ankles over to the bed." Joseph apparently had it figured out.

"Uh… okay," Jack said, "you'll have to hold the bag."

"I can't," Joseph answered, "put it on my stomach."

Jack did so, and dragged his dad from the bathroom into the bedroom. As they crossed over from the tile to the hardwood floor, it registered briefly in both of their minds that there was no carpet to create extra friction. That was good. Joseph the physicist probably even took it one step further, taking into account his body weight and the texture of his clothes vs. the floor.

"Now help me get on my knees, facing the bed," he said.

It took some doing, but Jack managed to rearrange this hulking rag doll of a man limb-by-limb until he lay in the proper position. "Okay, let's pull you up!" he said hopefully, taking his father's hands.

"I can't, you'll have to do it." There was an unspoken understanding that Joseph needed to save every bit of his strength for the last step.

As Jack pulled his father upright, both men groaned: Jack with determination and Joseph with pain. With a bit more arranging, the 'generic old man' finally ended up on his knees with the front part of his body resting on the hospital bed.

"Now help me the rest of the way," Joseph said, breathing deeply.

Jack held one of his dad's legs firmly and they both worked together to roll him into bed. The old man went limp as he landed on his back, and it was up to Jack to arrange his limbs, untangle the catheter bag, and replace the covers. Joseph's final engineering feat was a success, and he pulled it off as if he had been building a bridge or designing a rocket.

"Wow, that was a tough job," Jack said, out of breath.

"Yeah, that was awful," Joseph replied, and immediately fell asleep.

CR♦♦ℰℭ

Jack awoke suddenly. He'd become re-accustomed to the sound of the front door in the two days he'd been back, but this time it was a little louder and more forceful. It was his dad. Joseph carried a slender brown Samsonite suitcase and made his way immediately to the back of the house.

"Marie?" he called out, not even noticing his son was there.

The quick glimpse Jack got of his father was startling: this wasn't the old man he'd just seen in his sleep. Joseph stood tall, his hair was dark and full, and his gait revealed an inner drive. Someone in the Arts might call it the "creative urge," and an athlete might liken it to "St. Elmo's fire." But for a Renaissance Man, the innate desire to plan, build, repair and improve was so encompassing, it was hard to define it. In fact, something as generic as "inner drive" really didn't quite do it. "DNA" was probably better, since it was built into Joseph's very being. Even when he was dying, the engineer part of him had surfaced above all else. And here he was, true to form, barely in the door from a business trip and already on another mission.

"Marie?" he called once again.

"Are you home?" she replied, her voice coming from beyond the basement stairs.

That seemed like a silly response; of course he was home. But maybe Jack was just being his usual self: a bit too literal.

Joseph emerged from the back bedroom, minus the suitcase, and headed downstairs. He still wore his suit pants and a white shirt with a tie. "I know what we should do with the house!" He seemed excited.

Jack didn't know exactly how long his dad had been gone, but it was at least a couple of days. He thought it might have been nice for his mom to hear: *Hi honey, good to see you*, or words to that effect, before diving right into "what to do with the house." But that was Joseph, and though Jack hated to admit it, he could relate. Father and son had both eventually learned what was expected of them socially, and they managed to retrain themselves to fit.

Throughout his life, Jack had come to recognize two basic types of people; not divided by race or sex or class, or any other word that might be followed by "-ism." Instead, he identified "thinkers" and "feelers;" or perhaps more pointedly, those who acted logically and those who didn't. And though everyone seemed to be some mixture of the two, there was always one dominant trait that ultimately defined each person.

In general, the world seemed to be made up largely of feelers who saw themselves as the normal ones. To them, a thinker could seem cold or rude, or in a worst-case scenario, even diagnosable. That is, unless he learned to adapt and behave more like them. Jack had once heard about a jury who didn't believe a defendant's testimony because he "didn't show enough emotion on the witness stand." This seemed outrageous; maybe the witness just wasn't an emotional person! And yet that criterion, rather than the facts of the case, determined the outcome. Jack imagined an attorney speaking to a judge: *Your Honor, my client does not believe he can receive a fair trial with an all-feeling jury.* Perhaps "think-ism" should be added to the list of ways to discriminate.

Accordingly, Mr. and Mrs. Oliver seemed to live out those extremes, almost like two people who spoke different languages, but still managed to communicate through cues and gestures. Not that Marie was a total feeler; in fact, she had a very defined thinking side, which may have been one reason she and Joseph clashed so often. She would love to have had a co-nurturer in her husband, but Joseph wouldn't develop that skill for many more years. In the mean time, Marie had to compensate by suppressing her own logical side, and assuming the full-time role of caregiver. And so on this particular afternoon, it was one "thinker" and one "feeler" (with latent thinking tendencies) who emerged from the basement, embroiled in a head-butting discussion.

"That's so much work!" Marie said, carrying hangers of freshly-ironed shirts.

"It's work for *me*," Joseph answered, "*you'll* get a nicer house out of it!"

"Knocking out walls? It'll be a wreck!"

"Aw, Marie, don't start! You don't know what you're talking about. I can put up plastic and contain it."

"And how can we *afford* it?"

"We'll take out a loan. And it will add value to the house. It'll be worth it."

"Well, you're kind of springing this on me. Can't we talk it over later tonight?"

"I already sketched out plans I can show you…"

Jack knew exactly what was going on and how it would turn out. The big house addition was pretty much a done deal as far as his dad was concerned, and it would turn out to be a very good thing. But what Joseph didn't seem to 'get' was that his visionary mind moved perhaps a little too swiftly. His poor wife was putting up the only defense she could: asking for a little time to get used to the idea. After twenty years with Joseph she knew the drill: he planned things, he did them, and resistance was futile. Even the things that Joseph intended as gifts for Marie were sometimes construed as force-fed projects. Not that she didn't appreciate the idea of a new kitchen and a large master bedroom with a private bath and a pretty picture window; but she would like to have been included in the planning. Her reluctance was then perceived as ungratefulness, and the gap between the "thinker" and the "feeler" widened.

And Jack, who'd been happily oblivious the first time around, could now see both sides. He saw his dad's practical perspective because he'd received a full helping of engineer's genes himself. He also saw his mom's more organic point of view because over time he'd learned how. And in exercising those emotional muscles, he developed a genuine feeling side of his own.

"See what I mean?" Marie cried. "You've already got *plans* sketched out, and I'm just hearing about any of this for the first time!"

"That's why I'm trying to talk to you about it." Joseph said.

"I wish you *would've* talked to me about it! Now you're just throwing it at me. Why do you always do things this way?"

"For heaven's sake, Marie! You act like I'm some villain! Why can't you just listen?"

As the all-too-familiar argument continued, Jack automatically tuned it out and began to think about his own quest: to change one thing about his life. When he was talking to Francis he was so sure coming back was the thing to do, but so far he'd just been wandering blindly for two days, trying to identify random opportunities. He kept wondering if some little thing he did might be 'the one' that would send him back where he belonged. Up until now he hadn't really done anything differently other than getting in trouble at school and standing up to a bully, and neither of those could have been 'it' because he was still here. Oh, and he helped Candidate Charlie Blair get elected, but that probably would have happened anyway. But now as he listened to his parents fight, he thought he might finally see an answer. *Should they have stayed together,* he wondered, *and can I do anything to make that happen?* This was a much more practical goal than saving Nixon from Watergate; this was something Jack might actually be able to pull off! He'd seen how his father eventually developed a feeling side, so he knew the capacity was there. If only there was a way to accelerate the process...

But immediately, he had to stop and look at reality. After all, what would Jack's life be like if he were still married to his first or his second wife, and why was it fair for him to hold his parents to a different standard? He'd seen how Joseph ultimately changed for the better because he was allowed to fail. A relationship was the one thing he couldn't fix by thinking it through, and he was wise enough to learn from that. Things also got better for Marie once she was able to exercise her independent, thinking side again. Jack had to accept that his parents had new lives waiting for them, and nothing would have turned out the same if they hadn't seized the opportunity. What a way of looking at it-- the 'opportunity' to get a divorce!

He sighed and perched his young body on the couch, listening quietly while they traded volleys:

"I have to start supper. I really can't deal with this right now," Marie said.

"Prices are only going to go up. We can't sit on this very long," Joseph replied with the skill of a car salesman.

"What do you mean 'we'? It seems like you've already made all the decisions!"

"Oh, stop it! The whole reason I want to talk to you is to get your opinion!"

"Well okay, my opinion is that we shouldn't knock down the walls in our house!"

"You just can't envision what it will look like. Let me show you this..." Joseph followed her to the kitchen and continued to read his verdict, all the while believing he was just arguing his case.

Marie began to fix supper.

In between the sounds of the can opener, the refrigerator door and various pots and pans clanging, Jack could hear the occasional shots his mom and dad fired at each other. It really didn't matter whose voice he heard at any given moment; it was the words themselves that were important. Each one had a life of its own. "Why - stop - can't - selfish - money - ungrateful;" they were all jumbled together in an endless amalgamation of inflections and punctuations. Jack had forgotten just how well his parents could argue.

After several minutes Joseph walked slowly out of the kitchen into the living room. He breathed a sigh of disgust and said, "Women!" Then he noticed Jack for the first time. "Hey, Jack! How's my favorite boy?"

Jack wasn't sure how to respond. Having witnessed the foregoing argument, a normal son would have been confused by his father's quick change of demeanor, and probably resentful of having been ignored up until then. Jack however, had grown up with this kind of odd behavior being the norm. He just had to try and remember how he might have responded when he was twelve, before he developed a more acute social awareness.

Finally he decided on a reply: "Uh, I'm pretty good." That seemed safely non-committal.

"I want to build a nice big family room for you kids!" Joseph said.

"With a fireplace?" Jack asked.

Joseph was silent for a few seconds as he processed the thought. "Hmm... why not? I could do that!"

Of course Jack knew that the fireplace was eventually going to be part of his father's plan anyway, but this was an amusing means of taking credit for the idea. "Yeah, it could go on the back wall," he said. Jack was testing his dad here: he'd deliberately located the fireplace on the wrong wall just to see what would happen, and was stunned by the engineer's quick analysis.

"That would keep us from putting in a window to the back yard. The side wall would be better."

"Oh yeah, you're right. And I guess you'll build a split-foyer at the new back door?" Jack knew he might be pushing it, but he couldn't resist. "And the kitchen could have a walk-in pantry at the top of the stairs."

His dad looked at him strangely; much like Miss Kefauver had done following his little classroom pontification earlier that day. "Yeah, that's kind of what I had in mind," he said tentatively, "*how* old are you again?"

"I'll be thirteen next month!" Jack answered, knowing it wasn't a serious question. But when he was twelve he would have taken it literally, so he played the part.

Joseph sat in the armchair and grabbed the day's untouched newspaper.

Jack noticed the headline:

Excellent Turnout In General Election.

The front page was also peppered with smaller election-related story lines like *Beall defeats Tydings, Brock unseats Gore* and others. He didn't see anything about Charlie Blair, but since that was a local race, he guessed it would be elsewhere in Section 'A'. As his father opened the paper to read the inside, Jack saw a back page full of wedding announcements, and a big ad for free bars of Jergens Soap with a gasoline fill-up. He kept expecting his dad to continue the conversation about the house addition, but it was apparently over. After observing a few silent minutes of page turning, Jack rose and headed off to the kitchen.

Marie had arranged a cut-up chicken on a cookie sheet, and was sprinkling paprika and lemon juice on it. There was a box of instant mashed potatoes out on the counter next to a can of carrots. She seemed like there was a cloud over her head, and Jack wanted to try and lighten the mood.

He asked the stupidest question he could think of: "What's for supper?"

Marie's answer was automatic: "Baked chicken." Her mind was elsewhere.

"Can I help with anything?" Jack asked.

"Sorry honey, it won't be ready for forty minutes."

Hmm... that didn't answer the question. She obviously wasn't listening, and Jack knew why. "I think a house addition is a good idea, Mom."

She sighed as she slipped the cookie sheet into the oven. "So, I guess you heard all that."

"I heard enough of it," he answered.

"I think it would be good too, Jackie, and I know your dad thinks I don't trust what he says, but he can be like a charging bull sometimes."

"And you just want to run for cover until he slows down a little?"

Marie looked at her son curiously. "Yes, that's exactly it!"

"I think he's a lot like me, Mom. We mean well, but there are... I dunno; filters that keep us from feeling things the way other people do."

"You think you're that way, Jackie?"

"Oh, absolutely!" Suddenly Jack wondered if he was coming across a little too 'adult' for his physical age. He tried to adjust: "I mean, um..." but he'd already said too much. There was no way to retract his misplaced sagacity.

"Well," Marie interrupted, "you're in here talking to me now and your father's not. I don't think that's being very much like him."

Good, he didn't need a way out. Either his mother was so preoccupied that she didn't really pay attention to his sudden insightfulness, or he was just more mature at twelve than he remembered, and this was normal. To be safe, he slipped back into teen-speak. "He's just trying to... well you know, it's just how he is!"

"Yes, I do know. And of course he's not this way all the time."

Marie was trying to convince her son that maybe his dad wasn't so unfeeling after all, but he recognized that she was really trying to convince herself:

"Because, Jack, I've seen another side. You know, when your grandfather Oliver died and they played his favorite hymn at the funeral, your father cried."

"Yeah, you told me that." Jack deliberately refrained from adding any editorial comments; he feared that his interference could cause some change in the timeline of his parents' separation. He didn't want to alter the inevitable, especially when it had turned out for the best. This was not the time for his mother to know the extra bit of information that Jack knew: *why* his father had cried...

CR♦♦ൠ

Joseph took a bigger-than-normal sip of his Manhattan. He'd only ever been an occasional social drinker, but the beverage now seemed to be more of a painkiller than anything else. He was losing to the cancer, and nearing the day when he wouldn't be able to leave the house anymore. As he and Jack sat across from each other at a local pub, waiting for the last meal they would eat out together, the good-byes of two engineers began to progress quite logically.

"So, do you think it'll be a problem for you to plan the music for my service?" Joseph asked matter-of-factly.

"No, not at all," Jack replied. "I think I know just how you want it."

They couldn't discuss this topic in Joseph's house; it was too upsetting to his wife. Earlier in the week Joseph had even driven himself to the funeral home to make and pay for his own arrangements so that the family wouldn't have to do it.

"Other than the preacher, I just want you and your sister to speak. Keep it small and simple. And for the songs: 'Amazing Grace,' 'Blessed Assurance' and 'Does Jesus Care.'"

"I thought you might want 'A Mighty Fortress Is Our God.'"

"No, not for me. That was my father's favorite."

"I know. Mom always told the story of how you cried when they played it at his funeral."

Joseph sat back and sighed. "Those were tears of *relief*, Jack."

"Really… relief? Why?"

"My nemesis was finally gone."

"Well then, I guess I won't be crying at your funeral." Jack quaffed his beer, thinking about how he and his father hadn't really started talking until the past few months. He felt no resentment for the lifetime without a typical father/son relationship. He was simply grateful for what had finally come to be. Engineers are very outcome-oriented.

A few weeks later, Jack walked into his living room and found Joseph sitting contentedly in a wooden rocking chair. Even though his father had died the previous Monday morning, Jack didn't find it unusual that he was now here in the house, and thus knew it must be a dream. He didn't remember laying down to sleep, so maybe this was one of those waking dreams that people have when someone close has just died. The final exchange between the two men was brief:

"Do you believe in ghosts?" Joseph asked, maybe half-kidding.

"Define 'ghost,'" Jack challenged.

Joseph pointed at himself: "Me!"

"Yes, I believe in you," Jack said.

"That's all I wanted to know!" Joseph said slyly, and disappeared.

CHAPTER EIGHT

HOMEROOM STARTED at 8:45 and Jack was determined to be on time today. He tried to remember why he'd politely declined when Marie offered to drive him to school; something about wanting to be alone and explore his old neighborhood in the light of day. Now that he and his backpack had been afoot for twenty minutes and were little more than halfway there, the decision appeared to have been a rash one.

His shoes were wearing out and a little uncomfortable. He also didn't remember exactly what the best foot-route was; that is, the one that only took half an hour. It likely involved cutting through people's back yards and hopping fences. Jack just began to follow other kids who were out walking, figuring they knew where they were going. These were undoubtedly the same kids who had joined the procession to school in raincoats the previous day. Now Jack was one of them, voluntarily sharing in the plight of those he had seen as less fortunate because they didn't have rides.

It was a little bit chilly, and he could see his breath in front of him. Every time he exhaled, the little puffs of smoky humidity reminded him of the White Room and his short meeting with his great-great-grandfather, which he had again dreamed about the night before.

As he plodded down Tenbrook Street, he encountered a small brown and white dog whose barking seemed very familiar. The innocuous little pooch was tied to a stake in its front yard, struggling against the rope and yapping as if Jack were a dangerous invader, or even worse, a mailman. He knew this dog! Jack passed the yard regularly, and always noted the resemblance to Buster Brown's dog, Tige. Jack loved old comic strips. His favorite one in the newspapers was *Mutt and Jeff*, largely because of its old-style drawings and corny jokes. But *Buster Brown* was even older, and even more classic. When Jack occasionally ran across a vintage strip reprinted in a book or a magazine, he pored over it, examining each frame with interest. As he walked along, now thinking about old comic strips, he remembered that Buster Brown was also the mascot for a shoe store. His thoughts came full-circle, and again he focused on his worn shoes, and the fact that his feet were even more uncomfortable than they'd been just a minute ago.

He looked down at the worn asphalt as he walked, and for a few seconds, didn't pay attention to what was in front of him. A hard bump startled Jack as he found himself up against an obstacle that had moved into his path.

"Give me some money!" a voice said.

Jack looked up to see the lunchroom bully. For some reason he now remembered this kid's name. "Luther Howell! That's it!" he said triumphantly.

Luther seemed annoyed by the recognition, and by Jack's lack of intimidation. In fact, Jack was practically crying *eureka*!

"So, you know my name. So what? What are you gonna do, tell your mommy?" Luther chided.

"I'll tell whoever makes you leave me alone, Luther. Now get the hell out of my way!" Again, Jack had no fear. It was as if he were watching himself on television.

Luther bumped into Jack again, hard. "Give me some money or I'll kill you," he said.

"I don't think so. Now get out of the way or I will tell not only my 'mommy,' but also the principal, and if you annoy me enough, maybe even the police!"

Luther was obviously befuddled. Ordinarily his threats were enough to intimidate any seventh-grader into submission, but he wasn't sure how to respond to a kid who didn't seem scared, and in fact, had counter-threats of his own.

Jack watched with some amusement as the larger boy went through a visible thought process, coming out the other end without a viable solution.

Luther instinctively chanted one of his much-rehearsed lines: "Yeah, run and tell Mommy, you little pussy!" He didn't expect the articulate (though exaggerated) response that followed:

"You know that if I do that, *you'll* be the one who's dead in the water, Luther. If you're ready for some *real* trouble with *real* adults, go ahead, break my arm! Give me a black eye! They'll heal, but you'll be sitting in Juvenile Detention with a permanent criminal record!" As the target of bullies, young Jack was used to looking at the ground during episodes like this. Despite his natural tendency to avoid eye contact, he now looked defiantly right into Luther's eyes.

Surprisingly, it was the bigger boy who then looked nervously away, causing Jack's gaze to drift also. He was startled by what he saw. Bruises. They were on Luther's face and neck, and partially visible on his arms where they protruded from his shirt sleeves.

"How'd you get the bruises, Luther?" he queried.

Luther became immediately defensive. "Stop looking at me!"

Jack ignored the demand and probed further, "Did you get beat up by somebody else like you?"

"You better shut up!" Luther pushed Jack by the shoulders, sending him tumbling backwards. He landed on his behind, with his worn shoes sticking up in front of him.

Even with an engineer's mind, Jack was able to see what was below the surface of this eruption. He sat on the asphalt and brazenly continued his inquisition. "How many more bruises are there?"

Luther's eyes grew wide with disbelief. "You're being stupid," he half-whispered, his voice shaking. His expression betrayed an inner conflict as he looked down at the puny kid he'd expected to control, but the roles were reversed.

Jack ran with it. "Is that why you want to hit me? Because someone is hitting you?"

"You better stop talking *right now!*" Luther warned.

"Who is it, Luther? Your dad?"

"I said shut up!"

Jack was silent for a moment. He quickly reviewed what he hoped was good psychology. "You know Luther, if you hit me, I'll be brave enough to tell the people who can save me from you. You need to be just as brave."

Luther looked confused. "You're being stupid," he repeated.

"Your dad probably warned you not to tell, didn't he? Well, if you don't tell, maybe I will. He can't get away with it any more than you can."

"My dad died," Luther said, clenching his teeth and his fists.

Jack wasn't sure if he should fear for his life right now or be more concerned about Luther's. He reasoned that any damage he might do was already done, so there was nothing to lose by plowing ahead. "Who, then? Your mom? It's still wrong and it's not your fault!"

Wait, he thought, *how did I know to say that?* It occurred to Jack that he was the only person alive who had ever seen *Good Will Hunting,* so the script was fair game! "It's not your fault," he repeated.

With a growl, Luther gave Jack a swift kick on the side of the leg. For a moment afterward he looked stunned, unclenched his fists, and then ran off.

Jack sat there for a minute, his leg throbbing, wondering if he'd just made a mistake. He picked himself up and began to dust off the front of his pants, but his left thigh was tender where he'd just been struck. The left pocket was where he kept his house key and his lunch money, and the collection of metal objects pressed uncomfortably against his swelling leg. When he reached in to retrieve them and switch pockets, his hand brushed against the folded sheet of paper he also kept there. Something inside compelled him to take it out and read:

You'll be there when you need to.

Thinking he may have just been given a sign of some sort, Jack carefully folded the page and chose to return it to his left pocket despite the increasingly painful bruise on his leg. He straightened up his clothes and backpack, and started off to school again, with a bit of a limp. "Nothing like being fifty-two," he said under his breath. He didn't notice his sore feet so much now. He also didn't notice the dirty oil stain on the seat of his pants.

Even with the limp Jack made it to school by 8:45. The brief diversion, courtesy of Luther Howell, had really only lasted a couple of minutes. Jack easily located his homeroom and settled into his seat. As he touched down, he found that his left buttock was also sore from Luther's angry outburst. Maybe it would ease up as the day went on. When the late bell rang, Jack felt a slight sense of triumph for having made it on time.

The announcements started promptly, and the class stood for the Pledge of Allegiance. A few boys behind him snickered as the recitation began:

"I pledge allegiance
to the flag
of the United States of America..."
Now a girl was giggling as well.
"...and to the republic
for which it stands,
one nation..."
It was strange to hear this old familiar mantra again, recited so methodically by kids who probably didn't even understand what it meant. Jack figured the laughter came from the more immature ones who still thought it was cute to make fun of the words.
"...under God,
indivisible,
with liberty and justice for all."
Jack had recited some irreverent variations as a kid, such as "one naked individual," "one nation invisible," "with liver-tea and mustard," and "to the public's four sandwich stands." He laughed inwardly at this recollection as the laughter around him increased. Finally everyone sat down again, and the morning ritual continued. As was the custom, students made the announcements.

"This is Jennifer Pruitt with today's lunch menu. Spaghetti, French bread, salad..."

Jack's leg was beginning to hurt more, not less. He wished he could lose the backpack and stretch out somewhere for a few minutes.

"This is Dennis Ford with sports! Remember to come out and support our own Twin Springs Titans this Friday as they host the undefeated Kennedy Wildcats..."

Jack squirmed in his seat, trying to find a position that didn't hurt so much.

"This is Larry Berger reminding you about tonight's science fair, seven o'clock in the cafeteria..."

Something about that announcement jolted Jack's memory. For a moment he forgot about his pain. The science fair... this was the day Larry would be killed! Now he vividly remembered attending that fair, and being among those who wondered why Larry Berger's gyroscope project sat unattended on the display table. They all found out during the next morning's announcements. Larry was the passenger in his mother's car when it was broadsided by a large truck on the way to the fair.

How can I not do something? Jack thought to himself.

Larry finished reading his copy: "...so come one, come all, and see the scientific marvels this evening at seven o'clock!"

As Mr. Anderson took roll, Jack's thoughts began to swirl together. Larry, Luther, his painful leg... all of it seemed overwhelming. He knew too much and he could do too little about it. He'd already ruled out the possibility of warning Larry. Damn, his leg was stinging! Was there such a thing yet as Child Protective Services that could help Luther? Would Jack be intervening or interfering if he did anything about either boy?

He was in a lot of pain, and as he reached back to massage his bruise he felt a wet, slimy substance on his pants. Had his skin been punctured? The end-of-class bell rang and everyone stood again. Jack was sure he must have bled through the fabric of his trousers, and was prepared to head straight for the nurse. The laughter behind him started up once more, and Andy Norton turned around to see what was going on. All eyes were on Jack's clothing, and it was Andy who finally clued him in.

"Geez, what happened to your pants, Oliver?"

"I think I may be bleeding," Jack said tentatively.

"That doesn't look like blood all over your chair."

Jack looked down; his seat was smeared with a dark, oily film. "What the hell is *this*?" he snapped angrily, as he wiped a little of it on his finger and sniffed. "Motor oil! Crap!"

A few kids in the class seemed sympathetic, but largely the other students laughed. A couple of stray comments came Jack's way: "So which is it, motor oil or crap?" and, "You couldn't hold it till after class, Oliver?"

Mr. Anderson eventually took notice and came over to Jack's desk. "What's going on with you this week, Jack? Get to the office, and don't sit down!" Then he pressed the intercom button and announced to the whole school: "Custodian to room one-fourteen, please."

Jack felt less and less like he was watching himself on television: the embarrassment stung almost as much as the pain in his leg. Anyone in the nearby hallway could have seen this pathetic, gimpy nerd with soiled pants emerging from room 114. And for those who didn't happen to notice on their own, Mr. Anderson's announcement conveniently pointed it out to them.

Jack limped slowly down the hall, with students rushing by on both sides. Some of them brushed or bumped into him, but soon the bell rang and the hall was empty again. Jack was in no hurry to get to the office. He knew his poor mother would have to drop whatever she was doing to bring him another pair of pants. He also knew the oil stain probably wouldn't come out, and that the pants he had on were ruined. These were things he normally wouldn't have thought about at age twelve, but they were foremost in his mind now. With his sore leg he also really wanted to sit down, but he knew he couldn't. He turned the corner into the office and presented himself to the school secretary, Mrs. Browne.

"Hello, Ma'am. Mr. Anderson sent me from homeroom; I have to call my mom to get another pair of pants."

Mrs. Browne was an attractive, middle-aged brunette whose horn-rimmed glasses hung from a thin chain around her neck. She looked at Jack inquisitively: "Why don't you have a seat, young man?"

Jack turned around and said, "Probably not such a good idea!"

"Name and home phone number, please?" she stifled a giggle.

"Jack Oliver. 555-2409," he replied, impressed with himself for remembering a forty-year-old phone number.

As Mrs. Browne dialed, Jack fidgeted, bouncing on the balls of his feet within his worn shoes.

There was a long pause.

"Are you sure she's home, Jack?"

"She should be, but you could call..." for a split second he tried to recall his mother's cell phone number.

"Call what?" she asked.

"Never mind," Jack replied. "Nothing."

"I don't think anyone's answering at your house."

Jack had an idea: "Do you think I could walk home and change, then?"

Mrs. Browne had finally managed overcome her amusement. "Well, since you can't sit and wait... but you know I'll have to clear it with the principal."

"I'd appreciate that, Ma'am."

She walked into the adjacent office and briefly talked with a tall, professional-looking man in a brown suit. As they emerged together, the principal seemed to be hiding a smile. He approached Jack and said, "So, what happened to you, young man?"

Jack answered awkwardly, "I fell in the street on the way to school, and didn't realize I got this oil on me."

"His mother's not answering," Mrs. Browne added. "He'd like to walk home and change."

"I guess that would be alright," the principal said, "but be sure you're back as soon as possible, son."

"Thank you," Jack said, immediately turning to leave.

As he tried to establish a steady pace, his leg reminded him of the hard kick he'd received earlier, and Jack realized the trip home would not go as quickly as the trip there. He plodded along, feeling a dull ache in his thigh with each step and a stinging sensation in his behind as the oil-soaked cloth rubbed against his irritated skin. As he made his way back up Tenbrook Street he couldn't stop thinking of how he'd inadvertently read "The Rule" just after the encounter with Luther, and wondered if there was any meaning there.

Approaching the yard with the yapping dog, he looked around, half-expecting the bully to still be in the vicinity; so he was only half-surprised when he did in fact see Luther, sitting on the hood of a car. Jack crossed over to the sidewalk on the other side of the street, preparing for the larger boy to jump down and chase him, or at least yell out something derogatory. Neither happened. Instead, Luther simply watched him pass by. As Jack guardedly maintained his course, he began to feel overwhelmed by his day thus far, and by the looming responsibility of making a change without a clue as to how to go about it.

He rounded the corner onto Lark Lane and stopped in his tracks: right in front of him was Larry's house. With a tall privacy hedge separating most of the yard from the street, and twin magnolia trees flanking the front porch, the Bergers obviously had unusual tastes. But that was what made the house so distinctive, and so memorable. And there next to the hedge, parked along the curb, was a 1966 Dodge Dart: the car in which Larry would die that evening.

Jack didn't understand the fervid flood of feelings that suddenly engulfed him. The sight of that car triggered something he couldn't control.

"Francis, I hope I'm not destroying the world," he said quietly as he hatched an idea: the engineer's response to a feeling. He reasoned that if Lorenz' butterfly really could kick off a tornado, maybe it would only take a small change to save Larry's life. *If the Bergers' car reached the intersection just a few seconds earlier or later, the truck wouldn't hit it. That should be easy to do,* Jack thought.

It began to rain lightly as he considered his options, and a moment later he had it figured out: *The time it takes to fix a flat should be sufficient, but they might discover the problem and install the spare earlier in the day. So I need to create two flat tires. I'm sure they don't have two spares!*

Without further self-discussion, Jack looked both ways to see if anyone was watching. When he was satisfied that he saw no one, he ducked behind the Dodge to assess the situation. Shielded from view by the hedges on one side and by the car on the other, Jack sat his oily self on the sidewalk and removed the stem-cap from the front tire. It felt good to sit. He hadn't seen an old-style metal hubcap like this up close for a long time, and he tapped a little rhythm on it just for fun, enjoying the muffled, bell-like sound. He knew he would need something to help discharge all that air, so he went through the pocket where he'd put his small metal items. A penny was too large to get down in the stem; finally he decided to use the tip of his house key.

The light rain increased in intensity as Jack slowly bled the air out of the tire; it was a much longer procedure than he'd anticipated. He couldn't just let some of it out; the tire had to be so flat that the car wasn't drivable. Raindrops collected in his hair and rolled down his face as the cold, rubber-scented air spewed out through the valve stem. He continued to look around cautiously, hoping he wasn't being observed. It was probably close to five minutes before the front tire was effectively flat, and both of Jack's arms were beginning to cramp up from pressing down with the key for so long. And he was only half done.

Not wanting to be seen, he stayed low and scooted the length of the car to the back tire to repeat the procedure. It was now raining steadily as Jack removed the second valve cap and began his covert assault on the other wheel. After another five minutes, the Dodge had two flat tires and Jack's life-saving work was done. He lifted himself up off the sidewalk, shaking his arms to ward off the impending charley horse, and found that his sore leg was beginning to cramp as well. "And nobody will ever even appreciate this..." he said under his breath.

The remainder of the walk home was terrible. The rain was cold, Jack's clothes were soaked, his arms felt like rubber and his leg felt like burning wood. He limped slowly, helpless to defend himself against the wet weather. He began to shiver as he paced along.

When he finally arrived at his house a half-hour later, his mother's Buick wasn't in the driveway. Jack reached for his key to unlock the door, but it wasn't in his pocket. "Crap!" he yelled, checking the other pocket out of habit. He felt Francis' paper, which was now quite·wet, but there was no key. He must have dropped it on the way home from Larry's. Briefly he thought about retracing his steps, but he was too exhausted. He collapsed on the concrete porch where there should have been an awning. Instead there was a covering of clouds leaking cold rain. He sat and shivered, curled up in a little wet ball, until Marie arrived half-an-hour or so later with a car full of groceries.

"Jack! What are you doing here? What happened?" she shrieked, running to the porch in the rain.

"I lost my key," Jack answered matter-of-factly, barely looking up.

"Get inside where it's dry!" she responded, quickly sorting through the keys on her key ring. "Why are you home from school?"

"I got oil on my pants; I think they're probably ruined." Jack felt a familiar sickening ache in his muscles as he tried to untie his knotted body. This was how he felt as an overweight adult after shoveling an hour's worth of snow. It was also how he felt when he was coming down with the flu.

The front door flew open, and Marie offered both hands to help Jack stand up. "I'm going to run a hot tub. You get inside and get those wet clothes off," she said, as he awkwardly straightened himself.

His back hurt.

As they both went inside, Jack braced himself for his mother's cry of shock when she saw his pants. It never came. Instead, she went into 'total mom' mode, doing everything that was needed, quite automatically. She hurried ahead and started running the bath water.

Jack dropped his backpack and kicked off his wet shoes by the front door. He removed his jacket and shirt as he squished through the house, not thinking to also remove his wet socks. Once in the bathroom, he finally shed his trousers and got his first look at the bruise on his leg. It was large and purple, and there were tiny red spots where the skin was broken. Jack's coins and his key must have gotten in the way of Luther's kick.

Marie gasped when she saw it: "What *happened* to you, Jack?"

He had a decision to make here. Was this the time to tell on Luther? After all, he was the cause of everything. Well, actually not. If Jack hadn't stopped to commit his act of righteous vandalism, he wouldn't have lost the key, and this would all just be about a pair of dirty pants. There was also the issue of Luther's safety at home if he were to get into trouble for this. Standing there shivering in his underwear, Jack said, "I fell in a puddle of oil on the way to school." He hoped he'd just done the right thing.

"This doesn't look like just a fall," his mother remarked with concern.

"Uh... I bumped against a car on the way down," he responded.

Jack dropped his drawers, hurting too much to wonder or even care if he'd stopped undressing in front of his mother by age twelve. He stepped gingerly into the tub, which held about an inch of water so far. As he sat, the hard porcelain felt uncomfortable against his bruised thigh, but the heat from the running water made it worthwhile. He also noticed how big the tub seemed.

From the sink, Marie ran hot water on two washcloths, and applied them to Jack's shoulders while he waited for the tub to fill. The heat was a welcome relief. "Why didn't you go to one of the neighbors' houses?" she asked.

That had never even occurred to Jack. "I don't know. I was probably too cold to think. And besides, I had oil all over my pants. I couldn't even have sat down."

The tub filled, and Jack soaked and washed as and his mother went to the kitchen to cook a pot of Lipton's chicken soup. This was the soup mix that came in paper packets, and in this house, was considered the universal remedy. When Jack finally emerged from the bathroom clad in pajamas and a flannel robe, he found a hot bowl of soup and a cold glass of Tang waiting for him. As he hungrily finished them both off, he noticed that the acidic Tang was burning his throat just a little. He was definitely getting sick. But he couldn't let it happen yet; he had to make sure Larry would eventually make it to school.

"Mom, can you drive me to the science fair at school tonight?"

"Science fair? Are you sure you're going to feel up to it? I think maybe you should stay home and rest!"

"Aww, I'm fine," Jack said, beginning to feel a burning lump in his throat. "I have some friends who are doing stuff I want to see."

"Well, we'll see. I'm going to call the school and tell them you won't be back today."

Jack limped to bed and slept for two hours, feeling feverish when he awoke. He went into the bathroom to splash cold water on his face, which just gave him a chill. His throat was on fire by now, but he had to hide his symptoms. He snuck a glass and a salt shaker into the bathroom and managed to quietly gargle some hot salty water without his mother hearing.

This was how it went for the rest of the day, until 6:00 came around. Joseph had come home from work and gone right out again to price lumber. Jack got himself dressed, put on his healthiest face, and went to find Marie.

"Mom! I'm ready to go to school."

Marie looked her son over somewhat skeptically. "You look like you should stay home."

"No really, I'm fine!" Jack's throat burned. He held his body tense to try and keep from shivering.

"Well, I'll trust you on this one Jack, but you look sick. When does this thing start?"

"Seven, but I want to get there early. Can we leave soon?"

"Shouldn't you eat first?"

"No, I'm still full from the chicken soup." Jack lied. He was starving.

"Okay, I'll get my coat," she said.

"Thanks," Jack replied, his voice nearly trembling from the chills. He knew he must be running a high fever, but he couldn't risk his mother finding out. He ran to the bathroom one more time and splashed more water on his face, then headed to the front closet to find his coat.

The rain had let up and it was getting dark. Mrs. Oliver was already outside with the Buick running, trying to warm it up before her son got in. It hadn't been quite long enough though, and now Jack couldn't help but shiver from the cold air as he slid into the passenger's seat. The car backed out of the driveway and sailed down Salem Street, with Marie doing her best to get the heat going.

"Mom, go down Lark Lane," Jack said as they approached Larry's street.

"Why?" she asked. "Isn't Myrtle quicker?"

Jack had to think fast. "I walk down Lark 'cause I can cut through yards; I think that might be where I dropped my key today."

Marie didn't question the wisdom of trying to find a key in the dark; she turned onto Lark as she was asked. There was Larry's house, with Larry and his mother looking somewhat frantically at their disabled Dodge.

"Hey, stop at the Bergers' house," Jack said. "Larry's is one of the projects I want to see!"

She pulled up next to the Dodge and Jack rolled down his window.

"Hey, Larry! You ready for tonight? We're heading there now!"

Larry seemed a little puzzled; he and Jack didn't know each other all that well. "Uhh... well, it looks like I don't have a ride," he answered.

Mrs. Berger, a petite redhead in an overcoat and scarf, walked around the front of the car as Marie rolled down the driver's side window.

As the chilly cross-breeze assaulted Jack's senses, he noticed how little this woman resembled her son, with his curly brown mop of hair.

"Hello, I'm Doris Berger," she extended a hand which Marie shook tentatively. "Do you think you could give Larry a ride to the school? He needs to be there early."

"Well, I guess so..." Marie replied hesitantly.

Larry seemed rather uncomfortable: "Why can't we just wait for Dad?"

"He'll be along in a few minutes," Doris replied, "and I'll ride with him. But why don't you go ahead and ride with... I'm sorry, I don't know your name."

"Oh... Marie Oliver. And this is Jack."

"Hi, Jack!" Doris said brightly, peeping across the seat. "Larry, it's only a short drive, why don't you go ahead with the Olivers? Then tomorrow we'll figure out what happened to this car!"

Jack lost no time in opening his door for Larry to slide into the back. Even more frigid air was now spilling into the Buick. Jack wondered why they ever made such a big car with only two doors. He began to visibly shake with cold. "C-come on in, Larry!"

Larry scooted onto the large rear seat. "Thanks for the ride, Mrs. Oliver," he said courteously.

"Oh, no trouble at all, Larry," she replied. Windows and doors were now closed again, and the heat had finally started to kick in as the big old car lurched down Lark Lane and turned the corner onto Tenbrook.

"Hey, could we take Luther too?" Larry asked.

Jack was startled by the request. *Luther?* He looked out the window to see the bully slowly walking in the direction of the school, illuminated from behind by headlights. Marie slowed the car as Larry rolled down the undersized rear window.

"Luther! Wanna ride to school?" Larry yelled.

"I guess," Luther said a bit suspiciously. "Sure, why not?"

Now Jack was as confused as he was cold. Were these two friends? Little innocent nerdy Larry and big bully Luther were chummy? He thought Larry was the kind of kid Luther would have tormented. How could this be a viable friendship? And why would Luther Howell have any interest in the science fair? Marie opened her door to allow Luther to slide into the back seat next to Larry.

"Thanks for the ride," Luther said with surprising politeness.

"You're welcome," Jack replied, turning to show Luther whose car he'd just gotten into.

Their eyes met, and for a brief instant Luther seemed almost glad to see Jack. But just as quickly, he wrinkled his brow and turned toward Larry: "I guess everything's ready for tonight?"

Jack was amused by the odd reaction. The bully must have been caught completely off-guard.

"Oh, it's ready!" Larry said to his big friend. "The question is, are *you* ready to see... the 'All-Mechanical Inertial Navigation Operating System'?"

"So, you went with the A.M.I.N.O. system," Luther remarked. "Pretty big name!"

"Well, it needs a big name to distract from just how simple it really is!" Larry replied jokingly. "It's not like I had lasers lying around in the basement, so I kinda had to fake it. Besides, I'm just using models to explain the basic theory."

As he watched them interact, Jack tried to ascertain any logical link between Luther and Larry. Maybe this was one of those instances where a bully singled out a nerdy kid to 'protect' in order to atone for his mistreatment of the others. Jack had been in just such a situation back in the fourth grade. Or maybe Luther relied on Larry for answers to assignments; at least whenever he was in school. Jack guessed it didn't really matter. If they were friends, that was their business. He turned around and looked out the window.

"By the way, you better be careful with that gyroscope," Luther said. "My dad gave me that."

"It will be returned unharmed," Larry said, sounding a tad annoyed.

Jack couldn't make sense of the conversation. It didn't seem possible that "Poindexter" and the bad seed could be talking this way. He turned around in his seat once more and glared at them questioningly. There was an immediate change in Luther's demeanor, like maybe the 'bully mystique' had been compromised, and now he had to recover.

"Larry," Luther asked, "was something wrong with your car?"

"Yeah, there were two flats!"

Oh, here we go, Jack thought, *he saw me and he's going to try and extort my silence!* He just rolled his eyes and shook his head as he turned back around in his seat. He knew Luther would probably see this as a retreat, but he was starting to feel too sick to care.

"I'll drop you boys off at the main door, okay?" Marie asked, stopping the car before the conversation could go any further.

"Thanks, Mrs. Oliver," Larry said, as he slipped out of the back seat.

"Yeah, thanks," said Luther, sliding across and exiting from the same door.

Marie looked strangely at her son. "Aren't you getting out, Jack?"

"You know, Mom, I think you were right. I'm starting to feel pretty sick. I think I'd better go home."

"I thought so," she replied. "Larry and Luther: are you going to have a way to get home?"

"My mom and dad will be here later. We'll be fine," Larry answered for both of them.

The two boys went into the school building as Jack went limp on the car seat. *I did it,* he thought to himself. It became hard to breathe. Then he passed out.

CHAPTER NINE

"SO, IS it worth it, Jackie Boy?"

"Is what worth what?"

"You know, trading your life for his! I bet you feel really good about the decision, don't you? I know I would!"

Jack realized he was hearing Francis' voice from within himself again, but all he could see was darkness. "I don't remember making a decision. What happened? Am I dead?"

"Sometimes when life hangs in the balance, you have to choose which side is going to be heavier." Francis hadn't answered the question.

"Why is it dark?" Jack asked ominously.

"Open your eyes, Jackie," Francis chuckled.

Too disoriented to be embarrassed, Jack slowly, numbly lifted his eyelids and found he was in the White Room. Francis was in the same brown suit as before, but Jack saw the reflection of himself standing there in the twelve-year-old body he'd inhabited for the past few days. "I'm young this time," he said confusedly.

"Does that surprise you?" Francis asked.

"Yeah, no...I guess not. Did you say I traded my life? Do you mean for Larry's?" Jack was surprised at his own matter-of-fact acceptance of that idea.

"Well, this *was* Larry's time..." Francis said evasively.

Jack waited for his heart to skip a beat, but he was so weary that it didn't happen. And he didn't care. "I messed with something I shouldn't have, didn't I?"

"I can't answer that. Like I told you last time, I'm just the messenger."

"Francis, is it time for me to go with you? I think I'm ready."

The older man's eyes grew wide. "Just like *that*? You're 'ready'?" Then he squinted. "Exactly what is it you think you're ready *for*?"

Jack began to sob. "I'm so tired. I thought I might be able to make things better by getting a second chance, but I just seem to be making them worse. I really don't know what direction to take. I want to stop. I want to rest. I want to go."

"Well, where is it you think you're going, Jackie?"

"Heaven? Or wherever it is you came from."

"I didn't come 'from' anyplace. I'm here."

"Well I know that..." Jack sputtered. "But there's got to be another..."

"You mean a place beyond this cocoon?" Francis interrupted.

"Well, yes... I think."

"But why would you want to leave here, Jack?"

Jack wondered if he was being baited. "Oh, I like your company and all, Francis, but this can't be all there is."

Francis laughed out loud. Then he did it again. "Jackie, this is the *best* there is! I'm a little surprised you don't see that yet."

"See what?" Jack was exasperated. He felt like Francis was making fun of him, and he was in no mood to be a good sport. "You're so goddam cryptic, Francis!" He was becoming inwardly defiant, and didn't even care that he had just 'taken the Lord's name in vain,' possibly within earshot of the Lord!

Francis saw what was happening and knew how to deal with it. "So, don't you want to know why I finally got off the ship?"

Jack huffed. "If I wasn't so curious I'd be pissed off at you for changing the subject! Yes, please tell me."

"Remember I said my one change was up to me?"

"Yeah."

"Well, although that's true, I had no idea what I was changing. That's usually how it goes."

"I don't understand."

"See, Jackie, you're used to all those stories about 'time travel' where people go back and invest in the stock market so they'll be rich when they return to the present. Or they travel to the future to try and get inside information about how things *will* be. Either way it's the same idea. They're always trying to *cheat* just a little bit! But in reality, that's not how it works."

"Reality?" Jack watched his reflection as he shook his twelve-year-old head in disbelief. "This is totally *surreal*!"

Francis just smiled and went on. "What I didn't tell you is that after the first boat trip I made, you know-- the one that never really took place, I lived in Ireland for another ten years. America went to war a few years after I would've arrived there, so at first I thought maybe I'd been spared some horrible fate! But those next years in Ireland turned out to be as bad as ever. Potatoes were finally growing again, but the damage had already been done; and it wasn't really about potatoes anyway."

The conversation was developing branches, and Jack sort of liked it that way. "What do you mean, not about potatoes? Didn't people starve because the potato crop failed?"

"No. *Certain* people starved because they weren't allowed to eat any of the other crops. Do you really think there was nothing but potatoes in all of Ireland?"

"I never thought about it before…"

"We were growing wheat, corn, barley, beets… but we had to turn it all over to landlords for the privilege of growing a few potatoes for ourselves. That was our rent! And by the time I finally left Ireland, most Catholics had either died or gone elsewhere. Yet, when I got to America, I'm ashamed to say I was too frightened to stay. I saw Irish people living in New York in conditions that seemed even worse than where I'd been, so I turned around and I went back home. The ship was almost empty going back the other way; I guess I should have taken a clue from that."

"Wow…" Jack was fascinated.

"Of course I was having second thoughts while we were afloat, but by then it was too late. Any leftover money I'd had to make a start in America was spent on the return voyage, and I was a pauper once again. I couldn't get work, I couldn't find a girl, and I was ashamed of myself for being too much of a coward to stay in the States! I was good and ready to meet Liam when the time came."

"So, what happened?"

"Like you, I was given the chance to 'revisit' a part of my life and change something. And also like you, I had no idea when or where I'd end up or what I would do. But I was so miserable where I was, I figured any change was a good change."

"So *you* went back *ten* years…"

"Almost to the day, yes. I left in 1865 and found myself in 1855; May the twenty-third to be exact, ready to board the ship."

"And you made the trip again!"

"For the sake of argument I'll say it was 'again,' though I was the only one with any memory of the previous trip. At first I thought I might have just dreamt those ten years, until I started to recognize the people on the boat, and began to see the same ones dying of cholera along the way. That's when I realized that maybe I actually *had* been there before."

By this point Jack was completely captivated. "How do you… *handle* knowledge like that?"

"You've been doing it yourself, Jack. From Monday to Thursday you were a butterfly among caterpillars: knowing what would happen to the people around you."

"And foolishly trying to change their lives?"

"Who's to say what's foolish and what's not? Sure, I concocted a plan of my own! A voyage across the Atlantic gives a man plenty of time to think."

Jack smiled curiously. "What was your plan, Francis?"

The Irishman chuckled. "Well, I read about the death of Abraham Lincoln and I'd planned to warn him, though it wouldn't happen for ten years. In fact, he wasn't even president yet!"

"That's sort of what I did; I made lists…"

"I know! And why did you finally abandon them?"

"Because I was supposed to change one thing about… *my* life."

"You thought it through, in other words."

"Yes."

"And so did I. I realized I wasn't supposed to be a prophet to the world. Besides, prophecies can be prone to manipulation."

"What do you mean?" Jack asked.

Francis stroked his beard. "Well, all it takes for a 'prophecy' to be fulfilled is for one person to say it, and another person to do it. If I say 'Jack is going to sit down now,' and you hear it…"

Jack continued the thought: "...and I *sit* down, you've foretold the future only because I made your words true."

"Now you're getting it. So if I write: *Mr. Lincoln, in ten years a fellow named Booth will try to shoot you*, and later on a man named Booth reads it, maybe Booth really got the idea from me!"

Jack wrinkled his twelve-year-old forehead as he processed the idea. "So in that case, the 'prophet' doesn't predict the future..."

"He causes it!"

"But wait, Francis... you were there; you *saw* the future! You *knew* Lincoln would die!"

"No, I didn't see the future, from my perspective it was all in the present. But when I finally stepped off that boat to stay, the course of my life changed. And since I didn't even know what was going to happen to me, how could I presume to know what would happen to Abraham Lincoln? All bets were off!"

Jack shook his head. "But he was still assassinated..."

"Then it was meant to be. But no matter, *that* sequence of events wasn't mine to change."

Jack considered the idea. He'd crossed items off his list strictly for practical reasons; but maybe there was something more at play. "Francis, why were we both given this opportunity?"

"I can tell you this much, Jack: it wasn't so we could decide how to change the world. Lord knows, you and I aren't qualified!"

"Well, what if we do the wrong thing?"

Francis' eyes sparkled again as he smiled. "Well, we'll just have to concentrate on doing the *right* thing, won't we?"

Jack frowned. "Oh, *that* clears it up!"

"I detect a little cynicism, lad!"

"Well what do you expect? I go back to my boyhood with no instructions, I blunder so badly that I end up dead, and now here you are talking in circles... telling me what I should have done without really saying anything at all!"

Francis remained calm. "You want instructions? All right, do you still have that paper I gave you?"

Jack took a deep breath, partly to indicate his frustration and partly to help himself calm down. "You mean 'The Rule'? Yes, I have it. I'm afraid I didn't take very good care of it." He removed the folded paper from his pocket. It was dog-eared and rough from having gotten wet, and there were some spots where the oil from his pants had soaked through.

"It looks perfect to me," Francis observed.

Jack unfolded the sheet, carefully peeling apart the stuck surfaces. "I used it to make all my lists," he said.

"May I see it?" Francis asked.

Jack passed the paper to his ancestor, who carefully took it and looked it over.

"You'll be there when you need to," Francis read.

"Yeah, yeah. So, does that even mean anything?"

"Well, let's see. You have a list of ten things you could do to change the world, and four things you could invent before the people who actually invented them."

"That's why they're all crossed out."

"But there's something that's not crossed out!"

"Oh, that's just my school schedule. I guess it's the only list I actually used for anything."

"Jackie, this is stupidly obvious!"

"What is?"

"Oh, come on! 'You'll be there when you need to' followed by your school schedule? You needed to be in school."

Jack scoffed. "I think that's a stretch. School was abysmal; probably the worst two days of my life!"

Francis handed the page back as he spoke. "Well, there's one other thing on here that you might want to take a look at."

"What's that?" Jack asked, grasping the grimy paper.

"Down in the right corner. What do you see?"

Jack glanced at the area, quickly doing a double-take when he saw it in the once-empty bottom quarter of the page, formed by oil stains and the transferred impressions of a wet number two pencil. "It's a butterfly!"

"Indeed," Francis said.

"The image is perfect-- it could be the work of an artist!"

"I'll bet it's the work of several!"

Jack was dumbfounded. He blinked his eyes and spoke quietly, "Son of a gun..."

Francis interrupted with a chuckle. "Look, Jack, you're not dead. And you're not finished. And you're not ready to 'come with me,' since you seem so convinced I'm going someplace. Just follow your instruction manual there."

"I'm not dead? You told me I traded my life for Larry's!"

"I said no such thing! If this was a novel you could go back and read my exact words and you'd find I was being hypothetical."

A strange mix of feelings rushed through Jack's body. He understood the relief, but the disappointment came as a surprise. He realized for the first time how much he'd looked forward to the end of this hard-traveled road. And yet, in the core of his consciousness he knew Francis was right. It wasn't over. It couldn't be over, and he couldn't explain why. "Francis," he said, "why me? Why does it matter what I do?"

"Because *your* life is the most important life in the world."

Jack was perplexed. "No! I'm pretty insignificant in the big picture."

Francis raised his eyebrows. "Try telling that to your wife and your children."

The remark startled Jack. He absorbed it for a moment. "Touché. But still... I'm only important in their little part of the world."

"Really? Well then, why don't you tell me who's more important than you, Jack?"

"Ha! Okay, how about Newton, Einstein, Edison..."

"Stop right there. What's Edison got that you haven't?"

"I wasn't the one who invented the light bulb or the phonograph!"

"But do you understand how they work?"

"Well, yes..."

"Then you have some of his knowledge. Have you ever read any Shakespeare?"

"Well of course..."

"Prove it!"

"Okay," the young boy began to recite:

"What's in a name? That which we call a rose
By any other name would smell as sweet;
So Romeo would, were he not Romeo call'd..."

Francis interrupted: "So it seems you've absorbed a bit of *his* essence, too! What about the music of Beethoven?"

"Who *hasn't* heard Beethoven!"

"What's your favorite, then?"

"Probably the Sixth Symphony. He describes nature with music the way a poet might do it with words."

Francis scratched his head as he spoke, "And if you're anything like me, you sometimes hear that music when you're out in nature, don't you?"

"You mean you also hear Beethoven in your head?"

"Of course, Jack! He's a part of us both. So is Edison, so is Shakespeare! So are Mark Twain, Gandhi, Eleanor Roosevelt and Edmund McConnell."

"I don't know Edmund McConnell..."

"He's a fellow I grew up with-- starved in the famine. Not famous, but that doesn't make him any less important."

Thomas Edison's long-overdue light bulb finally blinked on in Jack's mind, but he wasn't overly excited by it. Instead he just sighed. "I get your point, Francis. We're all pieces of the proverbial puzzle."

Francis grew very serious. "But Jack, if one piece goes missing, even a small one, the puzzle will never be finished."

"Well, I sure can't see why my piece is of any consequence."

"I don't know why either," said Francis, "I just know it is, or you wouldn't be here. None of us would!"

"None of who?"

Francis seemed to be really good at not answering questions. "Remember Jack, once you understand enough of life's lessons you begin to see how they fit together."

"You said that before..." Jack felt strangely anxious, as if he were being watched.

Then Francis smiled broadly and his eyes illuminated from within. "I think you're ready to try again, Jackie."

Oddly, Jack knew exactly what that meant. He'd revisited the moment several times in his dreams, and was always left wondering what might be waiting for him when he again tried to "look into" Francis.

This time it happened so swiftly that he had no chance to prepare or even to think. Suddenly he was just there, lost in those luminous eyes; feeling like the universe was rushing at him from all directions. It wasn't a moving star field like a sci-fi geek might have expected; in fact this universe wasn't about space at all. It was about humanity: people arranged in rows and columns, side to side and top to bottom, each soul distinct, yet part of the whole. Jack couldn't really 'see' faces or bodies, yet there they all were, passing at lightning speed, but in an impossible way: each time a person seemed to go by, they appeared again right in front of Jack. After a few seconds, he was no longer sure if they were moving around him or if he was moving through them; everyone was just coming and going-- but staying in place, all at the same time. A feeling of utter elation began to swell up inside of his being.

Jack tried to speak out loud, but found that his voice was now simply integrated into his surroundings. "Francis! What *is* this?"

"This? This is the best there is, Jackie!" Francis' voice wasn't an audible entity either; Jack simply knew what he was saying as they rode the wondrous roller coaster together.

The universe of souls continued to swirl around as Jack 'spoke' again: "This feels impossible, but also like I've been here before!"

"You should recognize it. Everyone here is, in some way, a part of who you are, Jack!"

"I can see that; I can feel it! But there are so *many* people…"

"Let me show you something you'll really like! Name someone you'd like to see!"

"What? Anybody?"

"Anybody!"

"Um… Louis Armstrong!" Jack immediately wondered if maybe he should have chosen Jesus Christ or Galileo, but before he had a chance to second-guess himself, he felt his lightning bolt of a soul take a sharp right turn as it also remained in place.

And there was Louis!

"I've memorized your records!" Jack exclaimed, and he could sense Louie smiling that million-dollar smile. But the side trip didn't stop with Satchmo; Jack continued to rapidly glimpse the essence of his inner musician with Elvis and Ella; Bird, Bing, Bix, and of course Beethoven, who were all a part of the ride. And so was every other musician who had ever made music.

"Who else?" Francis asked.

"My dad!" Jack replied without hesitation. And there was Joseph. And they communicated without speaking. And they loved each other more than was humanly possible.

"Let's try one more," Francis said.

Jack hardly had time to react to the revelatory instant spent with his father. "You pick..." he said with a bit of confusion.

"Okay," Francis replied, "how about this fellow?" A person quickly flashed into view.

"That's Edmund McConnell," Jack said. "Wait a second; how do I know that?"

"You know him through me," Francis replied. "Everyone here is, in some way, a part of who you are."

And that was where it ended as quickly as it had begun. Jack felt as if he were spit back out of a vortex, and there he was again, a little boy standing with an Irishman in their quiet cocoon. He was suddenly conscious of his heartbeat: it was racing. He took deep, quick breaths. The feeling of exhilaration was unlike anything he'd ever experienced.

Francis spoke triumphantly, "So, that's the puzzle you need to complete. Do the right thing, Jackie!"

Before he could even start formulating a response, Jack began to feel faint as his great-great-grandfather disappeared into the hazy white walls. It became hard to breathe. Then he passed out.

ଔ✦✦ଝ

"Jack?" said a woman's voice, gently weaving through the silky, smoky clouds of unconsciousness. "Jackie!" she repeated more firmly.

Jack's eyes fluttered, then opened full. He saw his sister's face, showing a concern that seemed beyond her sixteen years. He gradually began to realize where he was: this was a hospital room. He tried to speak, but his breath gurgled so deeply in his chest that he just coughed.

Jeannie tenderly put her hand on his forehead and said, "Don't talk, just rest. You've got pneumonia."

Jack remained still as he watched his sister pick up the bedside phone and dial out. "Mom? He just woke up. Okay, I'll see you in a minute."

Jack recalled that St. Andrew's Hospital was within blocks of their house. He looked to his left to see an IV tube running into his arm. He was still so stunned by what he'd experienced with Francis that his observations stopped there, and he just lay quietly, trying to absorb what he could.

"You've been out for two days," Jeannie began, "they thought you might not make it, but you started to turn around last night. Mom finally went home a few hours ago to get some sleep; she's been here nonstop since Thursday." Then the young girl sat down in a wooden chair next to the hospital bed and took Jack's right hand, the one that wasn't connected to a tube. Her voice shook as she spoke, "You're such a 'tard!" She cried silently and pressed his hand to her cheek.

He heard the sound of distant traffic through the slightly open window behind her.

Marie entered the room with a nurse a few minutes later. Jack could only be still as the nurse checked his vitals and smiled. "I think we're on the upswing," she said.

Jack could tell that his mom was trying to remain strong and parental for his benefit, but being a parent himself, he saw through the act.

"You were pretty sick there, buddy!" she said.

He wondered where his father was, but strangely, it didn't really matter. He understood Joseph so much more fully from the brief encounter a moment earlier, that he didn't need any additional evidence of their relationship now.

As the three Olivers sat in the white room, mother and daughter gradually explained the goings-on of the past two days. Jack learned that the Buick had served as an ambulance to deliver him to the hospital after he passed out in front of the school. His temperature was nearly 105 degrees, and he remained unconscious despite heavy doses of antibiotics and attempts to bring his fever down. Jack listened somewhat casually as the saga unfolded, his mind flowing back and forth between where he was now and where he'd just been.

When Jeannie finally said, "...and Jack, there's something you should know," his interest suddenly zoomed in on the present.

Marie picked it up from there. "Jeannie, I was going to wait a day or so, but I guess we can tell him now."

Tell me what? he thought to himself.

As if in answer to his thoughts, his mother spoke. "Jack, your friend Larry was in a car accident on the way home from the science fair Thursday night." She paused. "I'm afraid he was killed."

"I'm sorry, Jackie," Jeannie said.

Marie just looked at Jack, waiting for an emotional reaction that never came.

Instead, he was absorbing the significance of her statement, and feeling Larry's presence just as he'd felt the presence of all the others in the universe of souls. He turned his head slightly when he sensed some movement elsewhere in the room. There in the corner, up near the ceiling, was a small blue butterfly slowly opening and closing its wings-- almost like a waving hand. Somehow, Jack knew all was well with the world as it fluttered out the window into the dusk.

CHAPTER TEN

"**BABY BABY** sweet baby..." the record started for the third time in a row. Jack could hear it from across the hall, through the closed doors of both his and Jeannie's bedrooms. Pneumonia had taken quite a bit out of him and he'd been home for well over a week, resting in bed. Somewhere, his father had acquired a small used television and set it up in Jack's room. This was how Joseph the engineer showed his caring side, and Jack now understood completely. With Pounce the cat as his constant companion, Jack's days had been filled with game shows and movie reruns and even a soap opera or two, as well as lots of Lipton's soup and canned ravioli.

In the evenings he saw a more memorable side of television: the prime time shows. Of course there were the old standards like *Gunsmoke* and *Here's Lucy*, but more interesting to Jack were the programs that were seldom if ever rerun in 2010. Shows like *Medical Center*, *The F.B.I.*, and *Mannix* were a big part of his childhood, yet they were all but forgotten until airing once more on the little black-and-white set in his room.

He'd also been watching the news for a week and a half, and as he saw the stories roll by about last Friday's tidal wave in Pakistan that killed tens of thousands, and Saturday's plane crash in West Virginia that killed the entire Marshall University football team, he couldn't help but feel a little guilty that there had been so much concern over his health while he lay in bed doing nothing. Of course, most of the previous week's reports had centered on the remembrance of Charles de Gaulle, who had died that Monday. According to the paper:

...the symbol of France-- its past grandeur, its genius, its eternal contradictions...

...had requested that his funeral take place...

...without the slightest public ceremony... without bands, fanfare or bugles.

Jack smiled as he considered that: yet another of France's contradictions.

Being confined to his bed gave Jack a lot of time to think; maybe even too much. The last thing he experienced before waking up in the hospital was the incredible revelation of "looking into" Francis. In some ways the encounter was like an answer to the ultimate question, but yet it also left Jack asking many new ones.

He began to have a recurring dream in which he asked Francis: "What is the meaning of life?"

To which Francis replied: "This!" and allowed Jack his brief glimpse into the infinite body of souls; or whatever it was.

Jack would then respond: "Wow, yes, I see! Now, what's the meaning of *this*?"

And then he would wake up with pillows clamped over his ears to try and drown out the sound of the question, which of course he couldn't do, because it was inside his head to begin with. If he was lucky, he would be waking from an afternoon nap, and it would be time for *Let's Make a Deal* or some other such show that would offer him a half-hour's worth of distraction from the persistent dream. Unfortunately, now it was almost 3:30 and the game shows were over for the day. Looking at his clock radio, Jack carefully calculated that he'd been back in 1970 for exactly two weeks and two days, and wondered how much longer he'd have to stay.

"Baby baby sweet baby..."

Maybe that was the distraction he was looking for! If nothing else, it reminded him that he wasn't alone in the house. To help combat his obsession with the meaning of "this," he decided an excursion to his sister's room was in order. The pajama-clad boy rolled out of bed and took the few steps down the hall, knocking twice before Jeannie finally heard him over the music.

She turned down the volume, cracked the door and peeked out: "What?"

Jack had now had more than two weeks to relive his relationship with his sister, and it wasn't very different from his recollections. They were not close siblings. Years later they would talk about growing up, and the mutual observation would be that their household often seemed less like a family than like four individuals who happened to occupy the same space. Since his homecoming, Jack had been able to observe the situation through different eyes, and in so doing, had validated some of his own recent self-assessments.

It wasn't important to young Jack Oliver that there was no closeness with his dad or his sister, and that didn't mean he was a selfish person; it was simply how he was wired. He realized that most of his life he'd been reaching for a bar whose height had been set by the people he perceived as the "feelers." According to their standard, he'd need to read emotions and social cues in order to be branded a 'good' person.

But as the father of Jack Junior, he'd intimately gotten to know a true angel-- who had a completely different kind of emotional makeup: one that was more like his own. For Jack, his son's autism made the height of anybody's bar irrelevant. And it was with this knowledge that he returned to his boyhood with a greater insight into his sister's twice-uttered one-word greeting:

"What?" she repeated.

"Can I come in?" Jack asked.

Jeannie looked a little confused. "You want to come in here?"

"Yeah, if that's okay," he said sheepishly.

"Um... I guess." She opened the door enough for him to slip by.

Aretha Franklin was still sounding quietly on the record player.

"So..." Jack fumbled, "...how are you?" *Well,* he thought, *that was dumb!*

"How *am* I? What do you want, Jack? I'm busy!"

Jack didn't see any homework spread out on the bed, or even an open book. There was a dog-eared copy of *Tiger Beat* with a picture of Bobby Sherman on the cover, but in Jack's mind that shouldn't have constituted "busy."

"I just wanted to talk," he said.

Jeannie seemed impatient yet intrigued. "About what? Is something going on?"

Jack could have reached into his brain and randomly pulled out any one of a number of topics:

*He appreciated Jeannie caring for him while he was in the hospital, and was moved by her brief, telling moment of tenderness there.

*He also understood how she felt about their family environment, much more than she realized, and maybe he could help her cope.

*Of course, he could have confided in her regarding his situation of being from the future… hey! Wouldn't it be a kick if Jeannie responded by divulging that she was in the same position? Then they'd be like super-hero siblings, figuring out their destiny together.

But he realized his thoughts digressed. He'd been twelve a little too long.

"What's the record called?" he blurted out.

"The record? You mean that one?" She pointed to the little 45 r.p.m. disc that was still spinning on the turntable. The tone arm was beginning to follow the spiral running groove at the end of the song, and picked up automatically.

"I know it's Aretha Franklin; but it's not just called 'Baby Baby Sweet Baby' is it?" Jack asked, unsure why he'd spontaneously chosen this line of questioning. Perhaps he'd forgotten just how uncomfortable the sibling relationship really was, and was subconsciously avoiding any really thoughtful topics. After all, he was normally just a "'tard."

"Um…" Jeannie hesitated, "I bought it a long time ago. I think it might just be 'Sweet Sweet Baby' or something like that. Is that all you wanted?"

Jack could have just looked at the label, but he didn't want to waste this opportunity by talking about records. "Thanks for watching over me in the hospital…" he spouted, changing the subject quite clumsily.

Jeannie was quiet for a moment. She blinked quickly, and her facial features seemed to get smaller, like she was trying to retreat into herself. Jack searched for something else to say, as he now realized he'd blindsided the poor girl. This was an instance that shouldn't have been awkward by any normal measure, and yet this brother and sister felt increasingly uncomfortable as they stood in each other's presence, strangely threatened by the menacing specter of affection. It just wasn't a part of their relationship, at least not yet. Jack had brought his additional forty years of emotional growth to the game table, but he'd forgotten that Jeannie was still holding the cards from their childhood.

And yet it was she who broke the silence first, shrugging her shoulders and gently shaking her head. "You're welcome."

Is that it? Jack asked himself. *Can't I say something more meaningful?* But he couldn't. Well, he could, but it would likely have made things even more complicated. "Okay, I just wanted to say thanks," he repeated matter-of-factly, and turned to leave.

"Jack?" Jeannie said.

He spun back around.

She looked at him for a moment before smiling. "You're a real 'tard!"

Jack returned the endearment: "Well *you're* a vampire!"

They both laughed, and Jack went back to his room having just learned another lesson: he and his sister had always loved each other.

Unlike Jeannie's bed, Jack's was strewn with books and papers. Of course, some of them were *Sad Sack* and *Archie* comics, but there was also a nice selection of school assignments that had been sent home, as well as a humorous kids' novel that the English teacher Mrs. Lewis had recommended for her student who was sick abed.

Jack had also been spending a lot of time looking at the butterfly image on Francis' paper. He wasn't sure how he could have had it in his pocket during their most recent encounter; his mother had washed those pants just to see if the oil would come out (it didn't), and the paper went through a hot cycle with bleach. When Marie found it afterwards, the four quarters had broken apart, and she returned them to Jack, remarking on the nice butterfly he had drawn, and asking what *You'll be there when you need to* meant. He made up an answer on the spot, something about just practicing his typing, and she seemed satisfied with that. After all, to her it was just a paper. Oddly, the butterfly image seemed even more vivid following the abuse in the laundry, and so did the school schedule, while the other lists (the ones he had crossed out) were so faded as to be barely readable. He kept the four paper rectangles in his nightstand drawer, taking the butterfly out every so often to examine it closely. He noticed new details each time. He thought about Larry.

After thirteen days of rest and nearly fifty doses of erythromycin, the congestion in Jack's lungs had finally cleared up. Since he was going stir crazy during the day, he looked forward to returning to school, and according to Francis, he "needed" to be there. For whatever reason, he wouldn't return to his rightful place in life until he'd "done the right thing." He approached his mother to ask if tomorrow, Thursday, might be a possibility for going back.

"You have a little of your medicine left," she replied. "Why don't you wait until Friday? I'd like to see you stay home a full two weeks."

"Aww!" Jack groaned. "It's so boring staying home all the time!"

"I know it, Jack. But you were seriously ill. It'd be best to play it safe. In fact, why don't we just wait until Monday? You can start the week off fresh."

As much as he hated to admit it, he knew she was right. Just because he felt better didn't mean he was ready to go back to Twin Springs, which was probably saturated with dust and airborne germs.

"You probably think I'm nuts, don't you? Most kids would love to stay out of school!"

"No, you're not nuts," Marie answered playfully, "you're studious. You get that from me! Well, *and* your father's a physicist."

"Oh all right," Jack said, "I'll figure out things to do for-- *four* more days!"

There was no Internet to surf, but since he was supposed to be "studious," Jack spent hours looking through various volumes of

the family encyclopedia: the 1962 edition of the *World Book*. By
2010 standards, all the information seemed so dated; he had to
remind himself that in 1970 the set was only eight years old. Jack
lingered on the same page he always favored as a young child: the
one with full color pictures of dinosaurs. He thought about the
famous "brontosaurus" skeleton, and how paleontologists
throughout the years would disagree about which head belonged
on the body. Maybe just for kicks he should write a letter to the
Yale Museum, claiming to be the ghost of the Great Thunder
Lizard, identifying the correct head and asking that it please be
returned! *Then you will surely see that I'm actually an apatosaurus... it*
would say. Whenever Jack had thoughts like this, or like the one
about Jeannie and himself being co-time-travelers, he wondered if
he was regressing to an alarmingly immature state, or if he was just
learning to have fun again.

Thursday, Friday and Saturday came and went, and Jack's
pneumonia was replaced by cabin fever. After days of looking for
excuses to be interested in dull things, he was overjoyed when on
Sunday afternoon he came upon his dad watching football on the
little color set in the living room...

"Who's playing?" Jack asked.

"The 'Deadskins' and the Cowboys," Joseph replied snidely.

It was true that the 'skins weren't having a very good year, but
nevertheless, this was always the game to watch. The twice-per-
season match-up would eventually be dubbed the "top NFL rivalry
of all time." Even if the game itself wasn't all that exciting, the
mere fact that it was Washington and Dallas made it at least
interesting. At one point during the game, the Redskins got their
only interception when Brig Owens returned the ball twenty-two
yards before finally being tackled. The final score was dismal for
Redskins fans: 45-21 in favor of Dallas.

"You know," Jack remarked afterward, "if Owens had been
wearing one of those tear-away jerseys, he would have scored a
touchdown. I bet that would have been the boost the 'skins
needed!"

Then Joseph said something that Jack found quite interesting. "Oh, I don't know; even if that had happened, the rest of the game would probably have gone the same."

Wait a minute; was the physicist disagreeing with *sensitive dependence on initial conditions*? Jack couldn't help but respond. "You don't think an additional score by one team would affect the rest of the game?"

"Why should it?" Joseph queried. "The Cowboys won by more than a touchdown."

"Well, what about all that 'butterfly causing a tornado' stuff?"

"Butterfly, eh?" Joseph replied. "I heard something similar using a seagull, but I guess the idea's the same."

Oops, Jack thought. The "butterfly effect" apparently wasn't a familiar concept yet. Time to dumb it down. "Well, you know... I heard about the basic idea... in school... I think."

"So you know something about chaos theory!" Joseph perked up, seeming rather impressed. "It's all hypothetical, Jack. We can't prove something if we can't re-create it, and the only way to prove *this* would be to go back and have Brig Owens *make* that touchdown."

Jack pondered his father's words. "Well, I guess that's true."

"And we don't have the capability of time travel yet," Joseph added.

"*Yet?* You think it's really possible?" Jack couldn't believe what was coming out of his own mouth! Who was he to question time travel?

His dad didn't answer the question, but continued his lecture. He loved that his son was interested. "And on top of that, we'd have to know the results of the first game in order to compare the data from the second one. But since a particular event at a particular time can only happen once, how could we get two sets of data to compare?"

Jack couldn't continue to act twelve any longer. "Well, what about the experiment of releasing a sled on an icy hill, and recording the path it takes to the bottom?"

"That's an interesting model," Joseph said, "did you come up with that?"

Jack hesitated. Had Lorenz not published that one yet, either? "Um, no. I think I heard it someplace, too."

"Well I think I see where you're going with it," Joseph said. "Can I assume that after the first run, we do it again by starting the sled in a slightly different spot, to see how greatly the path deviates on the second try?"

"Right!" Jack said. "And the deviation can be pretty large, even if all the other components of the experiment are exactly the same, right?"

"Not really," Joseph answered, "because there's one component that never *can* be the same."

"What's that?"

"Time."

Jack was wide-eyed. "How so?"

"Because you can't test the same sled from two starting positions simultaneously. Point 'A' has to be associated with one specific time, and point 'B' with another. And we can only guess what might have happened if we'd released the sled from one of those points at say, eleven fifty-nine instead of eleven fifty-eight!"

Jack picked up the thought, "...because the wind might have been slightly different, or the snow may have melted just a little more..."

Joseph interjected, "...or maybe just because it was eleven fifty-nine!"

Jack thought for a moment. "So you think time, all by itself, can be a factor in a physical environment?"

"Sure," his father answered, "just as much as the direction of the wind or the bumps on the snowy hill. In physics, time is sometimes called the 'fourth dimension.'"

What an intriguing thought! Jack had always considered time to be an abstract thing that had no meaning unless it was connected to events. But this was new to him: could time actually have an intrinsic value of its own? And correspondingly, could this be why he was still in 1970? Maybe the proper set of events had to happen at a specific *time*!

Since Joseph didn't seem to find his son's overeducated curiosity unusual, Jack posed another lofty question: "But if we *could* go backwards in time, we'd still have the memory of both outcomes, right?"

"Nobody knows the answer to that one!" Joseph replied with a glint in his eye. "And besides, even if that were possible, *which* outcome would be the one that would shape future events?"

"Maybe they both could!" Jack offered.

"Well," Joseph laughed, "if you ever figure out how Brig Owens can make a touchdown and also get tackled on the same play, please explain it to me!"

Jack's brain was whirring with ideas. He was living the scenario that his father described as possibly impossible! Still trying to clarify the concept in his mind, he offered one last challenge: "But... if we *could* test the same sled-- or the same football play, two different ways from the exact same point in time, you think the basic outcome would still be the same?"

"I can't say for sure," Joseph replied, "but you can't tell me that just changing one player's shirt would be enough to undo all the talent and practice that made the other team play a better game!"

Jack mulled it over. "So the losing team would have seven more points, but that would be it?"

"Well, actually six, unless Kurt Knight kicked the extra point."

He didn't mind his father's excruciatingly literal final answer. After all, Jack's mind worked the same way.

With a strengthened set of perspectives, he left the conversation and went back to his room to think. His dad had questioned, but not dismissed, the idea of time travel. Jack had one up on him there, he knew it was possible: he was doing it. But the questions that haunted Jack were more complex ones; things he hadn't let himself ask until now. For example, Francis had gone back ten years and started over again from that point. Did this mean Jack would have to relive the next forty? For that matter, was he actually in his past, or was this really the present, and he'd merely seen a glimpse of his future up through 2010? In other words, did this time travel thing work both directions?

The seesaw of ideas bounced up one side and down the other, with the elusive 'one change' being the fulcrum. And how would *that* play out? Would there be some 'winner takes all' moment when Jack realized: *This is it... this is the change!* as he pushed the flashing red "change now" button? Or would it be more subtle than that? He'd already learned one lesson in trying to change Larry's destiny. Larry died anyway, as did Abraham Lincoln. That event wasn't Jack's to change. And in retrospect, he wasn't sure what had come over him that even compelled him to try. It just seemed like the right thing at the time.

Then there was the brief but extraordinary excursion "into" Francis. What was that, exactly, and why did Francis take him there? It certainly didn't fit any description of Heaven Jack had ever heard of; and besides, Heaven was supposed to be a place where dead people went. Jack had a strange sense that the *living* were also in the place he'd been. But at the time he didn't have the presence of mind to ask, and it was over with so quickly!

Hey-- that raised another question. Jack had seen his dad amongst all the souls; the same man with which he had just conversed. Was that a confirmation that the living and the deceased were inter-mixed, or did it mean he went forward in time, after Joseph's death, for the experience? And wait a minute... what about Armstrong and Ella and Elvis and Bing? They were all still alive in 1970 as well!

Jack also kept mentally returning to something Francis had said in their first encounter: *...for the time being, Jackie, you're the reflection and I'm the substance!* What did he mean by that? Was Jack just existing in some mirror image of reality?

He managed to distract himself from the spinning array of questions as he watched *The Ed Sullivan Show* and *Bonanza*, and tried to turn in by 10:00. He tossed and turned all night, wondering what his first day back at school would be like, and also what the meaning of "this" was.

CHAPTER ELEVEN

WHEN THE clock radio clicked on at 7:30, Jack felt like pounding it to pieces with his fist. He hadn't begun to sleep soundly until almost 5:30, and he was exhausted from too little rest and too much thinking. Plus, it was playing that song again!

"Baby baby sweet baby…"

Normally, a person's relationship with their clock radio would be such that they could navigate the controls by feel; quite literally "in their sleep." But Jack had only used the alarm on this one two times since he'd been back: Wednesday and Thursday of that first week, and his fingers hadn't been reprogrammed yet. He had to sit up in bed, rub his eyes and focus on the noisy little device in order to find the alarm switch.

"Speak your name (bum bum bum bum bum…),

And I feel a--"

"Quiet, Aretha," Jack said, as he clicked off the button in the middle of her line. Even with the recent oversaturation, he still liked the song, but in his present state of mind it was probably the last thing he needed to hear. In fact, this morning it didn't even seem like a song, but more like a question: *What's it called, dammit?* Added to all the other questions that had kept him awake most of the night, the music may as well have been a blaring siren. And so the morning started.

"See? Aren't you glad you stayed home those extra days?" Marie chimed sweetly as Jack dragged his lifeless body into the kitchen. "How about an Instant Breakfast? Or I could beat an egg into it for some extra protein," she said.

He just sat, not wanting to complain, but feeling worse than he had in several days. "Okay," he mumbled. It took about a minute for his mother to mix the ingredients and set the glass in front of him. Jack reckoned the chocolate and egg drink might perk him up somewhat, but he was going to need more. Without thinking, he asked a really stupid question: "Can I have a cup of coffee?"

"Since when do you drink coffee?" she asked.

Jack was too tired even to worry about acting twelve. He sipped his breakfast drink and answered honestly. "I didn't sleep real well last night and I need to wake up."

Marie was confused. "Well-- you're almost thirteen; I guess I could perk some more..."

There must have been a little caffeine in the chocolate powder, because as soon as Jack took a sip he began to feel more alert. *That's it, fire up those neurons!* he thought. Only then did he realize the significance of the exchange he'd just had with his mother.

"Oh! Wait, don't make more coffee, Mom. I don't know what I was thinking."

"Are you sure, Jackie? I think you're old enough."

He would have loved a cup of java, but wasn't sure about this whole "perking" thing. He'd gotten used to modern coffeemakers that were quick and easy. On the other hand, the electric percolator that was in this kitchen was something Jack remembered as being slower and requiring more effort, elegant though it seemed. He didn't want to cause his mom any more work than was necessary; she'd just taken care of him for two weeks. "No, I'm fine. I was just zoning out," he said.

"'Zoning out'?" Marie repeated. "That's a new one! Are the kids finished saying 'groovy' already?"

Jack didn't even hear his mother's question. He was already thinking ahead: *Is this just the first day of the next forty years that I have to relive? If it is, I really will have the chance to buy charter stock in Apple Computers and write "Stairway to Heaven;" but I've learned better than to try and stop assassinations...* and he stopped himself from going any further. *I've already been through that thought process. I don't know why I'm here, but it's not for that.* And he felt a sinking feeling in his stomach as realized that he had not a single answer. Not even the name of that damned song!

He finished his liquid breakfast with very little conversation, and for the first time in two weeks he went to his room and quickly dressed for school. Jack was less concerned with trying to appear twelve; he actually made an attempt to match his shirt and pants. It wasn't easy. His wardrobe was such a hodge-podge of colors and fabrics that nothing really seemed to work well, but he managed to find a mustard-colored long-sleeved shirt and brown corduroy pants. It seemed like an outfit that would keep him warm, if nothing else. This was late November, and Maryland was cooling down for the year.

Marie drove him to school as she usually did, and the little bit of sun that managed to filter through the gray clouds shone on the fronts of the brick houses that lined every street. Many of them had brightly colored cardboard turkeys and/or pilgrims displayed in their windows, as Thanksgiving was coming up that Thursday. It had always been Jack's favorite holiday. He recalled that his boyhood friends generally preferred Christmas or Hanukkah, depending on their religious persuasion, because of the gifts received. One friend, Albert, even said he preferred his own birthday, which Jack thought was a bit selfish. But as he got older he realized that his love for Thanksgiving may have come out of a basic desire for family unity. It really was the only day they spent together without the distraction of gifts or church services or fireworks, and the food was certainly a bonus.

Jack walked into the school building for the third time in as many weeks, and headed straight for room 114. As he navigated the hallways, he felt as if he were separated from all the other students. He could see them, he could hear them, but he wasn't really in their midst. It was like he was watching it all from far away.

As Mr. Anderson took roll, Jack listened to himself answer "here" when his name was called. After homeroom he climbed the stairs to first period, hearing occasional bits and pieces of conversations from other students passing by. "…Everybody's gonna have a shag for the yearbook…" "…Nixon should never have gone into Cambodia…" "…I can't believe you didn't know the Beatles broke up…" and "…I'll trade you tuna salad for bologna…" all floated by like speech balloons in a comic strip.

Jack began to feel very sad, like his life was futile. He really didn't belong here any longer, and yet he didn't know what purpose he might serve if he returned to 2010. No matter what he did, it ended in failure. He shuffled into Miss Kefauver's science lab and found his seat with Paul and Hafeez.

"Hey, Oliver's back!" Paul said jovially. "Where you been, boy?"

Jack forced himself to speak. "Pneumonia. It was a drag."

"We missed you," Hafeez grinned, "we thought maybe we could get you to bet on the 'skins yesterday!"

"You're not getting any more of my cake," Jack replied. Hey-- he gave a snappy answer! Maybe he didn't feel quite as bad as he thought.

"You don't need more cake," Paul teased, patting Jack's pudgy tummy.

"Look who's talking there, Hoss!" Jack shot back, pointing to Paul's even rounder belly. Okay, this was getting easier. Suddenly the classroom seemed abuzz with life.

"I guess you heard about Larry Berger," Hafeez remarked.

"Yeah, but not much. Just that a truck hit his car. I was in the hospital for a couple of days myself, so I missed the news."

"A truck?" Hafeez asked. "Where did you hear that?"

Actually, Jack hadn't heard it. He'd only assumed it since that's what happened before. "I don't remember..." he answered cautiously.

"Oh wow," Paul exclaimed, "so you don't know the details?"

"Apparently not..."

"It wasn't a truck," Paul began, "it was his aunt's car, and she got killed too. I heard her boyfriend was driving and he was pretty drunk."

"What?" Jack was shocked. He sat up straight in his seat. Had he caused another death by meddling with Larry's destiny?

Hafeez jumped in: "Yeah, it was real close to their house, at Tenbrook and Lark Lane. The skid marks are still there."

Jack was still trying to make sense of things. "Wait, you said his *aunt*? Who was she?"

"She lived right around the corner," Hafeez said, "I think in the house with that little yapping dog, 'cause it's gone now."

"You know that kid Luther?" Paul interjected. "She was his mom. And I heard he was in Larry's car too."

"What? Larry and Luther were cousins?" Jack said with disbelief.

"Yeah," Paul replied, "but Larry never told anybody. I guess I wouldn't want to admit it if I was related to him either."

To Jack's surprise, that statement rather angered him. Even though Luther had been a major cause of his middle school miseries, the young bully was still a boy who'd lost his mother. How could Paul, who was a 'good kid,' not see that? But then again, Jack could easily have heard himself making the same kind of callous comment before he had grown up emotionally. He understood that despite the heartless sound of the sentence, Paul hadn't meant for it to hurt: he was just presenting it as a matter of fact.

Jack regrouped his thoughts and asked, "Well, what happened to Luther?"

"Don't know, don't care," Hafeez replied. "He hasn't been in school picking on anybody, so that's good."

Jack was able to let Hafeez' equally unkind words roll off his back as well. He wondered what this meant for his future, and if he'd somehow trapped himself in time by interfering with Larry's life. By the time Miss Kefauver began her first period lecture, Jack had withdrawn back into thought.

The rest of the school day might have been remarkable or mundane; Jack really wasn't a part of it. He moved through the building submerged in a sea of conflicting thoughts and questions. He could almost feel the salt water stinging his eyes. Only occasionally would he allow himself to surface, and even then, only long enough to respond to a question or react to his surroundings in some necessary way. Then it was back underwater, where both sight and sound gave way to introspection. Jack waded through the cafeteria at lunchtime, choosing not to eat, sitting quietly with his two friends. He scanned the room looking for Luther, who wasn't there. He would gladly have given him some lunch money.

When school was dismissed, Jack began to walk home alone. It may have been cold or unseasonably warm. He wasn't paying attention; he just walked briskly, heading for the intersection of Tenbrook and Lark Lane. He had to see the spot for himself.

There were the skid marks, just as Paul had promised. There were also tiny little bits of clear red plastic next to the curb; Jack wondered if they might be remnants of the accident that somehow still survived at the scene. Knowing that two people were recently killed there, one because of him, Jack expected to feel guilt, or some eerie sense of death in the air; but there was nothing. In fact, he even began to feel somewhat hopeful, though he didn't understand why. He just stood for a minute or two, 'absorbing' the spot, until he finally looked up and glanced down Lark Lane.

There was the Bergers' house, with a *For Sale* sign protruding from the privacy hedge. He moved slowly along the sidewalk toward the sign, stopping just before the opening where the hedge parted for the front walk. Jack peered around the corner, and sitting there on Larry's front step, between the two magnolia trees, was Luther, looking down at the ground. His right arm was in a cast. Mrs. Berger was there too, with one hand atop his head, offering comfort that Luther didn't seem ready to accept. When she went into the house, Jack stepped fully into view.

"Luther?" he said tentatively.

Luther looked up. "It's *you!*" he snapped.

"Is this where you live now?" Jack probed, searching for anything to latch onto.

Luther rose and strode halfway down the Bergers' walk. "Yeah, so?"

Closer up, Jack could now see that Luther's eyes were red and his face was puffy, like he'd been crying. Best to proceed with caution. "Listen, I heard about Larry, but I didn't know about your mom until today. I just wanted you to know I'm sorry."

Luther wrinkled his brow and looked quite annoyed. He took a few more short steps toward Jack. "Well maybe you *should* be sorry! I saw you messing with my aunt's car. Why did you do that?"

Jack certainly couldn't explain that one, so he tried to redirect. "Listen, I know what it's like to lose people you love. Especially all of a sudden..."

"You don't know *anything!*" Luther interjected with disgust.

Jack was at a loss. All he could think to do was to fall back on the old faithful mantra: "It's not your fault." But this time the words were meaningless.

Luther seemed bitter, and replied: "Then it's *your* fault!"

As he stood there across from his childhood demon, Jack's threads of thought began to unravel. He realized he was no counselor, and that *Good Will Hunting* wasn't meant to be a textbook. Nervously, his eyes refocused past Luther onto the glass panel in the storm door behind him. That's when the moment of realization came.

He saw part of his own reflection peeking out from behind Luther's round, real image, and immediately recalled the sight of himself in front of Francis, and the mysterious words: "you're the reflection and I'm the substance." Now, Jack was in Francis' position, and the substance simply began to flow.

"Luther, don't try to find fault in this, find a solution instead." Somehow Jack knew he'd just quoted Henry Ford, though it was through the filters of his own vernacular.

"A solution!" Luther said. "Okay, go back in time and don't mess with the car!"

Jack was struck by the choice of words. If he hadn't known the first outcome himself, he would have shrugged off Luther's response as one of the common stages of grief. But it was uncanny how he made such a definite connection, especially when the Dodge Dart Jack had vandalized was still in front of the house. It was obviously the Bergers' *other* car that was in the accident. Yet Jack felt like a hypocrite as he said, "How do you know that would make any difference?"

Luther hesitated before responding. "You changed the car! It wouldn't have happened that way if you didn't change the car."

"I guess that's possible," Jack said as the substance flowed once more, "but nothing ever happens all by itself. Everything is in relation to everything else!" Had he just unwittingly paraphrased the Buddha?

Luther stood ready with an answer. "But *you* didn't belong anywhere in relation to that car!"

Jack was shocked by Luther's insight: he was talking like he'd really thought things through.

Luther continued. "Larry was my best friend! If you didn't mess with those tires he'd still be alive!" He held back tears of anger.

"But you don't *know* that!" Jack said. He knew Luther had it wrong, but there was no way he could say so.

"...and then maybe only the *other* car with the *drunk* driver... would've..." Luther couldn't bring himself to finish the sentence.

In the recesses of his being Jack heard his father's voice: *...those were tears of relief... my nemesis was finally gone...* and he realized that he probably understood much more than Luther was ready to hear. "I'm sorry," he said. "I know you can't see it, but I was just trying to do the right thing."

"You don't know what's right! What's gonna *happen* to me now?"

As Mrs. Berger stepped into view through the glass of the storm door, Jack could again feel some inner force taking control of his speech, and he was shocked by the seemingly harsh words that came out of his mouth.

"Luther, once or twice in your life, fate taps you on the shoulder. If you turn around and look, he'll show you the direction you're supposed to go." That was General Patton speaking. Where had *he* come from?

Luther burst into tears. "Well this is for fate!" He punched Jack in the stomach with his good arm, knocking the wind out of him. The bulky cast on his other arm caused Luther to spin around, and he found himself looking through the glass, right into the eyes of his Aunt Doris.

Meanwhile, Jack felt all the air leaving his body. He reeled backwards and sensed himself falling, but he never hit the ground. Instead, he began to see strange things. He knew he must be hallucinating from a lack of oxygen, but it was all still very real. Luther was gone. There in front of him instead, he saw his father Joseph holding the small television set from Jack's room. On the screen, Brig Owens was running into the end zone with half of his jersey missing, while Joseph said, "The rest of the game will go the same!"

Then the image quickly changed to Marie, with a Stratego game in one hand and a flier in the other, which she held out to Jack, saying: "Please vote for County Blair for Charlie Council!"

Next he saw Jeannie, who just giggled as she handed him a 45 r.p.m. record. The label read:

What's it called, dammit?
by Aretha Franklin.

By the time he looked back up to share the joke, his sister's image was dissolving into a sparse field of orange sparks that silently flickered in front of him. He was sure he was suffocating. Nevertheless, his soul spoke effortlessly:

"Is this my life passing before my eyes?"

"Only the parts of it you missed!" It was Francis.

"So this is it, Francis? This is my change? I don't even know what I changed!" He could sense, but not see, the White Room around them, and their communication was entirely through thought.

"The last puzzle piece is in place, Jackie Boy!" Francis seemed very self-satisfied.

Jack could feel all the souls he'd seen inside of Francis; every one of them a part of who he was, watching and listening; but he was particularly aware of Henry Ford, Buddha, General Patton, and of course, his dad. The unlikely foursome seemed to be quite pleased with things.

Jack was just confused: "It can't be finished; there are so many answers I don't have yet!"

Francis spoke with very calming thoughts. "Jack, you won't need answers. What you'll find from here on is that there's no more need for questions!"

As Jack considered what may have been the most comforting thing he'd ever heard, he found he could now see the White Room. It was different than it had been before; the walls were quickly closing in, quietly surrounding him like bandages around a mummy. But the white fluff didn't stop; it continued to press in, to squeeze, to engulf Jack, who just hung there in mid-air, limp and helpless, waiting perhaps to die. Even his mind was now stopping. It was the end.

Silence.
Darkness.
Peace.

It was the beginning! The recent memory of a loud sound, a quick snap into awareness as he gasped for air, and the white walls suddenly letting go of his body, all greeted Jack as the world might greet an infant being pulled from its mother's womb. He was disoriented enough to expect some kind of ethereal music to be playing as he crossed into Heaven, but instead he heard a familiar song:

"...Since you've been gone,
(why'd you do it, why'd you have to do it...)"

His eyes began to focus on his whereabouts as the white airbags deflated around him, releasing Jack from their tight, lifesaving protection, and Aretha began to sing verse two:

"Baby baby sweet baby,
I didn't mean to run you away..."

And there he was, sitting in the remains of his little Ford Focus, with the radio still miraculously playing and the front end of a dump truck peering through an opening that used to be the passenger's side window.

The truck driver jumped out and ran over to Jack. "Hey! You okay? Lucky you had a new car!" he shouted.

Jack thought this was an odd first thing to say to someone who had probably nearly been killed! "I *think* I'm okay..." he tried to move his limbs. "Everything seems to work." He slowly became aware of the fact that he was in his fifty-two year old body once more.

Almost immediately he heard sirens in the distance. He looked up at the truck driver and tried to remember what had just happened, but he could not. "Where are we?" he asked.

"Still in the middle of the street! I didn't see you around that tall hedge!" That didn't answer Jack's question.

Within a few seconds a police car arrived. The officer got out and walked rather nonchalantly over to Jack. "I wouldn't have used the siren if I knew you were driving one of these," he said jokingly.

Jack had no idea what he was talking about. He tried to open the door, but it wouldn't cooperate.

"Just sit tight," said the officer, "we'll pry it open, or cut you out if we have to. Emergency vehicle's on the way. You think you'll be okay for a few minutes?"

Jack was stiff and still a little out of breath, but all-in-all he felt surprisingly well. "Yeah, I think I'm good," he said.

Some residents came out of their houses to watch the rescue in progress, and it took several minutes for the emergency crew to free Jack from the shell of his crumpled compact car. Once out, he managed to walk by himself, and when he had gotten his bearings he looked around to see just where he was. It was his old neighborhood-- the corner of Tenbrook and Lark Lane.

CHAPTER TWELVE

"**D**ELIVERY FOR a Mr. O'Lantern?" A police officer stepped into the cubicle where the doctor on call at St. Andrew's Hospital had been checking Jack over.

No broken bones, no concussion, no major scratches. He was now just waiting to be discharged.

"Yes, that's what it says: 'Mr. Jack O'Lantern,'" the officer repeated, as he held out Jack's briefcase. "I found this at the corner of Tenbrook and Lark Lane."

As was his tendency, Jack avoided eye contact. Instead, he focused on the visitor's name tag, which read: *Sgt. T. Edwards*. The quick, quirky feeling of déjà vu was too much to resist, and Jack looked up and into the face of his old school chum. "Tim?" he said cautiously.

"Yep!" the officer confirmed.

"Tim Edwards!" Jack exclaimed. "Sonofagun!" He took the briefcase.

"Hey, long time no see, buddy boy! I showed up to make a police report after they brought you here. That briefcase got thrown from your car; when I looked inside I couldn't believe who it belonged to!"

"You're a sergeant now?" Jack asked.

"Only for the last seventeen years! Boy have we been out of touch."

"I probably haven't seen you since high school...?"

"That sounds about right. Wendy and I'll be celebrating number twenty-nine next year. Five kids!"

"You mean *Wendy* Wendy? Majorette Wendy?"

"Man, you really *did* move out of the loop, didn't you, Jack? I heard you married Kate... you still together?"

"Oh, no-- we divorced almost..." Jack calculated, "twenty-five years ago! I'm married to a California girl now."

"Well," Tim said more seriously, "your California girl should be very glad you had the HAL 9000 on board. It saved your life, man."

"HAL 9000?" Jack asked bewilderedly.

Not realizing he'd been asked a serious question, Tim continued. "I've seen a lot of accidents, Jackie. If this had happened five years ago, there's no way you would've survived getting hit by that that dump truck! The HAL System's made my job a lot less depressing."

"What HAL System?" Jack said, still a bit loopy from the accident.

Before Tim had a chance to respond, he was summoned by a call to his portable police radio. He answered and quickly decided he needed to be elsewhere. "Wish we could talk longer, Jack; it was great to see you, and I'm real glad you're okay!"

He left Jack alone with his briefcase.

While waiting to be discharged, Jack took a look through his attaché. He recognized everything: letters, documents, computer storage paraphernalia, even a half-bag of Halls cough drops. "Hmm..." he remarked, "I guess everything else *did* go the same." And there was his cell phone, which reminded him that he hadn't yet spoken to Violet. Had anyone called her? She was listed in the phone address book as an I.C.E. contact, but if Tim had made that call, he undoubtedly would have said so. And besides, Jack was healthy and conscious, so it probably didn't constitute an emergency anyway. He needed to make the call himself.

But that brought up some other issues: Jack didn't remember why he was in his old neighborhood to begin with or where Violet might be. He wanted to assume they still lived in Florida. He took out his wallet and checked his driver's license: they did. So where would she be when she received this call? He swallowed hard and started to dial Violet's mobile number, just as a nurse walked by the cubicle and reminded him that cell phone use was prohibited inside the building.

"But I have to call my wife, and I haven't been discharged yet," he said.

She led him through a lobby area to another cubicle with a computer and a land-line phone, which he used to dial out. The conversation with Violet seemed strange and almost dreamlike: from Jack's perspective, he hadn't heard her voice in over two weeks, and it was like feeling the first rays of sun after having been locked away in a cellar for that long. Violet on the other hand, spoke as if he'd never been away; and after talking for a couple of minutes, Jack was able to confirm that he had seen her just two hours earlier. They were in Maryland visiting his mother, and he took the car to cruise his old neighborhood while Violet and Marie took care of some other things. Jack remembered none of this, and was a little disconcerted by his wife's seemingly nonchalant response to the news about his accident. Her simple exclamation: "Oh gosh honey, are you alright?" wasn't what he would have expected after surviving a wreck that totaled a vehicle!

Violet told him that she would drive Marie's car to the hospital to pick him up and then they could see about renting a car for the trip home. They exchanged 'I-love-yous' and the call was over. Jack was now even more puzzled by the seemingly cavalier attitude of everyone around him; especially his wife. He also began to wonder if the time spent in 1970 had just been a dream that occurred in the few seconds he lost consciousness during the accident. It had all seemed so real.

Then his eyes fell on the computer which was next to the phone. "I wonder if this has got Internet access?" he asked himself. Locating the browser, he typed in *www.switchboard.com*, and looked himself up. He was at the same Florida address that was on his driver's license. He visited *yahoo.com* and was able to access his email account just as he always had. Jack checked a few more familiar websites, and when they all turned out to be as he expected, he began to believe that he had in fact just emerged from a dream.

But with a computer at his disposal and no explicit instructions not to use it, Jack followed the nagging urge to check one last item online. He 'Googled' "HAL 9000," with the hope of discovering what Tim had been talking about. There were thousands of results, mostly having to do with the famous *Space*

Odyssey computer. No real help there. But Tim had also used the term "HAL *System;*" perhaps that would yield more of an explanation. Immediately, Jack saw several results, and clicked on the first one, which brought him to a *Wikipedia* article:

HAL System

An advanced automobile safety system credited with saving thousands of lives and preventing countless injuries. The name is borrowed from the fictitious "HAL 9000" computer in Stanley Kubrick's 1968 Film *2001: A Space Odyssey*. Introduced on a limited basis in 2003, the HAL System has since become standard equipment on most new cars.

Jack began to read faster, and with increasing interest.

Unlike traditional airbag systems which simply deploy on impact, the HAL System uses laser technology to register the size, weight and current seating position of the driver and each passenger, 256 times per second. Additionally, a gyroscope-based sensor reads the slope of the vehicle (uphill, downhill, left and right), and the direction and intensity of any impact, to determine the proper deployment pressure of each airbag, for each occupant. An average of forty-eight airbags is installed in a typical system, targeting passengers' feet and legs as well as chest, head and torso. Twelve airbags per-person allows an individual to be literally surrounded from head to toe with evenly-distributed protective cushioning in the event of an impact, regardless of their seating position or movement. The seats themselves also become airbags, providing a safer rear body cushion.

A chill of anticipation ran up his spine as he continued to scan the screen.

Originally thought too expensive to be practical, tests of the system worked so well that mass-production began in 2005, greatly reducing the cost, and allowing auto manufacturers to include the HAL System even on compact cars.

And like the big reveal in a whodunit novel, he braced himself for the end of the article, though he already knew what it would say.

Although the name "HAL" is a Science Fiction reference, it is also a play on words, resembling the name of the system's inventor, Luther Howell (b. 1956) who in 2009 was awarded the National Medal of Technology and Innovation for his life-saving work.

Jack sat in stunned silence. It suddenly made sense. All of the events, past and present, had worked together toward the moment of impact-- when Jack would be unwittingly saved by the person he had unwittingly saved. But the implications went far beyond just that. If not for a very specific sequence of events, his precious Violet would have been notified as an I.C.E. contact by a stranger bearing bad news, and Jack's *widow* would be on her way to the hospital now. He began to delve into some of the more complex details of that scenario when his thoughts were interrupted.

"Mr. Oliver? You shouldn't be using that computer!" It was the nurse again, bringing Jack his discharge slip as she politely scolded him.

"Sorry, I didn't realize..." he half-lied, taking the paper and turning toward the lobby.

"Do you have a ride home?" she asked.

"Yes thank you, my wife is on her way." He found that idea to be quite exhilarating. *My wife,* he reiterated to himself, *not my widow!*

On his way to the main lobby, he stopped in the gift shop. In a refrigerated case there were flowers for sale, and he was delighted to find some purple roses. They were expensive, but they were

Violet's favorite, so he bought them. She of course would have no idea why this was such a significant event, but Jack couldn't resist giving them to her to celebrate the future they now had before them.

He sat in the lobby and waited amid the fragrance of Violet's flowers, when a sudden salvo of questions burst into his mind. For starters, was this the whole of his change? He'd expected some great alteration of his quality of life, but what he'd apparently gotten instead was a prolonging of his life as it was.

Also, how could it be that *his* one change had actually caused a change for Luther? Could it even work that way? And the fact that an additional person had been killed certainly should be figured into it as well-- shouldn't it? Then again, did Jack really even cause that to happen, or would Luther's mother eventually have died anyway, like Larry did? Maybe *time* was the only factor that Jack modified, and the different mix of dimensions simply brought about a different outcome. Perhaps he really just helped to make two otherwise meaningless deaths count for something. That was a more pleasant thought than the other extreme: that he might be guilty of involuntary manslaughter!

And what about the thousands of other people who now remained alive because of Luther's invention? Not to mention their children... and *their* children? Was Jack partly responsible for all those lives being saved?

And the questions kept exploding all around him. He buried his face in the bouquet and took a big whiff to try and mask the odor of the smoke from each blast. With the sweeter fragrance came a reminder of Francis' final words to him: "What you'll find from here on is that there's no more need for questions." If that was indeed true, then why did he still have so many?

It was something he noticed first through the corner of his eye that made Jack lift his head up out of the roses and look toward the front door: a very familiar vertical motion. At best, strangers found it curious, and at worst, they saw it as pathetic or even threatening. But for Jack it was a confirmation that God existed: it was Jack Junior, awkwardly toe-walking through the lobby in all his autistic glory, his fingers splayed tightly, and his face beaming with the innocence of the angels. The gentle giant towered almost a foot above his equally angelic traveling companion: the love of Jack's life and the center of his world. Jack's heart nearly jumped from his chest when Violet's gaze met his from halfway across the lobby. He burst into tears. The beautiful brunette smiled and led JJ over to the bench where his father was sitting, weeping, holding a briefcase and a bouquet of purple flowers. He set them both aside as he stood slowly to greet his two loves.

"Don't worry sweetie, I'm not mad at you for wrecking the car!" Violet teased, not quite sure how to take Jack's unusual display of emotion. She was trying to put him at ease by being more like him; but for the moment he couldn't help but be more like her. The embrace that followed was the same one that Jack always expected to occur when he first arrived in Heaven and met Jesus. It was a spiritual moment; combining not only bodies, but souls. And when JJ spontaneously added a bear hug of his own to the two lovers as they held each other, Jack realized that Francis was right: this was the best there was!

Being the feeler that *she* was, Violet had no choice but to absorb some of Jack's overwhelming emotion, and soon she was crying with him. "Jack, my goodness, sweetheart! Whatever it is, it's going to be okay!"

He kissed her face several times. "It already is! Oh, it's so good to see you!" He looked up at Jack Junior, "And you too, Sonny Boy!"

"Sonny Boy," Jack Junior echoed.

"You just saw both of us a little while ago," Violet said through her involuntary tears.

"It seems longer," Jack replied, "and I guess the accident kind of made me think."

"Seems more like it made you *feel*…"

"And what's wrong with that, my love?"

Violet smiled contentedly. "Nothing. Nothing at all… my love."

"My love," Jack Junior echoed.

Jack picked up the flowers and presented them to his soul mate.

Violet's doe-eyed reaction confirmed that he still knew where her soft spots were.

"Here, these reminded me of you," he said.

"They're beautiful," she half-whispered.

"Isn't that what I just said?" Jack replied with a little wink.

After a few more moments of loving each other, the three Olivers made their way to Marie's borrowed car, which Violet had parked in front of the hospital. When Jack offered to drive, his wife was hesitant, thinking he may still need time to decompress after the accident. Jack felt otherwise; wanting to return to the normalcy for which he now had a fresh appreciation.

He joyfully took his usual place in the driver's seat and began to remember more things as they headed back to his mother's house. It was just the three of them: Jack, Violet and JJ, who had made this particular trip. The two girls were away at school for the semester, and Will was now sixteen and old enough to stay on his own. Of course he jumped at that chance. It was the first weekend of September: three days long because of the Labor Day holiday, and the brief window of opportunity was open just long enough to allow a visit like this one.

Violet held her roses in one hand while she turned on the radio with the other. A song was playing:

"Baby baby sweet baby,

There's something that I just gotta say…"

"Hey!" she said. "How long has it been since you last heard this?"

Jack couldn't even answer.

Violet began to softly sing along. "Since you've been gone, (why'd you do it, why'd you have to do it…)"

Jack just chuckled to himself and thought: *If you only knew!* He'd probably never be able to tell her even that he *had* been gone, much less why. And he guessed she really didn't need to know anyway. All that mattered now was that they'd been given more time together.

And nineteen-year-old Jack Junior just looked contentedly through a Dr. Seuss book in the back seat as they rolled along.

Marie's house wasn't the same one in which Jack grew up, but it was just as inviting. For the past twenty-six years it was the place where the various kids and grandkids came on holidays and Sunday afternoons; and Carl, her husband during those same years, was as much of a grandpa as Joseph had ever been. As the Olivers stepped into the house, returning from Jack's unexpected escapade, both parents greeted him with more curiosity than concern. By now Jack was growing used to the notion that a 'fatal' car accident was no longer a big deal. His old nemesis Luther had seen to it that usually the only fatality was the car itself. So rather than becoming alarmed or offended by their lack of worry, he began to feel a bit giddy over it.

He was also struck by his mother's almost regal silver-haired appearance. Having just spent two weeks with her as a much younger woman, the physical contrast was a bit startling; but even more remarkable was her aura. Marie exuded a feeling; this was no longer the woman who put her hopes on hold until her children were independent. Rather, this person offered her life experience, her education, and all the other things she'd accumulated in the past four decades, anytime she offered herself. Maybe the feeling Jack sensed the most in her now was one of fulfillment. After all, she had found *her* soul mate and lived happily ever after; and she seemed to recognize the fact that her son had been just as fortunate.

"You can borrow my other car if you need it," Carl began, practical as always.

"The Ford was insured to the nines," Jack replied, "so we should get a replacement pretty easily. Besides, the police report said it was the truck driver's fault!"

Jack's tall, bearded step-father responded: "That still doesn't give you a car to drive in the mean time. Here's the key to the Toyota."

"Well thanks, Pop!" Jack said, gratefully taking the key. "I'll have her home by midnight!"

They laughed.

This was how Marie and Carl were: they liked to take care of people. It was also the way Joseph had been, though his approach was even more pragmatic. Jack now thought about the people who had been role models all his life, and how long it had taken him to follow suit. But he was finally starting to get there, and like his various parents, he had a lot of experiences that could now be translated to wisdom. And that wisdom might someday contribute to happy endings for his and Violet's children, and the cycle would begin again.

But how did someone like Jack Junior fit into this picture? He would certainly never become a father, and would likely require residential care when he grew older. Jack just looked at his son sitting there on the couch with Violet next to him on one side and Marie on the other. Everyone knew that he had a limited understanding of the words that were spoken to him; yet everyone seemed to seek him out to talk to. It certainly wasn't that he offered lively conversation; in fact he certainly did not. No, he offered much more! And having spent a brief time "inside" Francis, Jack now understood what it was that drew people to Jack Junior.

It seemed like a paradox until someone experienced it: the boy that barely spoke was actually a master communicator. His interaction came from the deepest level of his humanity: straight from the soul. He joined the extremes of thinking and feeling by simply *being*. This was what Jack had experienced in the White Room: communication that was beyond any logical or emotional boundaries. And he now understood. Jack Junior was born into a state that most people strove to achieve: he had *always* been a butterfly!

"Jack, you've had the hardest day today," Marie said, "so you get to decide what's for dinner. We could carry in Chinese, I could cook..."

"I hate to make you cook," Jack answered, "but for some reason I would *love* to taste your baked chicken again!"

"I'll be glad to help you, Marie!" Violet chimed in.

"Well, we'll need a few things from the store then," Marie replied. "Chicken, lemons..."

"I'll drive if you like," Jack offered.

"You've done enough 'driving' for one day," Violet teased. "Why don't you stay here and relax, and we'll be back soon with ingredients!"

Jack accepted the offer, and the ladies went off. It was now Carl's turn to communicate with JJ for a while, and as the pair worked on a jigsaw puzzle, Jack felt the urge to explore. He made his way upstairs to a room that had once been part of the attic, before it was finished off. The small space was now used mostly for storage. There was an old sewing machine, a mattress set, and many framed pictures, most of which had been painted by Marie's mother. In the afternoon light that filtered through the pink window curtains, Jack could see them all on the floor, leaning against the walls, stacked two and three deep.

His attention was drawn to one much smaller, plain black frame that was hanging up and out of the way. He didn't recall it specifically, but he instantly recognized the small piece of artwork that was in it. Jack blew the dust off of the glass and looked at his butterfly-- the one that used to be part of Francis' paper. Marie thought he had drawn it himself, and must have preserved it in that little matted enclosure. The glass had a sort of a chalky glaze; the kind that glass gets when it's been sealed in a frame for a very long time. The picture inside now seemed quite colorful; more so than Jack recalled. Maybe it was the oil in the image that had cured over the years, or maybe it was just magic, but there was a beautiful deep blue tint to the wings.

"I wonder if Mom would let me take this?" Jack said to himself, as he set it aside. He'd just begun to casually flip through some of the other paintings and pastels when again he stopped short. There it was!

"Oh my gosh..." Jack exclaimed quietly, as he pulled a very old frame from the stack. It was the charcoal portrait of Francis; a beardless, smooth-skinned old man with a rather stern expression. Not at all like the person Jack had met.

"You look better with the beard," he said to the flat, lifeless image.

"I never liked that picture," Francis replied.

Jack didn't think twice about the response. He knew the words weren't coming from the picture, but from within himself. After all, just like Edison and Beethoven, Francis was a part of who Jack was. "So, what do you think of my one change?" Jack asked himself.

"Very clumsily executed; but a very elegant outcome!" the Irish voice answered with a chuckle.

"That's okay, Jack. Engineers are outcome-oriented anyway," Joseph added.

Jack smiled. He took his butterfly picture and headed down the stairs, just as Marie and Violet were returning with two small bags of groceries.

"Dinner will take about an hour," Marie announced. "Miss Violet, I think we'll just be in each other's way in this little kitchen; why don't you relax? You've had a long day too!"

"Are you sure, Marie?" she asked politely.

"Yes! I don't get to cook like this very often."

"Well, thank you!" Violet smiled.

Having been virtually banished from the kitchen, Violet joined her husband in the living room. They stood together and looked briefly at JJ, who was happily poring over puzzle pieces with his grandpa. He was in good hands (and so was JJ).

Without speaking, husband and wife relocated to the spacious property outdoors, where the sky was beginning to turn orange as the sun slowly danced away to share its warmth with other parts of the world. Jack gave Violet the little picture frame.

"Did anyone ever show you this?"

Violet looked it over with interest. "No... it's beautiful! Where did it come from?"

This was no time for Jack to try and share the real story, so he carefully abbreviated his explanation. "I made it... in 1970."

"Really? You were, let's see... thirteen when you painted this?"

"Twelve actually, but I didn't paint it. It's mostly pencil."

"But it's so colorful!"

Jack examined the little image once more. "Yeah... that just happened to it over time. I haven't really looked at it for many years."

"Well I think it's too beautiful not to display," she said.

"Funny, I feel the same way about you!" he replied.

Violet batted her eyelashes playfully, like butterfly wings. "Flattery will get you everywhere, kind sir!"

And they kissed under the setting sun.

Jack's life started over as the day came to an end. Rather than looking backwards and lamenting *what if...* he found himself looking forward, and anticipating *what's next?* In time he would come to fully appreciate the gift that he'd been given, though he would never fully understand it. And he didn't need to: for as he had learned from Francis, when you're seeing the world through the eyes of a butterfly, there's no more need for questions.

BOOK TWO: LUTHER

… you don't know how great you can be! How much you can love!
What you can accomplish! And what your potential is!

--Anne Frank

CHAPTER THIRTEEN

LUTHER HAD been lifting boxes most of the afternoon. When the produce trucks arrived, he was always the first one to get pulled from the floor to come and help unload. As the wooden pallets rolled out one by one, stacked with crates of cantaloupes and bananas and celery, Luther would intercept them and quickly distribute their contents to the proper location. He always kept a mental tally of what was on display in the store versus what was in the back waiting to be brought out: if anyone ever needed to know what to reorder they could just ask him. It had been suggested more than once that he might eventually make a good produce manager, but the owner, Mr. Murphy, said Luther simply wasn't smart enough. Murphy once imitated Foghorn Leghorn and mimicked: "That boy's about as sharp as a bowlin' ball..." behind Luther's back, or so he thought. Actually, Luther overheard him, but didn't understand that he was being made fun of. He just thought it was amusing that his boss was imitating a cartoon character.

Every Tuesday a particular lady customer would come into Murphy's Mart to do her weekly shopping. Luther always knew when she came in because her rubber-soled shoes chirped on the tile floors as she navigated her cart up and down the aisles. There were also other customers with chirping shoes, but the tall woman with the plaid purse was the only one that had this *particular* chirp, and something about it just made Luther feel good. Maybe even hopeful. He could keep track of her position in the store just by the sound, and when the chirp stopped for a few minutes it meant she was checking out. When it started up again, Luther would leave whatever he was doing and go up front to help her with her bags. It wasn't part of his job, and the woman certainly didn't need the help; but Luther was drawn to the sound, and in his mind it was just the commonsense thing to do. He liked taking care of this customer, and no one ever questioned the particularity of his politeness.

Today it was 2:40, and Luther's favorite shopper hadn't yet made her usual Tuesday appearance. Knowing he'd be off work at 3:00, he grew anxious at the thought that he might not get to 'hear' her this week. Gingerly arranging a display of peaches, he looked at his watch once a minute or so, a little confused. Finally at 2:48 he heard it:

Chirp!

His friend had arrived.

Chirp chirp... she moved through the store.

A very reassuring sound it was, and for the moment all was right with Luther's world. He found busywork to do, lining up cucumbers and rotating eggplants, waiting for the woman to check out.

"Luther, it's after three! You can go now," Murphy said, half-sneaking-up behind him.

"I know it is; it's okay," Luther replied. The chirping had moved to aisle eight. The tall lady must have needed toilet paper. Or Dixie cups.

"I ain't payin' you overtime," Murphy said soundly.

"Okay," replied Luther. There had never been any thought of overtime, he was just waiting to complete his expected routine. He "fluffed" bunches of grapes, listening intently as the shrill squeaks resounded through the small mom 'n' pop grocery.

Chirp chirp chirp... she must have been in more of a hurry than usual. The sound seemed to move straight from paper products to the cash registers. Luther looked at his watch: 3:14. Time to man the lookout post. He hurried to the candy aisle where he could see both registers without being too-too obvious himself. Standing patiently next to a display of Pez dispensers, he glanced at the designs. There was one with the head of Uncle Sam, another with the head of an Indian chief, and Luther's favorite: a red one with the head of a giraffe. He thought that if he weren't twenty-one years old he might actually buy that one for himself, but he knew everyone else would think it was childish. Plus, the budget was tight, and a plastic candy dispenser wasn't a necessity. He peeked around the corner, waiting quietly while his favorite customer checked out her fewer-than-usual items. Murphy's cash registers were the old fashioned kind with a dinging bell, and when Luther heard the cash drawer open and close, he took that as his cue to step into view.

The plaid-purse lady expectantly glanced toward the apron-clad worker as he approached the front of the store. "Hello, Luther!" she said with a smile.

"Can I help you with those sacks, ma'am?" Luther asked, quite automatically.

"Always appreciated," she replied, allowing Luther to take over the navigation of her cart. He pushed it onto the large ribbed-rubber mat in front of the doors, waiting patiently for them to open. Once outside, he instantly located her familiar car and loaded everything into the back seat. She preferred it to the trunk.

She knew better than to offer him a tip. She'd tried it once, but Luther simply handed it back to her with a rather confused expression, saying, "This is yours." He wasn't expecting anything in return, and in fact he felt he was paying her back for having gotten to hear the sound of her shoes!

Once she was gone, Luther retrieved his jacket from the back of the store and began the sixteen-block walk home.

Maxine Howell didn't even look up when her son came in the door just before 4:00. As always, the frail, defeated redhead was engrossed in her book: a paperback novel with a cover picture of a beautiful woman being ravished by a handsome, shirtless pirate. Or maybe she was being rescued by a handsome, shirtless swashbuckler; either way Luther thought it looked the same as every other book his mom had brought home in the past six months. They came from the library, thrift stores, yard sales, and anyplace else she could find them, as long as they were cheap. Or free: she had to save the rest of her money to buy cigarettes, which had just gone up to forty cents a pack.

Luther never did entirely understand his mom. Her lifestyle was a reflection of the hopelessness that saturated her soul, and he was resigned to the fact that there was nothing he could do for her. He worked at the grocery store all day and went to school some nights. Maxine collected welfare, sitting in a dining room chair where she endlessly chained cigarettes and ran away from her life into the pages of those books. But soon there would be no more need for novels: her story was in its last chapter.

"How was today?" Luther asked, trying to get her attention.

"Mm. Fine..." his mother replied, turning a page. She seldom talked about anything anymore. The cancer had taken over her body, and Luther knew she looked forward to the end of her misery.

"I have to leave for school in an hour," he said flatly, now noticing that even with the saturation of smoke in the room, something just a little bit rotten was cutting through it.

"M-hm. Good, honey." She wasn't even paying attention.

Luther took off his jacket and went into the bathroom to wash his hands. He'd handled some overly-ripe cantaloupes that day, and though he knew that wasn't what he smelled, he still had to rule it out. His mother hadn't moved when he returned to the dining room, shaking water from his fingertips. Of course the odor was still there: the 'cancer smell' was in the room, not on his hands. Though he knew it was pointless, Luther still asked the next question. "You want dinner?"

"There's, um-- probably leftovers," she turned another page, reading feverishly. The cigarette that dangled from her mouth had a rather long ash that looked like it might fall off. Smoke spewed out. A plastic tumbler of sweet tea sat on the table next to her, with a couple of mostly-melted ice cubes floating up at the top. That was good: it showed that she'd gotten up at least once in the last couple of hours.

Luther blinked, his eyes stinging from the smoke. "I'll get something before I go," he said, and headed to his room.

The apartment only had one bedroom, and when the two of them moved in three years earlier, Maxine insisted that Luther take it. She said he was eighteen and needed his own space, and that she was perfectly happy to sleep on the sofa bed. That's what it was for. Of course that also meant that the tiny living room was cluttered with bedroom-type items: there was an alarm clock on the end table and the front coat closet was stuffed with hangers of Maxine's clothes. An assortment of tissue boxes, over-the-counter medicines and little egg-shaped packages of panty hose were scattered around the other surfaces, including the floor, and all of it was blanketed with a thick layer of dust. The rest of the place was in a similar state of chaos: the kitchen appliances were covered with grease, and the white porcelain sink was stained brown. In the bathroom, the toilet hadn't been cleaned for months. The tub was filthy and would barely drain, and the shower didn't work. The carpeted areas hadn't been vacuumed for a long time, and everything in the unit was covered with the brown film that only non-smokers ever seem to notice. Maxine hadn't done any cleaning and rarely left the apartment since she'd been diagnosed. Instead she just sat there smoking and reading: waiting for her escape.

Luther anticipated an escape of his own as he crossed the threshold into his bedroom. It was the one place he could get away from the organizational anarchy. His room was very much the opposite of the rest of the apartment. The bed was made, the furniture was dusted, and his clothes were neatly folded in his dresser drawers. His small closet held only a few items, including the suit he'd worn to his cousin Larry's funeral more than six years earlier. It was now much too small, but he kept it anyway. On the walls were three posters: a team shot of the 1976 Champion Pittsburgh Steelers, another with the members of Led Zeppelin, and of course, Farrah Fawcett in the famous red swimsuit. These images were probably Luther's equivalent of the beautiful woman and the handsome swashbuckler that had become his mother's obsession: they were like imaginary friends who allowed him a glimpse of a different existence. And though to anyone else they might have emphasized the disparity between that world and this one, to Luther they were simply enjoyable to look at. Among other things, he thought Farrah had pretty eyes. He really didn't see the need to acknowledge his own eventualities either, and the fact that even *this* meager excuse for a life would soon be taken away. He had no idea what would happen to him when his mother was gone: when the handsome, shirtless angel of death finally came to her rescue.

Luther had to bend down in order to see himself in the mirror that was attached to his dresser. He'd always been the biggest kid in school, and now he'd grown into a rather large man like his father had been. The world around him sometimes seemed like it was in miniature. Especially his furniture: it was the same bedroom set he'd had since he was six, and everything was little-boy-sized. The reflection that stared back from the glass still reminded Luther of the youngster who'd grown up with that furniture, with straight, dirty blond hair and round, knobby facial features. His eyes were the same nondescript shade of gray they'd always been, but adulthood had blended in the redness of fatigue. Anyone else who looked at Luther would have seen it too. Yet he never thought to ask why his world was this way: his oversized left brain just didn't work like that. It was never about the idealism of what life ought to be, and Luther never felt entitled to anything more than what he already had.

Exhausted, he lay on his bed and rested his head on a pillow, though he knew he dared not fall asleep. Night classes only met once a week, and if he missed even one he might not pass. At the urging of his Aunt Doris he'd managed to secure a small grant based on financial need from a local university, and was currently in his second semester, exploring the possibilities of higher education one class at a time. In this, the spring of 1977, it was Physics 101; and though Luther found it interesting, his real dream was to enter some field involving microscopes. Ever since Christmas of 1963 when his dad presented him with his first one, Luther had been fascinated by all the things that were too small to see without it. He learned the names of the various parts of the instrument: the eyepiece, the tube, the stage... and he loved peering into the tiny secret world that lived on each little glass slide. Even something as mundane as 'diatomaceous earth' could captivate the young boy, who didn't know, and wouldn't have cared, that he was basically looking at a close-up view of cat litter. A bird's feather or a butterfly's wing was even more of an adventure, and Luther would sometimes daydream about becoming small enough to walk around on the slides and touch the things that he saw. If he could reach out and put his arms around one of those little branches that made up a feather, would it feel as soft as it looked? His favorite slide was a thin slice of cork. When he viewed it just right, Luther thought it looked like the surface of the moon, and in the days before Neil Armstrong he would imagine himself being the first human being to go there.

But that was when he was seven. Now he was twenty-one and running late. Though he hadn't fallen asleep, he had lapsed into a rogue daydream that stole away the few minutes he would have had to eat something. No matter; Luther was used to being hungry. It was ironic that someone who worked around food all day got so little of it for himself. He jumped up and grabbed his jacket on the way back out the door: he had a bus to catch.

Maxine just turned another page, squinting to see the print through the smoke. Six months ago she might have paused to occasionally ponder how things ended up this way. But no more. She'd thought it through too many times, and always reached the same conclusion: God was angry with her. She believed she probably knew why, but short of hearing from God directly she couldn't be entirely sure. Regardless, her transgression was obviously pretty serious considering the length and severity of the punishment. The retribution began with an infectious outbreak in the spring of 1964...

શ♦♦ଈ

"Do you think Luther understands what's happening?" Lou asked.

"I'm not sure *I* understand what's happening," Maxine replied numbly. "Rubella? People don't *die* from rubella!"

"Well, with the epidemic, maybe they just assumed it was rubella. It could've been something else; maybe the regular measles," he replied.

"That's enough, Lou!" Doris said loudly under her breath. She grabbed her husband's arm and pulled him away from the casket. "Ben's gone and Maxine doesn't need to hear your amateur diagnosis right now!"

"Well," he whispered back, "I think they should have done an autopsy!"

It was impossible for Maxine not to overhear. She approached her sister and brother-in-law. "It's okay, Doris," she said. "I've actually had the same thought. And Lou, I'm not letting Luther see any of this. I don't think he would be able to handle it." She was still in that early stage of widowhood where the reality of death and the permanence of separation hadn't completely sunk in. In the first four days her focus had to be on the immanent practicalities: organizing a wake and a funeral, and somehow shielding Luther from it all.

"Are you sure that's the best idea?" Doris asked. "He may need to see his dad one last time."

Maxine sighed. "I think Luther's got enough troubles without this too. He's the only seven-year-old in kindergarten and he's struggling. The only friend he talks to is Larry, but he's in the other class, and I think Luther's lonely enough. This would just devastate him."

Normally Doris would have been sympathetic, but she found this disturbing. "So you're going to try and hide it from Luther that his dad died? That doesn't seem..."

"It's a big mistake, Maxine!" Lou interjected.

The widow sighed again, and was quiet for a moment. "Well no, I'm not trying to hide it, but..." she wrung her hands, "...I suppose I do have to tell him, don't I? But I am *not* letting him see his dad in an open casket!"

Doris began to cry. She embraced her sister and said, "I'm sorry sweetie. I'm so, so sorry..."

Maxine cried too, her first real cry since it all began. Her voice quivered, "People don't *die* from rubella..."

Lou just stepped away, a bit uncomfortable with the emotional display. He tried to blend in with the others attending Ben's wake: mostly work colleagues. Other than he and Doris, there was little family left.

Later in the day, Maxine asked the funeral director to close the casket, and Luther was brought in. A hush came over the room as the little boy and his mother slowly approached the coffin. She explained that "...daddy is in the box, and he has to stay there."

Luther's response was to smile broadly and look all around the room, mostly up at the ceiling.

"He doesn't get it," Lou said.

Doris added: "Sweetie, are you sure you don't want to open..."

"No!" Maxine snapped.

Luther still smiled. "That's a coffin," he said.

The hush got quieter.

Maxine agonized for a moment, before saying, "Yes, it's a coffin. And Luther, Daddy is inside the coffin."

Without hesitating, Luther began to slowly shake his head. "No, Daddy's inside here."

"Yes, sweetie, Daddy's inside there..." Maxine pointed to the casket.

"No, in here," Luther reiterated, closing his eyes and grinning.

Maxine just couldn't bring herself to say *daddy's dead*. She thought it was for Luther's sake, but perhaps it was she who wasn't ready to hear the words.

And as Luther's beaming face continued to illuminate the room, everyone else supposed that he just couldn't comprehend what was happening.

But they were the ones who didn't understand.

ca♦♦so

After that, the wrath of God just kept on. Ben's death caught Maxine unprepared. She often said that her husband did her no favors, leaving only a small savings account, no life insurance, and a house payment she couldn't afford. In 1964 she was considered "just a housewife" with no other work experience. The dollar-twenty-five-an-hour she could have made at a minimum-wage job was nowhere near what she needed to survive. Much too soon (out of desperation) she took up with Darrel: a carpenter who appeared at first to be a blessing out of the blue. She met him in Murphy's Mart one Saturday morning, and after they saw each other only a few times, he moved in with her and Luther, and took over the mortgage payment. All 108 dollars of it. He also took over everything else, and by the time Maxine realized what she'd done, she was trapped: kowtowing to an abusive alcoholic and completely dependent on him. Luther rarely saw the man without a can of beer in one hand and a cigarette in the other, and eventually Maxine became a smoker as well.

With the proper underpinnings in place, everything was now on Darrel's terms, and he could be very unpleasant if he didn't get what he wanted. At first, Maxine managed to absorb all the abuse herself, keeping young Luther safe. But by that first Christmas, both of them had become regular targets for Darrel's physical wrath, and each new bruise was a confirmation of his true character. And that was how things were for nine years, until Luther was almost eighteen, and one day realized he wasn't just bigger than the kids at school: he was also bigger than Darrel.

He hadn't planned it; it just happened one night when the mean drunk came home and started in with all the usual swearing and name-calling that preceded a violent outburst. Luther's response was swift, decisive, and entirely logical. In less than a minute, he ensured that this demon would never again touch him or his mother. He brutally pummeled the older man, blackening both his eyes and knocking out several teeth. Luther might have unwittingly killed him if his mother hadn't intervened, but she did; and once Darrel was able to stand his drunken, bloodied self up again, he left the house for the last time, taking his clothes, his dog, and his car with him. His control had been taken away, and there was no more reason to stay.

And mother and son were free from the tyrant. And nobody was left to pay the bills. And despite help from Lou and Doris, within a year they lost the house and had to move into the tiny subsidized apartment.

That was early in 1974, when the minimum wage had climbed to two dollars per-hour, and that's how much Maxine earned while her son finished high school. He managed to graduate with the bicentennial class of '76, and immediately began working days at Murphy's Mart. For a brief time the ends did more than just meet: they actually overlapped a little bit. It was a time of pitiful prosperity, when Luther was able to buy occasional treats like posters for his room. But just before Christmas that year, Maxine was diagnosed with inoperable breast cancer: the doctor said it must have been growing for at least seven or eight years to be as advanced as it was. So she gave up and began to read. And she never stopped, even just to say goodbye to her son as he left for his night class.

CHAPTER FOURTEEN

"So LET'S suppose you're watching a football game. The quarterback is just fading back to pass, and right at that moment you turn to the hot dog vendor to request extra mustard. Now-- you'd probably realize you chose a really stupid time to take your eyes off the field..." (the class laughed) "...when you turned back around and found the *defense* had just scored!" Ms. Fuller had a very animated style, and the class seemed to enjoy her presentation. Luther certainly did; and beyond that, he had a bit of a crush on her. The athletic-looking young woman had her short blond hair pulled back into a ponytail. She continued: "You'd obviously wonder what you missed while you were concentrating on your lunch, and some possible scenarios might include... what?"

"He got intercepted," one student chimed in immediately.

"Maybe, yes," she replied, "but are there other possibilities?"

"He could've fumbled the ball... or the receiver might have," another person added.

"Okay, that's two and three. Any others?" Unlike the other respondents, Luther raised his hand. "Yes, Mr. Howell, what do you think?" she inquired.

"I have two questions:" he replied, "what was the starting field position, and how many points were scored on the play?"

About half the class muttered a simultaneous *oh, yeah...* as Ms. Fuller reacted: "*Excellent* questions! Now we're getting somewhere." A few students picked up pens or pencils, and sat poised to write in case some noteworthy tid-bit was about to be shared. The teacher further baited her student: "Why would those things matter, Luther?"

"Because," he began, "there's only three ways to score on one play... it was just one play, right?"

"That's a safe assumption!" Ms. Fuller was beaming. This was the kind of moment teachers lived for.

Luther continued: "Then two points is a safety, three is a field goal and six is a touchdown. A field goal is impossible on the same play where the ball changes possession. A safety becomes less likely the farther downfield you are."

"That's sound reasoning," Ms. Fuller said. "So let's explore your model and put the ball, say, on the *defense's... thirty* yard line."

Luther didn't hesitate. "Then the ball was intercepted or fumbled and run back for a touchdown."

"So, which was it? A fumble or an interception?"

"Well, I don't know... you'd have to see the play."

"Correct!" she said, addressing the whole class once again. "And relating this back to the idea of chaos, we see outcomes and possible alternate outcomes, but we don't necessarily know how they came to be. A lot of factors, both seen and unseen can influence them, and as we observe in this case, the same six-point score could be reached in two different ways."

But Luther wasn't finished yet. "But the number of points isn't the only thing that matters about the play."

"Give an example..." Ms. Fuller said, humoring her student. Luther sometimes went off on tangents and she suspected this might be one of them.

"Okay..." he thought for a moment, "if the fumble was because the quarterback got sacked and sprained his leg, the other team gets six points, but he's out for the whole rest of the game. But then if he *broke* the leg, he's out for the season. Or maybe even his career..."

Ms. Fuller politely interrupted Luther's enthusiastic micro-analysis, "...good observations, and football is just one example of where we can see this. If you all remember from your text, Edward Lorenz was the meteorologist who used a computer to document how the tiniest change in a numeric sequence, even the fourth or fifth decimal place of a single number, could result in a completely different weather prediction." She pointed to the phrase she'd previously written on the blackboard: "In 1972 he gave a lecture titled: *Does the flap of a butterfly's wings in Brazil set off a tornado in*

Texas?; and please note that this title is phrased as a *question,* not as a statement!"

Luther nodded his head: "A question because we don't *know* for sure..."

"We *can't* know for sure," Ms. Fuller interjected, "because we are finite beings in an infinite universe. There's way too much out there for any of us to keep track of; yet it's still human nature for us to try and explain everything. Chaos theory suggests that not only is it impossible to make predictions with perfect accuracy, it's also impossible to explain known outcomes with perfect accuracy."

A balding student who looked to be in his forties put up a hand, but didn't wait to be called on before he spoke: "It seems to me that if I paid attention to the whole game from start to finish I'd be able to explain the outcome."

The class buzzed a bit, but the energetic adjunct regained control immediately. "Good! That's a legitimate challenge, Fred. Let's take a single play from this hypothetical football game and see if we can explain it completely. Somebody describe something that happened."

Three or four students spoke at once, but the anonymous voice that cut through the din said: "Incomplete pass!"

"Okay. Incomplete pass," Ms. Fuller repeated. "Quarterback throws to a receiver downfield; the ball goes right through his fingers. Let's explain why..."

Fred chimed in: "Because it was poorly thrown."

"Do you all accept that?" Ms. Fuller asked. "Was it poorly thrown?"

"It could've been," a heavy-set girl replied, "or it could have been poorly caught."

Luther's mind was spinning with ideas. He put his hand up, reluctant to just start talking because he had so much to say. He wanted the teacher to clear the way for him, which she unsuspectingly did: "Yes, Luther?"

"There could have been a gust of wind, the sun could have been in their eyes, a slippery patch of grass, um... one of them might have been worried about something ..."

Ms. Fuller normally would have interrupted Luther when he started making a list this way, but he was helping her make her point, so she let him continue...

"...somebody could have yelled out something from the sidelines..."

Fred busted in: "...or Martians could have fired an invisible anti-football ray down to Earth at that exact moment! C'mon, these NFL guys are very well paid, and should be able to adjust to anything like that."

A girl's voice cut through the sarcasm: "Who said this was an NFL game?"

It was Brooke: a brown-haired beauty who always sat toward the front by the window. She didn't say much in class, but when she did speak, she made it count. And the myopic, bald-spotted cynic had gotten her goat: "You assume an awful lot, don't you think?"

"I don't think I've 'assumed' anything!" Fred answered, acting offended. "I'm just stating the obvious."

"Oh, c'mon! How was it 'obvious' that this was a professional game," she pointed to Luther, "and how can you be sure anything *he* said *didn't* take place?" Brooke knew her looks could be intimidating, and she was about to use them to put this drip in his place. She could get away with a lot when it came to guys: they always seemed to want her to like them. Even when they were forty-ish, and probably married. She turned around in her seat to confront her opponent.

"Well, I mean... I... guess anything's t-technically possible..." the cynic retreated, suddenly diffused.

Luther marveled at the potency of the gorgeous green eyes that had so quickly and efficiently unraveled his detractor.

Brooke had to keep herself from laughing. That was just *too* easy! But she didn't really want to be the focus of the class; Fred had just ticked her off, that's all. She turned back toward the front, hoping Ms. Fuller would open an escape hatch.

The teacher, who had been rather amused by the whole exchange, somehow managed to extrapolate a lesson from it: "I think what we're seeing here is the classic struggle between deterministic theory and chaos theory... and the inevitable attempt to combine them."

With the feminine spell now broken, Fred tried to get in one last dig. "Well, two and two is four no matter how you look at it."

"Unless you convert it to binary!" Brooke spouted, now looking down at her desk.

A few people snickered.

"Okay, boys and girls," Ms. Fuller cut them off. "Methinks we digress. I'm going to let everyone go a few minutes early this week. Read chapter fourteen and answer the study questions for next Tuesday. Don't forget: the final is in *two* weeks!"

Sporadically, the twenty-five-or-so students began to rise from their desks and head for the door. A few, including Luther, remained seated long enough to copy down the assignment that had just been dictated. Most of the class would simply memorize it. It was always the same: read the next chapter and answer the study questions, but Luther always felt better if he wrote it down. Somehow it just seemed a little more scholarly that way. As a person who'd only recently learned to appreciate school, he felt he needed to take education as seriously as possible, and that meant copying down his assignments. When he finished writing in his yellow spiral notebook, he sensed someone standing next to his desk. He peripherally recognized the light blue jeans and faded denim jacket that Brooke was wearing. Though Luther's 'crush' was on the teacher, he still always noticed how nice Brooke looked, and what she had on. Everybody did. He looked up cautiously into her hypnotic eyes, drawn in like a sailor to the sirens. This girl was *way* out of his league!

"Hi!" she said brightly.

"Oh, uh... hi," he answered clumsily, trying to extract his oversized body from the dinky little desk. He stood up, now looking down at his pretty classmate.

"I just wanted to tell you how much I liked what you said a minute ago," she began. "You have a great mind to be able to see all those alternative possibilities."

"I do?" Luther was a little embarrassed. He wasn't accustomed to compliments, especially from girls. "Well... uh, thanks."

There was a brief, awkward pause before Brooke spoke again. "Okay! So, um, you're welcome." The conversation was apparently going to require a bit more work than she was used to. Normally, guys would grab the reins straight away and begin trying to impress her. But Luther was oddly reticent. She took the next logical step: "I'm Brooke."

"I know. I'm Luther..." pause, "...Howell."

"I know." She smiled.

Another pause.

He just stood there, all six-foot-five of him, becoming drenched in the greenness of her eyes, wondering what to say next. Wondering why he ought to say it. After a three-second eternity, he put his hand out. That's what you were supposed to do when you met somebody new. "Pleased to meet you, Brooke."

She shook his hand, politely stifling a giggle and slowly blinking her eyes in disbelief. She knew Luther was a little odd, but she hadn't expected this degree of social immaturity, and for the first time in a long time, she was at a loss. College boys typically offered more verbal reciprocation, and she found it strange yet charming that Luther didn't have more to say.

Meanwhile, he wondered why the classroom darling was talking to him at all.

The encounter could have just fizzled from there, but Brooke was determined not to let that happen. She pushed the conversation forward: "You know what, Luther?"

"What?" he answered guardedly.

"I bet we could make a list of at least fifty things that could have gone wrong with that pass play!" She brimmed with enthusiasm.

That did it. Luther picked up right where he left off before Fred had so rudely interrupted him. "Oh yeah... there could have been an imperfection in the ball that made it spiral funny, the... cold weather could have made the receiver's knee stiffen up..."

Brooke interrupted him: "Well, maybe we should sit over a cup of coffee and write some of this down!"

Luther was clueless. "Oh, I don't drink coffee. Only iced tea..."

She found his naïveté to be as endearing as it was frustrating. She recognized this type of personality, and expected no offense to be taken at what she was about to say. "Luther?" she asked.

"Yeah?" he answered.

"Um... when a girl says 'let's go have coffee...' it's not about the coffee. It means she's asking you out."

Luther froze in place as a glut of thoughts clogged the passage from his brain to his mouth. He'd always wondered what would happen if any girl ever took an interest in him. He was well aware of his social shortcomings, though he had no idea what to do about them. To further complicate things, his life was in a miserable state: he had no money and no car, and lived in subsidized, substandard housing with his dying mother. He hadn't anything to offer any girl, much less a stunner like Brooke who probably could've had anyone she wanted.

"Luther...?" she probed gently, now wondering if she had perhaps offended him.

"Oh, sorry..." he sputtered, finally managing to squeeze a sentence through the congestion of excess brain waves. "Um, you know, since there's a coffee shortage and everything... I just thought... you meant..."

He didn't have an ending for the sentence and Brooke knew it. She realized she'd just put Luther very much on the spot, and felt obligated to make this as easy as possible for him.

"I guess I'm asking if you'd like to go someplace for a few minutes and just talk," she offered. "It doesn't have to be for coffee."

"We could talk right here," he replied.

"Sorry, no you can't," Ms. Fuller interjected, standing by the door jingling her keys. "I need to lock the classroom!"

"Oops, sorry!" Brooke said sheepishly, now noticing that everyone else had left. "Come on Luther, how about downstairs by the vending machines?"

As they began to walk out together, Luther realized he needed an excuse *not* to spend any money. He only had enough for his bus fare home. "Well, we can talk," he said, "but I'm not really hungry." He was actually famished, but after nine years of living with Darrel and having most of the household budget going toward beer and cigarettes, meals were something he'd learned to do without. And because hunger was such a familiar foe, he was able to ignore his growling stomach with relative ease as he walked slowly down the stairs beside Brooke.

The "snack room" (as it was called by students) was a very inelegant spot, resembling a Laundromat more than a place to eat. Luther had never been inside it before: he never had any money to spend there. For just a moment as he stepped through the doorway, his attention was diverted from his lovely companion by the gently buzzing lights inside the various vending machines. Luther was always conscious of the flickering of fluorescent bulbs (120 times per-second, his dad had once told him) and he wondered why more people didn't notice it. The distraction of fluorescent lighting in the classrooms was something Luther constantly struggled with. Sometimes it even gave him a bit of a headache, but here in the snack room someone had turned off the overheads, and with the dusky natural light filtering through the windows, the atmosphere was actually rather pleasant. The only artificial lighting passed through colored signs that read *Fresh Coffee* and *Pastries* and *Dr. Pepper*, and they served to dampen the flicker. It was late April, and the sun didn't fully set until after eight-thirty, and both boy and girl enjoyed the subdued, restful ambiance, though neither of them said so.

Brooke dropped a quarter and a nickel into the coffee machine and waited passively as it performed its mundane, repetitive job. Meanwhile, Luther delighted in the mechanism, taking special pleasure in the sounds it made: two coins clinking into the cash box, the dry *pock* of the empty cardboard cup as it dropped into place, and the wet trickle of the "fresh" instant java that filled the waxy container. It made him wish he drank coffee.

"I really hope I'm not being too forward," Brooke said, claiming her little cup and sitting carefully in one of the plastic chairs that lined the perimeter of the room. She lightly blew across the surface of the hot liquid, trying to cool it down enough to take the first sip.

Luther focused on the steam that skittered away from the cup and rapidly evaporated in the subdued light. He thought to himself: *When water evaporates, it removes heat, reducing the surface temperature.*

Brooke spoke again. "I hope I can talk candidly to you... *about* you."

Luther finally sat down, leaving one empty chair between them. "Well sure, but... I don't think there's much to say." If Brooke had wanted to talk about physics or sports (or microscopes) he would have been much more receptive to a conversation. He used those things to escape from the uncertainty of his world. But she said she wanted to talk about *him*, and that was confusing. Anytime Luther spoke of himself it was a clumsy undertaking. Granted, he wasn't very articulate to begin with, but at least when he talked about his *interests* he felt he had good things to say. Not so when it came time to share things personal.

"Have you ever read about a psychologist named Bettelheim?" Brooke began.

"No."

"...or taken abnormal psych? Or any psych classes?"

"No."

"Oh..." she hesitated. "This might be harder than I thought, then."

Luther didn't want it to be hard. "No... it's okay. You're okay," he blurted. Caught unprepared, he was concerned only with the conversation itself; and hadn't paid that close attention to her questions. He thought if he could make this dialogue about her instead of him, it would become more 'external,' and less daunting. Trying to grab onto anything he could think of, he said: "It was really cool how you just um... disabled Fred like that!"

"Fred?" Brooke queried. "Oh, the creepy guy. Yes, that *is* his name, isn't it! I 'disabled' him, huh? That's an interesting way of putting it." She blushed just a little.

Luther hoped he was salvaging things. Not realizing just how blunt his words tended to be, he went on: "Your green eyes really give you an advantage!"

Brooke was silent for a moment while she mentally dissected that candid statement. Then her green eyes became a bit damp as she looked at her coffee cup. She laughed to herself, not with derision, but with a familiar appreciation for what she was gradually confirming about Luther. Still focusing on the coffee, she said, "You think he was looking at my *eyes*, don't you?"

Luther was confused. "Well, I guess... yeah..." He couldn't tell if maybe he was being challenged. What did that question mean?

Now Brooke knew exactly how to proceed: ask direct questions, expect honest answers. She smiled sweetly and gave a semi-honest opening: "I um... get a lot of compliments on my eyes. I guess you must like them too, to have noticed."

"Yes, they're very pretty. Beautiful." Luther's guard seemed to be slipping down just a bit as he sensed some level of understanding.

Brooke beamed and fought back a tear. "Thank you, Luther, that's really sweet. Are you sure you wouldn't like a soda or something?"

"No, I really can't..." he didn't want to say why, but Brooke knew. Anyone would have been able to tell from just a quick look at Luther: his clothes didn't match and were threadbare in spots. His shoes were very worn. His hair was uncombed and his eyes were a little glazed. This person obviously had limited resources.

Brooke carefully set her coffee down on the roundish seat of the chair next to her. She stood up and dropped two more coins into the pastry machine.

Luther noted that she pressed the buttons for selection A-3 as a cellophane-wrapped sweet roll slowly began its journey toward a free-fall, propelled by a spiraling rotor. The little tartlet sounded a soft thud as it landed in the bottom of the machine.

"Shoot!" she cried out. "I meant to press *B*-3! Would you like a cherry Danish?"

"What... you don't want it?" he answered.

"No, I don't like cherries!"

"Well, um... I guess. Sure." Luther stood and reached into his pocket to grab his change, already planning his route now that he'd be walking home. "How much was it?"

Brooke was taken aback by the gesture. "Luther! I don't want to *sell* it to you!"

"But it's not the one you wanted..."

"And that was *my* mistake! *You* don't need to pay for *my* mistake."

Luther stared at her uncomprehendingly. "Uh... okay. So...?" He had no idea what to do or say.

Brooke finally burst into giddy tears. "I'm just *giving* you this sweet roll, that's all. Take it, enjoy it! It's a present!"

Smiling, half-giggling, she held it out and he reluctantly took it.

"God, you're just like Philip!" she said, now sniffling as well.

"Philip?" Luther asked, utterly confused. What had he done to make this girl cry? Or was she laughing at him?

"He was my brother. He passed away four years ago."

Luther carefully unwrapped the pastry. The sweet flavor and bready aroma began to revive his senses as he took a bite. With his mouth full he said: "Thanks!" followed by, "oh, sorry about your brother."

The dichotomous response didn't faze Brooke at all. She answered similarly: "You're very welcome. And thank you for the condolences."

They both sat again as Luther took a second bite. "This is really good," he said as he chewed. "I thought you were going to get yourself a B-3."

"I guess I'm not hungry after all," she said, picking up her coffee again. She pursed her lips, cautiously anticipating the temperature of the first sip. Her face became mildly contorted when it was indeed too hot.

"Careful, that's hot..." Luther offered a belated warning.

"*Now* you tell me!" she joked.

He didn't get the joke. "Oh... I'm sorry..."

Brooke blew cool air over the cup one more time and answered: "It's not your fault. I'm a big girl and I should know better than to drink something that's too hot."

"Okay." Luther was becoming perplexed as to the purpose of this meeting. Thus far it had largely been small talk, and that was where his verbal skills were weakest. Yet, he didn't want it to end.

Brooke realized that Luther wasn't able to move the conversation forward, so she did: "Like I said, you really remind me of my brother. The things you say in class are always so... special; so different! It's like you see things from an alternate perspective or something."

Luther hoped she was being complimentary. "Thanks..." he replied, just in case.

"And the way you talk in a regular conversation," she continued, "is kind of the way Philip talked. This is really hard for you, isn't it, Luther?"

Now unable to discern positive from negative, he simply answered honestly. "Yeah."

"I'm sorry; forgive me if I'm making you uncomfortable. You've already answered a lot of the things I wanted to ask you." Brooke looked straight at Luther with probing eyes.

He was now even more puzzled. He didn't remember having answered anything. He wordlessly finished off the pastry in a couple of big bites.

She continued: "Philip had autism. Do you know what that is?"

"I don't think so."

"He had trouble talking to people, but he was also, like, a genius!"

Luther could now open up a little. It wasn't about him anymore. "A genius? That's cool! Was he like Einstein? Einstein was a genius."

"I guess, maybe a little. He always had a way of taking unrelated things and bringing them together to make something new."

"Like what?"

She thought for a moment. "Like once he found an old golf ball in the back yard and he balanced it on the brass end of the garden hose..."

"That's called a coupling," Luther interjected.

"Yes, of course you'd know that!" she replied. "Anyway, he spent half the afternoon turning the water on and off, trying to get the golf ball to lift up slightly and land back in place without falling off. When my parents found him he was soaking wet, saying he was testing a valve for an artificial heart."

"That makes sense," Luther said very matter-of-factly. "Except that the dimples in the golf ball would keep it from making a really tight seal, so he'd probably need something smoother."

Brooke laughed with delight. "Yes! That's exactly what he figured out! The next day he was out there again with a ping-pong ball..."

Luther interrupted once more: "...but it was too light-weight and he needed to control the water pressure better than he could do with the spigot."

She breathed deeply, as if this was the first fresh air she'd had in a long time. "And I'll bet you know how he did it, don't you?"

Luther never hesitated. "There are lots of ways, but the easiest would be just to kink the hose and control the pressure by squeezing."

Brooke could barely set her coffee down without spilling it. She buried her face in her hands and began to sob uncontrollably.

Luther was utterly bewildered, wondering what he had said to upset her. "Well, I'm sorry..." he said quietly.

Brooke's makeup was running as she looked up into his eyes. "You have abso-*lutely* no reason to be sorry!" She stood up and kissed him on the forehead. "Luther, I'm sorry I'm such a mess, but you have no idea what a gift you've just given me. Can we *please* talk again next week?"

"Well, sure..."

"I promise to have regained my composure by then. I'll see you after class, okay?"

"Okay..." he stood up as she quickly scurried out of the room. She smiled back at Luther one more time through the doorway.

He returned the smile, taking a last look into her beautiful, mascara-smeared eyes.

A college boy passing in the hallway ogled the rest of the buxom girl, in her scoop-neck top and open denim jacket.

Luther noticed she'd left a nearly-full cup of coffee on the chair. "Why not?" he said to himself, trying a sip, which he ended up hating. He tossed it in the trash along with his pastry wrapper, and headed off toward the bus stop.

CHAPTER FIFTEEN

"**B**EDDLE-HIME. Battle-hime. How did she say that?" Luther mumbled to himself as he plodded up the front steps of the campus library building. He had no idea how to spell the man's name, and wasn't entirely sure of the pronunciation. But Brooke had mentioned him the previous day, and Luther wanted to be sure they had something to talk about after the next class. He was going to do a little research.

"Can I help you?" The woman behind the counter said.

Luther appeared rather aimless standing there looking around, overwhelmed by the vastness of it all. He'd never been in a library this large before.

"Hello? Young man?" she rephrased her inquisitive greeting.

Luther stared briefly at the tall gray-haired woman before gathering his thoughts enough to speak. "Are you the librarian?"

She raised her eyebrows and answered with amusement: "One of them, yes."

In his usual oblivious way, Luther continued: "I'm trying to find out about a guy whose name I can't remember all the way."

"A guy?"

"A psychologist."

"Well, that narrows it down a little," the librarian said. "Do you know any more than that?"

"Um… he's an abnormal psychologist. I think."

The woman burst into laughter.

Luther was just confused.

"The *field* is called abnormal psychology, young man! I'm sure the psychologist himself is quite normal."

"Oh, okay," Luther still didn't understand what was so funny. "His name is 'Battle-hime,' or…"

"Bruno *Bettel*heim!" the woman trumpeted triumphantly. "A name well-known to me."

"So it's 'Bettel-heim?'"

"That's correct: it's 'Bettel' like 'nettle' or 'kettle.' Do you want to read *about* him or do you want to read what he's written?"

Luther was confounded. "Well, I don't know…"

The woman looked at him for a moment and said, "Please follow me."

The library seemed to Luther like a huge warehouse, with an endless number of mysterious, anonymous tomes, identified only by the abbreviations and strings of numbers that adorned each bookshelf. Awestruck, he followed the librarian up a staircase and down a long aisle as she brought him right to the desired spot.

"Here's a popular one," she said, pulling a cellophane-encased volume from the shelf and reading aloud: "*The Empty Fortress: Infantile Autism and the Birth of the Self,* by Bettelheim. 1967; it's a few years old, but still definitive."

The title triggered something else Brooke had said. "Ought-ism!" Luther declared. "That's another thing I want to look up."

"If I were you, I'd start here," she handed him the book. "Dr. Bettelheim is the one who discovered what causes autism and how it should be treated."

Luther took the book with apprehensive interest, noting the correct spelling of *autism.* "Can I check this out?" he asked.

"Are you a student here?"

"Only on Tuesdays this semester," he said.

"Well then you'll need to come back next Tuesday and check it out…" the librarian jested.

Luther didn't get the joke. "Oh, okay… that won't give me much time to read before…"

"I was only teasing you, young man!" By now she was beginning to see that there was something different about Luther, and perhaps she should be a bit more straightforward with her answers.

Luther remained practical: "So I *can* check it out?"

"Yes, of course. You just need your student I.D."

Luther pulled out his wallet and held out his I.D. card.

"We need to go back to the front desk first," the woman said, stifling a smile.

Back to the _front_ desk? Luther thought. After a few more minutes of social awkwardness, he was on his way home with his book. This was Wednesday, not normally a day he went to school, so he'd used up one trip's worth of bus fare unexpectedly. When next Tuesday came around, he'd probably have to walk to school straight from work. But it would be worth it: it was only about four miles, and he'd get to see Brooke.

Maxine Howell didn't even look up when her son came in the door just after 6:30. Luther thought it was neat that for once he had a book of his own to complement the one his mother was reading. Her paperback had a cover picture of a man and a woman in white tennis clothes, looking quite affluent. He had an arm around her waist, clutching her forcefully. To Luther it just seemed like a variation of the shirtless pirate. Maxine's tumbler of iced tea was no longer iced, and Luther realized he was more than two hours later than usual.

"Sorry I'm late," he said.

"Okay, honey. Mm-- oh, are you late?" She hadn't even noticed.

Luther headed straight for his room and turned on the lamp that sat on his miniature nightstand. He lay down and began to read, starting at the _very_ beginning: a title page which simply said, _The Empty Fortress_. The next page repeated the words, but in much bigger letters. In the back of his mind, Luther questioned the redundancy, and the practice of wasting paper that way. But since the page also included the subtitle, the author's name, and information about the publisher, he figured maybe it wasn't really so bad. Turning the page, he read:

To Ruth Marquis.

Who was that? Luther had never examined any of his college texts this closely, always reading only the required pages. But since this book was a link to Brooke, he thought it best to study it very carefully. Even so, he did elect to skip over the detailed copyright and publishing information, advancing to the next page:

Acknowledgements
First and foremost I wish to express my gratitude to all
staff members of the Sonia Shankman Orthogenic School...

"Ortho-genic?" he asked himself. He read some more, occasionally coming across other words he didn't know. He got a pencil and a scrap of paper, writing them down as they occurred, with the goal in mind of looking them up in a dictionary once he'd reached ten. The list became populated quickly:

1.   *orthogenic*
2.   *feral*
3.   *intellectually*
4.   *solipsistic*
5.   *manipulative*
6.   *evoke*
7.   *pathology*
8.   *ambiguities*
9.   *schizophrenic*
10. *dehumanization*

...and he was only on page seven! Maybe this was going to be more difficult than he first thought. There was a dictionary in a box in the front coat closet: it never got unpacked after they moved in. The folding metal closet doors were rusty on the edges and had many layers of old paint. They squeaked as Luther opened them wide. The storage carton he wanted was on the shelf up top, above his mother's hanging clothes. A little dust storm engulfed his head as he lifted the heavy box of books and set it on the sofa his mom used as a bed. The gritty dust made him cough, and he made his way back to the kitchen/dining area to get a glass of water.

Maxine had finished with the tennis couple, and had started yet another novel. Luther, feeling particularly erudite, this time read the title before looking at the picture. *Passions of the Fire* was adorned with the predictable, familiar image of a shirtless man roughly caressing a beautiful flowing-haired woman. At least his mom was consistent.

Like everything else in the kitchen, the glass Luther chose was covered with the brown smoker's film. He cracked a few cubes from the aluminum freezer tray into his lukewarm tap water, all the while feeling compelled to talk to his mother. About what, he wasn't sure, but all the reading had stirred up something inside of him. He innocently began with, "Mom, have you ever heard of autism?"

Maxine stopped reading. She closed her book, set it on the table in front of her, and put out her cigarette. Acting as if she'd just been doused with cold water, she looked straight at Luther and said, "Where did you hear that word?"

"I heard it from a girl at school, and in a book I'm reading," he answered.

Maxine trembled inside. "What book?"

"It's by Bettelheim. 'Bettel' like in 'nettle' or 'kettle.' It's called *The Empty Fortress*."

His mother was silent.

"I'm reading it!" Luther said, smiling.

"I know it's my fault, Luther. I wish I could've been a better mother."

Luther was confused. "What's your fault?"

Her sunken red eyes began to tear up. "I didn't think you'd ever realize what I did, sweetie; I'm so sorry!"

Luther furrowed his brow and sat down at the table across from his mother. He shooed away the last of the active smoke and stared perplexedly at her.

For a few moments there was just silence as she regrouped her thoughts: this was Luther after all, and he probably didn't understand nearly as much as she suspected. But this conversation was inevitable and long overdue, and her son had unwittingly lit the dormant fuse. Her only quandary was how to present things.

At the same time, Luther's mind had drifted and he was thinking that he'd inadvertently left the kitchen light on, and the fluorescent fixture was flickering 120 times per-second. And he thought Brooke had beautiful eyes. And she kissed him the day before.

"Luther," she began, "I probably should have told you this a long time ago, but when you're reading that book, you're reading about yourself." There. She presented the most important point right out of the gate, just as Luther would have done.

"Myself?" he said cluelessly.

"I believe *you* have autism, Luther."

"No I don't," he replied. "I'd have to be, like, a genius. That's what Brooke's brother was."

Maxine realized she was in for a challenge. This could be like trying to describe shades of color to a blind person. "There's more to autism than just, um… being a genius. It happens when your parents--" she sighed, "no, not your parents, your *mother*-- doesn't take good enough care of you. And you react by going into a shell."

Luther looked around. "I'm not in a shell."

"You sort of are, son. Well, you used to be a lot more than you are now."

"And you take care of me. You're my mom!"

Maxine smiled pitifully; she appreciated the vote of confidence, though she doubted its veracity. "Luther, I don't think I've been able to really… take care of you… since your father died."

"Well… sure you have…"

"I brought Darrel into our house and let him steal our lives away! I will never forgive myself for that!" She thought Luther would bristle at the mention of that name; it had rarely been spoken since the night the demon left.

Luther's reaction was surprising: "At least he paid the bills."

Maxine was unsure how to follow such a response. Luther wasn't trying to be offensive, he was just naïve, and well… autistic. Social graces weren't logical, so he didn't employ them. She turned the topic around. "So who is this 'Brooke' girl?"

"Brooke! She's beautiful. She kissed me!"

"She kissed you? Really?"

"Yeah, right here!" He pointed to a spot in the center of his forehead.

"Oh…" Maxine said with some relief. "I thought you meant a *kiss*; like on the lips."

"It *was* a kiss," Luther explained, "and she said I reminded her of her brother, and she said he had autism and was kind of like Einstein. And I'm meeting her after class next Tuesday."

The plot now became clearer. Someone else had figured it out. Luther was autistic and his mother's awful secret was exposed. After all, it was all right there in Dr. Bettelheim's book: autism was the result of parents (particularly mothers) who were emotionally cold toward their children. By the time Maxine read the work, Luther was a strapping fourteen-year-old in public school, but she still saw similarities between her son and the 'case study' children in the book. Almost from birth he seemed listless and disconnected, and he didn't have any functional speech until he was four. Around age six, Luther very suddenly demonstrated some big gains in aptitude that allowed him to be mainstreamed into age-appropriate classrooms, but he always seemed rather confused by his teachers, and never sought social interaction with other children. It became apparent that he could learn from those who understood how to get through to him, especially his dad and his cousin Larry. But public schoolteachers didn't have the expertise or the resources to devote to someone like Luther, and he was considered a problem student. At one point in the seventh grade he even began bullying other kids and taking their lunch money. When Maxine talked to Luther about it she discovered that he didn't realize he was doing anything wrong. He'd seen other bullies at work and was imitating what they did and said, but to him it was just a way to get a meal. That kind of social disconnect was a part of this "autism" Maxine was just learning about, and after reading Bettelheim she had decided it was essentially her fault. In fact, the doctor even went so far as to write: *...the precipitating factor in infantile autism is the parent's wish that his child should not exist.* And now with Bettelheim's book thrust into her life once again, this time as Luther's literary discovery, Maxine was all the more certain she knew why God was mad at her...

ᘓ✦✦ᘔ

"It's not that simple, Ben!" Maxine said as she knelt, scrubbing the carpet with a sponge and a pan of water. It was the third time in a week that Luther had spilled fruit juice on that exact spot. She addressed her handsome, grey-eyed husband, who stood over her. "How can you say he'll just 'grow out of this'?"

"He's *three*, Maxine! Some boys just take longer to develop." Ben Howell worked for an engineering firm, and as a budding supervisor he was seldom home, leaving his wife to take care of the house and of Luther. "I think Luther's bright; just look at how meticulously he likes to arrange things! That's not normal for a three-year-old," he said.

Maxine wore an old pair of plaid pedal pushers and a worn-out white blouse as she tried to remove the stain. At twenty-four, she was quite a pretty young woman: fair-skinned with red hair and freckles. She said, "Well, all I know is that he only ever spills the purple grape juice, and always in this same shape. It's like he's making a mess on purpose! I don't see what's so 'bright' about that!"

Despite the discord, Ben found himself enjoying his wife's superlatively domestic pose. This was 1959 after all, and even in those old clothes Maxine seemed to embody the ideal of the day. Her husband scanned her form as he replied: "Just be patient, okay? We know he's not retarded or he'd have those Mongoloid features. So just let nature take its course." He was half-kidding when he followed with: "Now stop picking on *my* son!"

Maxine stopped what she was doing, leaving the sponge on the carpet instead of in the pan. "His" son? *She* was the one who took care of Luther ninety percent of the time! In response to the rude remark, she stood up in her bare feet and attempted to confront her husband. Yet, as often as she'd tried in six years of marriage, it had never worked: he was brawny and six-foot-five while she was a fragile five-foot-nothing. She found herself face to face with his ribcage.

Ben playfully took a step forward, forcing her to take one backwards. He'd just won any argument that might have been about to start.

"You're such a big… lunk!" she said in a childish voice, as her frustration began to scatter. The normally docile housewife realized she'd just challenged the authority of the resident alpha male.

Ben smiled and took two more steps, pushing his wife further back.

Maxine pressed against his stomach with her flat palms. "Stop it, Ben!"

Her insistence only egged him on, and soon she found herself pinned between the living room wall and her husband's massive body. And just that quickly she was his for the taking.

"So, me captive beauty," Ben teased in a pirate voice, "perhaps I should take ye to the captain's quarr-ters!"

The vanquished redhead looked up into the eyes of her "captor," instantly aroused by his suggestion. "Whatever you say, Captain..." she flirted. Her hands fell limply to her sides as she prepared to be ravished...

Crash! The sound came from Luther's room, startling both the pirate and his ruby-haired prize.

"*Damn* it, Luther! Now what'd you do?" Maxine wiggled her way out of the captain's clutches and hurried upstairs to the source of the sound. "Ben! He broke a tumbler and there's pieces of glass on the floor. I'm barefoot, I can't go in there!"

"I'll get a broom and a pan," Ben replied.

Even at three years old Luther still slept in a crib. But now he stood up in it, gazing over the side rail toward his dresser. He rocked gently.

"Luther! Bad boy!" Maxine shouted.

Luther ignored her.

"Luther, you're supposed to be asleep!" Ben said, carrying a whisk broom and an aluminum dustpan into the bedroom.

Luther ignored him too, continuing to stare at the dresser as his father swept the floor.

Once a safe path had been cleared, Maxine made her way to Luther's crib and picked him up, holding him at arm's length and scolding: "No! You don't *break* things! Shame on you!"

The youngster had a blank expression as he hung there limply in his white flannel pajamas with little multicolored footballs printed all over them. He was still fixated on the dresser.

"How'd he get a glass tumbler in the first place?" Ben snapped.

Maxine felt a twinge of guilt as she answered, "I left it on the dresser. He must've reached over the side of the crib."

Luther silently reached out a splayed hand toward the dresser. His mom glanced over and saw what he apparently wanted: a plastic butterfly with purple celluloid wings: a piece salvaged from an old a baby mobile. She sighed forcefully and shifted her son to one hip so she could reach the toy with her free hand. When she passed it to Luther he immediately began orally exploring its surfaces. He still hadn't outgrown the infantile practice of putting things in his mouth, and the Howells had become so used to it that they didn't try to stop him anymore.

Maxine placed Luther and the butterfly back into the crib while Ben finished up the sweeping. Once his parents had returned to the living room, Luther sat up and inspected his pajamas while he rocked. There was a seam where two of the purple football shapes came together in such a way that they resembled the outline of a butterfly. It was the same shape as the purple grape juice stain on the carpet... that he would have to re-create tomorrow.

"Why does he have to be this way?" Maxine lamented, once again on her knees scrubbing. The spontaneous pirate moment would apparently need to be rescheduled.

"Don't worry so much, Maxine! It'll work out."

"Really? *When*, Ben? *When* will this be over? It's so much easier for you, you're never here!"

"Hey, *I* just swept up the glass!"

Maxine scrubbed harder. "You want to know what all *I* did today? While you were gone I cleaned up two more of these grape juice stains, which don't come completely out, by the way. I hand-washed three pairs of Luther's soiled underwear, because *you* won't let me put him in a diaper..."

"He'll get the idea! Just stick with it!"

"You always say that. And he never does." Exasperated, she began to get teary-eyed. "And you know what, Ben? You know what?"

He knew that setup. When Maxine began repeating words, it meant she was about to say something of consequence. He voluntarily took the bait. "What, Sweetie?"

She trembled. "I never wanted a kid this soon! Luther was *your* idea!"

ल♦♦१०

Eighteen years later, those words still haunted Maxine. She'd shuffled them in her mind until they became *I never wanted Luther*, which was even worse. Over time she became convinced that the rearranged version was probably what she really meant, so when she read Dr. Bettelheim's thoughts on "the precipitating factor of autism," she knew it was her fault. She had caused her only child to be autistic, and the whole rest of her life was punishment for that. There was no other explanation.

"Mom?" Luther said, his voice cutting through her brief daydream.

"Huh? Oh, I'm sorry, honey. I was just... um... thinking about something. Yes, your new girlfriend! Tell me about her!"

Girlfriend? Luther thought. That seemed like a sudden step. But maybe his mother was right. After all, Brooke kissed him, and that's what girlfriends did. "She has beautiful eyes. And she's smart. She's in my physics class!"

Suddenly Maxine realized that this was the first conversation she'd had with her son in a very long time, and despite the ominous mention of autism, it felt really good. She reached for another cigarette: a smoke seemed like it would somehow validate the event. "You said her name is Brooke? Brooke *what*?"

"Well, I don't know..." it had never occurred to him that she had a last name. "But I hope she's my girlfriend like you said!"

Uh-oh. Apparently she'd opened a can of worms by using the word "girlfriend." "Luther, I didn't mean..."

Luther interrupted: "And maybe we could be in love!" He almost never interrupted, so the idea must have been quite an exciting one.

But Maxine knew it wouldn't be fair to let him get his hopes up. "Now Luther, love isn't just when a girl kisses you on the forehead!"

"I know," he said. "Love is like..." he thought for a moment, "...it's like the people on your books!"

Maxine looked at the picture of the shirtless Casanova she'd positioned on the table between her ashtray and her watery tumbler of tea. She sighed. "Luther, that's not love, that's 'romance.' It's not real."

Luther was confused. "Not real?"

"Look son, we've talked about how..." she paused, "...you know, I won't be around much longer."

Luther didn't react, so she continued: "And even now, I don't really *live*, I just sort of *exist*. And these books just help me escape."

"Escape? Where?"

She was quiet for a moment. Then a thin, wistful smile crossed her lips, and long-absent spark seemed to flicker in her eyes. "I escape to where I used to be when your father was alive; when it was just me and him."

"You mean the books are about Dad?"

"I suppose in a way they are!" She decided not to light the cigarette after all. "I don't know if this will make sense to you or not, but when your father died, half of me died too."

"Was it the half with the cancer?"

Maxine laughed out loud at the innocently macabre remark. "It wasn't literally 'half' of me!" She took her first deep breath in a while. The movement caused a stabbing pain in her chest, but the air felt good. "When you lose the people you love, you lose your purpose."

"Yeah, like you when you couldn't go out on dates with Dad anymore."

Obviously her philosophizing was largely lost on Luther. "Sweetie, love isn't about going on dates with someone. It's about taking care of them."

Luther thought that over for a bit. "Brooke took care of me. She gave me a cherry Danish."

A little light went on, and Maxine smiled. Why shouldn't Luther be allowed an escape of his own? "Well, maybe she *does* love you, then."

Luther beamed. "Thanks, Mom!" he said, grabbing the dictionary and heading back to his room.

She just sat for a few minutes, thinking about the people in her life she'd taken care of. Maybe God wasn't really so mad at her after all.

CHAPTER SIXTEEN

"**M**CCLOSKEY,**"** Brooke said. "It's Irish!"

Luther's first thought was that the name had a neat "sound" to it. It was sort of like the sound of the word "clock," or the *pock* of a cardboard cup loading into the coffee machine. In an instant he started to mentally look for other oblique rhymes (*epoxy, hockey, Mr. Spock...*) but he stopped just as quickly as he'd begun. He knew his mind tended to wander pretty far pretty fast, and people didn't like it when that happened. Plus, Brooke deserved a timely response. "Brooke McCloskey!" he said with a smile. "I really like that!"

She found the simplicity of his reply refreshing. "Thanks! It's actually Brooke Laine McCloskey. L-A-I-N-E. Everybody always forgets the 'I'."

Luther immediately memorized the spelling. "Brooke Laine..." he repeated.

"People say it sounds like a city in New York," she giggled. "Like 'The Brooke-Laine Dodgers!'"

"The Dodgers moved to Los Angeles in 1958," Luther spouted. "You know, they were originally called 'The Brooklyn Atlantics.' And Jackie Robinson was the first Black major leaguer to play and he was with the Dodgers. That was 1947!" Wow! Already Luther had found more to talk about than he thought he would. This date had started off well!

Brooke, meanwhile, was very patient. Having heard Luther speak in class, she'd learned that he was just doing what he did best: sharing information, however extraneous. And last week she'd also learned to let the vending machine coffee cool off a little longer before trying to drink it, so she held the recently "pocked" cup in both hands and blew across the surface.

The steam dispersed into the snack room just as it had the week before, and just as *he* had the week before, Luther thought:

When water evaporates, it removes heat, reducing the surface temperature. But this week he continued his mental deliberation: *So... the heat must be defying gravity if it's going "up" out of the liquid...*

"Luther?" Brooke said. "Are you in there?"

"In where?" he responded, and his little mental detour came to a sudden stop.

She lightly "knocked" on his forehead: "Hel-lo! Don't forget I'm here, too!"

All Luther could think of was that she was once again touching the spot she'd kissed last week. Maybe she was trying to remind him!

"Thank you, Brooke!" Pause. "Brooke Laine."

Her patience gave way to a bit of frustration. She sighed. "Okay, Luther: let's stay on task tonight. I'd really like to ask you some questions if that's alright."

"Sure it is. And I brought a book to talk about!" He dug through his backpack and held up the library copy of *The Empty Fortress*. "I started reading it."

Brooke looked curiously at the cover, then back at Luther. "You're reading Bettelheim?" she asked.

"Yeah, you said your brother had autism, so I wanted to learn about it. My mom thinks I have autism, but I don't. I'm not a genius like Einstein."

"That's a pretty intellectual book, Luther!"

"'Intellectual!' That means 'involving the mental processes of abstract thinking and reasoning.' I looked it up because I saw the word in *The Empty Fortress*. Well, it really said 'intellectual-*ly*,'" he said proudly. "That's an adverb."

Brooke's beautiful eyes were already getting misty. "You are *so much* like Philip!" she marveled. "Look, Luther, I just wondered if you could describe some things to me."

"Describe what?" he replied.

"Like... what it *feels* like to be you! And what things *look* like; and *sound* like..."

Luther suddenly shut down. The conversation had shifted to *him*: the one thing about which he had the least to say.

Brooke looked at him, anticipating some response, but it didn't come. After a moment she gently took the book out of his hand. "Luther? Did I say something wrong?"

"No... it's okay. You're okay," he said.

She recognized that exact phrase from their last conversation. Something went *click* in her head, and she realized what she'd done. "Wow," she apologized. "You're so much like my brother, and I should know better! Here I am just running slipshod all over your feelings! I didn't mean to make anything hard for you! I'm real sorry..."

"It's okay, you're okay," he answered, not knowing what else to say.

The normally confident girl seemed at a loss, and her carefully-calculated questions gave way to a flowing stream of thoughts and feelings: things that had been bottled up for a long time. Maybe Luther wouldn't even understand them, but they needed to be said. "It's just that I miss him so much, and I loved him so much... and he was really the nicest person I ever knew! And I always thought that if I could just get inside his head for even *ten minutes* I might be able to figure out what things were like in there, and maybe find some way to help him. Or who knows, maybe it would have helped me? And then when I met you, you reminded me so much of him, and..." she stopped short and shifted her focus: "I'm sincerely sorry, Luther."

Luther's mind scrambled; he knew he should say something to make her feel better, but had no idea what that might be. So he just said *something*: "I don't know what to say, Brooke." He grinned. "Brooke *Laine*!"

And that smile was all it took. She sniffled, smiled meekly back at him, and suddenly felt more peaceful than she had for a long while. That's how it had been with Philip: there didn't need to be an agenda. Sometimes it was okay just to *be*. She leaned over and gave Luther a bear hug; reaching as far around his massive shoulders as she was able. "You must think I'm a nutcase! All I ever do is cry."

The hug felt good, but Luther sat there stiffly, and his reply was simple: "You're not a nutcase. I really like you."

Brooke felt like she was hugging a giant teddy bear. And also like she was with her brother again.

Just then, two male students from Ms. Fuller's physics class hastily entered the snack room, interrupting Luther and Brooke in mid-hug. Heading for the Dr. Pepper machine, the boorish one said quietly to the clueless one: "Man, what's *she* doing with that retarded guy?"

Luther replied matter-of-factly: "I'm not retarded or I'd have those Mongoloid features." The sentence had been filed away somewhere in a very distant memory, and retrieved spontaneously for this moment.

Brooke was embarrassed on Luther's behalf. "Hey, why don't we go talk outside?" she said. "The weather's getting nicer out there and nastier in here!" She shot a scornful glance at the impolite pair as she and Luther rose and started for the door.

"Don't you want your coffee?" Luther queried; noticing she'd left her nearly-full cup on the chair once again. "I can throw it out for you if you want."

"No... it's okay. You're okay," she said with a knowing smile.

Luther sensed a spark of understanding that delighted him.

The coffee remained on the chair.

With summer just ahead, the campus landscape was quite picturesque. Neatly-trimmed shrubs and lush green grass filled the spaces between the various academic buildings. The sky hinted of the coming sunset: it would likely be a pink one this evening. The unlikely couple strolled silently for a bit, until they came upon an inviting oak tree that sheltered a park bench.

"Let's sit here!" Brooke said.

"You know," Luther began, "cows and horses can't eat acorns or they get sick. And sheep too."

She basked in the long-lost luminosity of autism as they parked themselves amid the flow of student traffic that passed on the nearby sidewalks. Her reasons for wanting to question Luther now seemed unimportant. There was no more need for questions. She just let him talk.

"And you know what else?" he went on. "An acorn is a *real* nut case."

Luther had accidentally made a joke! Brooke laughed out loud with delight, feeling an incredible release of tension and anxiety.

Luther responded to his favorite girl's blissful laughter by splaying his fingers and rocking slightly back and forth; something he rarely did anymore. He'd learned not to. But this time he couldn't help it. "Sorry," he said.

Brooke just laughed all the more: those behaviors were very familiar, and very dear to her.

Luther realized he had only a limited knowledge of oak trees, so he moved on to another topic. "I think that book is interesting, Brooke."

Her giddiness had settled a bit. "You mean the Bettelheim book?"

"Yeah, *The Empty Fortress*. I got up to page thirty-one last week. That's where I learned 'intellectually,' and some other words. 'Feral' means you're like a wild animal, and 'solipsistic' means that I exist but you may not. That's what my mom said."

"Your mom sounds smart," Brooke said.

"She is! She reads all the time. Mostly books about my dad."

"There are books about your dad?"

"Yeah, I think before I was born he took his shirt off a lot and acted like a pirate."

Brooke felt a little awkward, and tried to nudge the conversation in another direction. "So Luther, can I see the book?"

"Sure, here…" he handed it over.

She took the volume and began flipping pages. "I remember reading a lot of this in my psych class; did you see the pictures yet?"

"No, I don't remember any pictures," Luther said.

She stopped on a page showing two large dark blobs against a light background. "Here's one drawn by an autistic little girl. Bettelheim thinks it's supposed to be two breasts." She showed it to Luther:

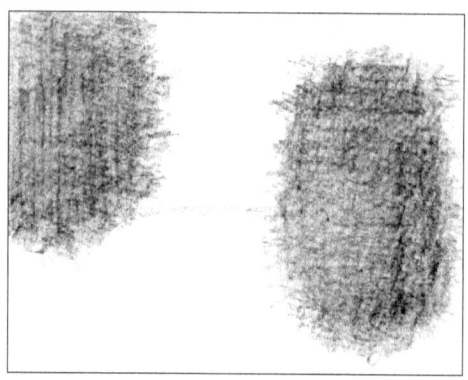

"That's two eyes," Luther said.

"Eyes?" Brooke asked. "How do you know that?"

"Well, it's like the inside of somebody's head looking out! Eyes!"

"Really..." she was intrigued. She flipped a couple of pages ahead to another picture of two light blobs against a dark background. "Well what about this one? Bettelheim also thinks this is two breasts!"

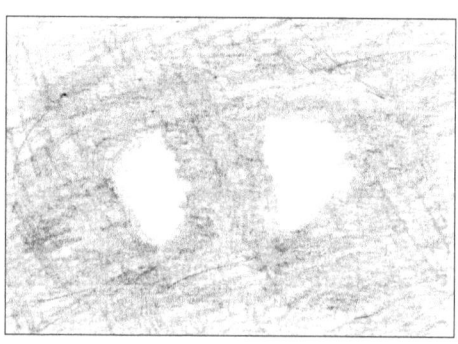

"Same eyes from the outside," Luther said unhesitatingly. "It's somebody looking into somebody else's head!"

Brooke got a chill. "So the light is *inside* your head?"

"I guess," Luther responded. This wasn't the same as being asked to talk about himself; it was more like just talking about something that was there: "The light is all over everything inside."

Brooke stood up and faced her seated friend. She crouched slightly and stared into his dull gray eyes. "Is that what Philip saw?" she asked. "Is that what it's *like* in there?"

She'd just made two inquiries that had no answers, and Luther could only respond again with, "Well, I don't know..." as he stared back at her.

She felt like a treasure-seeker, inches away from a long-sought cache of gold. "Help me out, Luther!" she pleaded.

And Luther wasn't sure why he said it; it was almost as if another voice was speaking through him, saying, "I'll take care of you, Brooke."

And at that moment everything changed, and the beautiful green color seemed to fade from Brooke's eyes, and Luther's mind was overtaken by the two pictures he'd just been shown. They merged, becoming superimposed: the dark blobs covered the light ones, and the light background covered the dark one, and the whole image blended into a solid, subdued gray: like the gray of Luther's eyes. And the grayness grew into a cocoon-like shell all around him, dimming the light just enough so that for the first time he could focus on a single thought. And there was also something else he'd never experienced before: silence.

After a few seconds, a gentle voice seemed to say, "You want to take care of her?"

Luther replied, "I want to love her."

The communication transcended physical language, and even after such a short exchange, the depth of understanding was beyond anything Luther had ever experienced. There was a complete transparency of being between him and this other soul. And from the very start, their silent conversation unfolded without any of the verbal barriers that normally existed for Luther.

"Where's everyone else?" Luther asked.

"They're outside," the silent voice said.

"They're supposed to be inside!" Luther responded.

The fuzzy image of a person slowly began to materialize, saying, "Yeah, this is weird, isn't it?"

Luther couldn't make out any facial features, only the outline of a body floating like a bubble in the ambient grayness. "What's happening?" he asked.

"Good things!" it said. "This is where you start over."

"Start what over?"

"What you're destined for."

Luther was puzzled. "I just want to love Brooke…"

"Oh, you're going to love a lot of people! You're going to take care of us all!"

Now Luther was downright mystified. "Me?"

"Sure! You learn new things every day, and after a while, all that knowledge adds up. If you just figure out how to organize it, you can do great things with it!"

"Like what?"

"You'll find that out as you go. But there is one thing you should think about."

Luther just stood still, waiting for the rest of the thought.

"Remember when your dad gave you that microscope?"

Unaffected by this abruptly-introduced topic, not to mention the apparent omniscience of the other being, Luther perked up. "The microscope! Is that my destiny?"

"Well no, not really. Do you remember what else he gave you that Christmas?"

"Sure I do. I also got a deck of magic cards and a gyroscope."

"Do you still have the gyroscope?"

"No… Larry borrowed it before he died and I never got it back."

"Well, get it back. And don't stay too attached to the microscope, okay?"

Luther was bewildered. "Well, okay… but how can I get the gyroscope back? That was a long time ago."

"How long?"

Luther calculated briefly, "Six years, five months and… twenty-eight days."

The figure replied, "Okay then, that's where we'll start over!"

Again Luther asked: "Start *what* over?"

The entity became more distinct, and now had a face of sorts. It reminded Luther of one of his microscope slides coming into focus through the eyepiece. "It's all good, Luther. You'll be there when you need to," it said.

"Be where?"

The eyes on the face continued to increase in clarity, and Luther was able to discern that they were green in color. He wondered if, and hoped that, they might transform back into Brooke's eyes, but instead they began to sink down low, and the mysterious body attached to them quickly grew smaller and assumed a sitting position on the ground. "It's not your fault," the now distinctly adolescent figure seemed to say.

"What's not my fault?" Luther asked, feeling his own body shrinking as well. He realized he was suddenly unable to control his movement as his right leg administered a hard, swift kick to the left leg of the green-eyed person, and he silently demanded: "Who are you?"

"Jack Oliver!" was the silent, ardent reply.

And all at once the cocoon cracked open and fell away, and all the lights and sounds and thoughts of Luther's normal existence once again filled his head. And he found himself staring into the green eyes of a young boy he recognized from long ago-- evidently one Jack Oliver, who was down on the ground. Luther had just kicked him pretty hard, and Jack Oliver cringed with pain. Luther was abruptly reminded of a time he'd done that sort of thing, back before his mother explained that it was called "bullying," and that it was wrong.

He became confused and panicked, splaying his fingers and turning around to try and get his bearings. But this was no longer the rolling green landscape of an evening in May. Now the familiar barking of a Boston terrier punctuated what had become crisp fall air, and Luther found himself staring at his childhood house. Not knowing what else to do, he ran into his yard, almost tripping over his newly shortened legs. The front porch of the small Cape Cod was poured concrete with black metal railings, and Luther scrambled up the steps and into the house as quickly as he was able. The door slammed behind him.

His mother scurried into the living room: "Luther? Shouldn't you be on your way to school?" She wore a faded blue house dress and had a white bandana tied around her red ponytail. Luther remembered the exact outfit, and how it had made him think of an American flag, even as he watched his mother break down at the news of Larry's death... and now Luther knew what day it was. November 5, 1970. Six years, five months and twenty-eight days earlier than where he'd been a moment ago.

He remembered everything about this house in excruciating detail; every picture, each piece of furniture, every crack in the wall; and of course the remains of a purple juice stain on the carpet (one of his early masterpieces). Ideas began to flicker through his brightly-lit brain: all the possible reasons why he was suddenly back in this place. The one thing he knew for sure was that somehow it would be good for Brooke. And it involved a gyroscope. And apparently not a microscope.

"Luther!" Maxine half-shouted, pulling him up out of his pool of thought. "Why did you come back home?"

She wasn't crying, so it was obvious that nothing monumental had yet happened that day. Luther recalled the street scene from a moment earlier, and remembered the position of the sun. It was still early in the morning: that meant Larry was still alive!

"Luther!" his mother now yelled.

"Mom! You look young!" he yelled back.

Not sure if she'd just been given a compliment or if Luther was just being Luther, she sidestepped the impending 'thank you' and gripped him by the shoulders. She had to reach up a little to do so; even at fourteen Luther was bigger than she was. In a somewhat quieter tone she said, "Son, get to school! You know Darrel's in one of his moods!"

Luther almost said: *No, Darrel's gone...* but he quickly reassessed things. If Larry was still alive, then Darrel would still be around too. No problem: Luther knew how to neutralize the older man using his size advantage. But then again, looking at his mother, he realized that he was now only a few inches taller than she. Maybe there was no advantage after all.

After three consecutive wanderings-of-thought with his mother waiting for some germane response, Luther finally got his wits together enough to say, "Mom, I'm just here for the gyroscope, and to help Brooke!"

"Who's Brooke?" she said, growing increasingly anxious.

"The girl in my physics class that kissed me..."

Maxine threw her hands up in the air and spun around 180 degrees. "Luther! What the *hell*! Stop with the nonsense! You're always talking nonsense..."

"Goddam it, Luther! I told you to get outta here!" The voice was one that Luther hadn't heard in several years. Darrel swaggered in from the kitchen, opening a can of beer that was obviously not his first of the day. Beer for breakfast was standard on days when the dark-bearded ectomorph didn't go to work. "You and your mother are both so goddam stupid, you can't even follow simple orders! Maxine! Tell this stupid-ass boy of yours to get to school!"

She twirled back around quickly with panic in her eyes. "Luther, get out! Please..."

He remembered that look in his mother's eyes. He glanced at the visible parts of his own arms where they protruded from the too-short sleeves of his sweatshirt. There were bruises on his wrists. He felt an aching sensation in his back and chest, and his neck was stiff: things he hadn't noticed in the initial confusion of his return. But now he suddenly remembered the way it felt to live with Darrel.

Without questioning, he turned and quickly made his way back out of the house. Through the closed front door he heard a familiar *crack*; the sound of Darrel slapping his mother across the face. She'd probably have a black eye when he saw her next. Muffled male profanity followed, mixed with the whimpering of a defeated, terrified woman. Not knowing what else to do, Luther wandered back into the street just in time to see the distant dot that he knew was Jack Oliver, limping over the crest of the hill on Tenbrook Street.

CHAPTER SEVENTEEN

HE CAME home in the fall. It wasn't like May in Maryland; Lark Lane was sparsely ornamented with brown and orange leaves: remnants left behind by the county leaf pickup a couple of days earlier. Luther stood on the corner of Lark and Tenbrook, gazing up at the olive green leaves of the Bergers' twin magnolia trees. *They normally grow in more southern regions*, he thought to himself, *and they don't drop any leaves until spring*. He also thought about what was likely happening in his house right now, and wondered if, even with his smaller size, he ought to go back and try to confront Darrel. He remembered how very easy it had been when he was seventeen, and how the older man had collapsed almost instantly when Luther started striking him. He also thought about his physics class, and Newton's Three Laws of Motion.

I. *Every object in motion will remain in that state of motion unless an external force is applied to it. So if I rush toward Darrel, his body is the external force that will change or stop my motion.*

II. *The greater the mass of an object, the greater the amount of force needed to accelerate it. So when I was seventeen I had greater mass than Darrel, and the force required for me to hit him was enough to stop him. But now I have less mass.*

III. *For each action, there is an equal and opposite reaction. So if I'm smaller than Darrel, and his body exerts a force to counteract my force, it would probably hurt me more than him.*

And with that brief analysis he determined that going after Darrel was an impractical idea. He should focus on his instructions instead: Larry had the gyroscope and Luther was supposed to get it back. So he walked up to his cousin's front door and rang the bell.

His Aunt Doris answered. "Luther! Shouldn't you be at school?"

Before speaking, he took a moment to look at her. Doris and Uncle Lou had moved away soon after Larry was killed, and

Luther and his mother saw very little of them after that. Doris very much resembled her younger sister, with the same petite figure, red hair and freckles. When young, they'd often been mistaken for twins. The woman who now stood before Luther possessed a vibrancy reflecting her thirty-something years of life; a vibrancy that Luther had seen disappear within a week of her only child's death. The same vibrancy that had gradually left his own mother after a few months of living with Darrel. But right now, Aunt Doris still had it. It was in her eyes.

"Luther? Are you alright?" she asked.

"You look young!" he said.

"Well thank you!" she replied.

"Um, is Larry home?"

"Luther, Larry is in school! And you should be as well."

In light of the circumstances, Luther was too keyed-up to think about school. "Um, do you know if he's got my gyroscope? I need it."

Doris smiled curiously. "Of course he has it... you loaned it to him for his science fair project. Don't you remember?"

To Luther, this created a dilemma. On one hand, of course he remembered that Larry still needed the gyroscope. On the other hand, he knew that if Larry died today, he wouldn't see his gyroscope again, and Jack Oliver had indicated that Luther needed it. "Yeah, I remember," he said with some confusion.

Doris knew how things were in her sister's house, and sensed some kind of need on Luther's part. "Um, Sweetie, do you need a ride to school? I'd be glad to take you over right now."

"No... it's okay. You're okay," he replied.

"You're *sure*, Luther? Really, I'd be glad to..."

He didn't even hear the rest of her sentence. He glanced across the yard to the privacy hedge, remembering that just on the other side was the Dodge Dart in which his aunt was offering to drive him to school. It was also the car in which Larry would be killed later that day. "Wait, yeah. I'd like that." He had no idea why he'd just said what he said, but there was a sudden compulsion to ride in that car. "Yes! Can we go to school?"

Doris was surprised by Luther's reaction. She was used to him being much more withdrawn than this, so she seized the opportunity to interact. She'd always loved her nephew, even as a non-responsive little boy, but because of the oppressive atmosphere at Maxine and Darrel's house she got few opportunities to take care of him. "I'll get my coat!" she said enthusiastically.

The drive to Twin Springs Junior High School took only about three minutes. Luther looked all around the interior of the car he'd ridden in a handful of times before, trying to come up with some plan of action. Bit by bit he began to remember details and blend ideas, recognizing that in order to get his gyroscope back he would have to make sure Larry's car accident wouldn't happen. Riding along wordlessly, Luther mentally addressed the question of whether some change to the vehicle might make a difference, but he quickly acknowledged that the accident wasn't due to a defect in the car, so any modification he might come up with would be irrelevant. When Doris dropped him off in front of the school, he was so deep in thought that he didn't even remember to thank her for the ride. As soon as her car was out of sight, he began to walk back home, following the same path that the Dodge would be taking later on, hoping to find a clue or two along the way. He even considered just warning Doris and Larry not to drive that night, but figured they would just think him foolish.

For about twenty minutes Luther slowly, methodically paced along the route, his head holding even more simultaneous ideas than usual. Unable to stand it any longer, he finally stopped, splayed his fingers and jumped up and down in place for several seconds. As much as he tried not to do that sort of thing anymore, especially in public, it was sometimes unavoidable. And it felt *good!* Now with his head cleared a bit, he could resume his investigative reflection. So why *did* the accident happen? Luther mentally listed the details as he walked:

1. It was on the way to the science fair, about 6:25 p.m.

2. Aunt Doris was driving, Larry was in the front passenger's seat, and nobody else was in the car. Uncle Lou was to have met them later at school.

3. The dump truck that hit them belonged to Reed's; a local paving company.

4. The truck driver said he swerved to miss a dog that had run into the road.

5. The Dodge Dart was struck from the passenger's side as it turned right from Lark onto Tenbrook.

And that was all he could remember. By now he was almost back at his house, having traced the entire route with no new insight. Not wanting to be seen by Darrel, he pulled himself up onto the hood of a car parked a couple of houses down from the Howells' lot, and sat there to think. There was nothing obvious that could be done with the route itself; intersections and trees and fire hydrants were all permanent. If the hedge around Larry's yard weren't so tall, maybe Aunt Doris would be able to see the truck coming before she pulled around the corner. But he couldn't cut all those bushes down. Hmm...

A distant dot appeared at the crest of the hill on Tenbrook Street. As it increased in size, Luther was able to confirm that it was Jack Oliver. *Maybe he's going to tell me what to do*, he thought.

Jack Oliver limped slowly up the street, looking up only once at Luther before crossing over to the other side.

Puzzled by the apparent avoidance, Luther just sat there and watched. It began to rain lightly as he considered his options. *Maybe I could do something about the truck if I could get to Reed's Paving, but there might be more than one truck there. Wait... the truck swerved to miss a dog...*

Shielding his eyes from the drizzle, Luther looked up and down the street, taking stock of which neighbors had dogs. There were none. And as the solution dawned on him, he gradually became re-sensitized to the yapping of the Boston terrier tied up in his own yard. It was Darrel's dog; he'd never even given it a name. Luther always just called it "Boy" since "here boy" was how Darrel summoned it. Boy's barking was so incessant that Luther learned to tune it out. It just blended in with all the other sounds that were always in his head. Now listening more keenly to the yapping, he had a realization: *Boy* was the dog that was going to run into the road! Now with a plan, Luther slid off the car and proceeded stealthily toward his own back yard, hoping not to be seen through a window. Peering over the chain link fence, everything was as he remembered: a big grass-free area that encircled a steel stake where Boy stayed tied up at night. This is where the dog needed to be: a place where he couldn't get out of the yard even if he got loose from his tether. All Luther had to do was move the dog to the back, but it had to be done without Darrel's knowledge. The drunken demon couldn't know that Luther was skipping school.

The light rain increased in intensity as Luther walked toward the street once more, pondering when he might be able to move Boy unnoticed. Since this was apparently one of those days Darrel didn't have any work, he'd be home all day drinking and barking abuses at Maxine. Maybe that's why Luther never minded the dog so much; at least it made a nicer sound than Darrel. Lost in thought, he meandered across Tenbrook Street toward the corner of Lark Lane, assessing the scene of the upcoming accident. He stopped abruptly when he saw something unusual. Seated on the sidewalk next to Aunt Doris' Dodge was Jack Oliver, busily performing a task of some sort. Luther watched with curiosity as Jack Oliver lingered there in the rain. He briefly considered approaching the other boy but thought better of it, instead waiting around the corner until the mysterious undertaking was complete. Luther must have stood in the precipitation a good ten minutes before the coast was clear enough to investigate. When he finally got a look, he saw two flat tires on the passenger's side of the car, rendering it temporarily un-drivable.

That's it! Luther thought. *That will work. It should delay the time they leave by enough that the truck will already have passed when they go through the intersection. I don't need to move Boy; Jack Oliver's idea is better.*

And he began to look around for a way to get out of the rain himself. He had no coat and no umbrella. He certainly couldn't go back to his own house, and Aunt Doris had just dropped him off at school, so going back to her place wasn't an option either. The rain was cold, and Luther hastily made up his mind to wait in the Dodge until the sky cleared up. He thought the back seat would be safer, since he could duck down if Aunt Doris got into the driver's seat for some reason. As he opened the passenger's side door he noticed a key lying on the sidewalk next to the rear wheel. *Jack Oliver was here before, maybe this is his*, he thought. Luther pocketed the key before slipping into the vehicle and quietly closing the door. Cold and wet, he curled up on the back seat and began to think about all that had happened to him so far that day. Up since 5:00 to be at the grocery store by six, he had worked until 3:00, walked four miles to school, sat through a nearly-three-hour physics class and met up with Brooke; all before being sent to the place he was now. Exhausted, he fell asleep to the patter of raindrops on the roof of the car.

He awoke several hours later to the sound of a memory: it was Larry's voice! Luther perked up when he heard it through the car window, passing by on the sidewalk.

"Yeah, I still haven't decided what to call it," Larry said to somebody.

"Well, I like acronyms, so I'd vote for 'A.M.I.N.O.,'" somebody said.

"I've gotta decide by tonight," Larry replied. "See you at seven!"

Luther sat up. Peering through the rear window he saw his cousin turn left onto his front walk, disappearing behind the hedge. He could also see the back view of whomever Larry had been talking to, continuing down the sidewalk. It was a short boy who still wore his yellow hooded rain slicker even though the rain had stopped. Obviously school was out. Luther got out of the car and followed behind his cousin, managing to catch him before he got inside. "Larry!" he shouted.

Larry stopped and turned. "Hey! Did you skip school or something?"

"Huh?" Luther fumbled. Larry might blow his cover with Aunt Doris, who had taken him to school. "Don't tell anybody, okay?"

"The sacred pact cannot be broken!" Larry said with a comic formality, holding out three fingers to initiate the "secret handshake" he and Luther had invented when they were younger.

Luther instantly recognized the gesture, and offered three fingers of his own to complete the rite.

They brushed their fingertips together and intoned: "Nyuk, nyuk, nyuk," imitating the Three Stooges.

The "sacred pact" had been an important method of bonding for the boys; especially for Larry, who was sometimes at a bit of a loss to understand Luther. He liked his cousin but always felt a bit awkward when confronted with his peculiarities. The secret handshake and reference to the (actually nonexistent) oath of loyalty, provided a formal procedure that gave Larry a bit of a buffer. He could interact with Luther without having to delve too deeply into his odd mind. It was a bit like a churchgoer embracing religious rituals to make up for a lack of theological comprehension. There was comfort in just knowing what was coming next.

Luther on the other hand, used the little routine not as a buffer, but as a way of connecting more deeply with his only playmate. At age fourteen Luther hadn't fully understood who the Three Stooges were and why he and Larry were imitating them. But now with the insight of his twenty-one-year-old self, he found the practice rather funny. Luther laughed.

Larry looked at him oddly. His cousin didn't laugh often. "Wanna come inside?" he asked.

The two boys entered the family-friendly dwelling together, heading straight for the kitchen.

Doris heard them talking and hurried to the kitchen as well. She seemed very surprised to see Luther. "Well hello, boys!" she said. "Let me make you a snack!"

"Nestlé's Quick!" Larry spouted. "And Nilla Wafers!"

"Is that okay with you, Luther?" Doris asked.

"Well, sure!" he replied. He hadn't expected to be fed; he just wanted to check on the welfare of his gyroscope. But some chocolate and vanilla certainly sounded good, and he was starving.

Both boys sat down at the kitchen table as Doris quickly mixed up two tumblers of the chocolate milk. In the time it took for Larry to take his first sip, Luther had downed a whole glass.

Doris stared, wide-eyed. "My goodness! Are we hungry, Luther?" She took his glass to mix another serving.

Luther realized too late that he'd just done something impolite. "Oh, I'm sorry," he sputtered, clumsily pointing at the empty glass. "No... it's okay. You're okay."

Doris just smiled. "Hungry boys need to be fed!" Within a minute she'd stirred up another glass of Nestlé's Quick and set it before her nephew. She also arranged about two dozen vanilla wafers on a plate and placed it graciously on the table.

"Thank you," Luther said, this time remembering his manners.

And this time Larry's mouth was too full of cookies to respond.

After a couple of minutes of mutual wordless feasting, Luther opened the conversation with: "Where's my gyroscope now?"

"At school of course, with the rest of my project," Larry replied.

"I want to see your project," Luther said.

"Are you gonna be able to get out of the house at that time?" Larry asked. "I know Uncle Darrel's pretty strict about everybody staying home at night."

This jogged Luther's memory. Larry was right; "Uncle" Darrel enjoyed having Maxine and Luther home together in the evenings, so his abuse could be doled out fairly. Luther realized he might have to sneak out when it came time. "I don't care what he wants," he said.

Larry opened his eyes wide with surprise, and smiled. "Good for you, man!"

Doris had been only a few feet away listening to the boys talk. Neither Maxine nor Luther had ever dared to speak disrespectfully of Darrel, so this was quite a departure. She recognized the dysfunction in that household as well as anyone, and knew it was an environment in need of major change. At the same time, Doris had a rather stoic response to it all, demonstrating a strangely abnormal respect for what she saw as her sister's chosen path. So the boys' exchange seemed impudent: "Watch your manners, fellows," she said with polite disapproval.

"Sorry Mom..." Larry replied robotically.

Luther was still thinking about the safety of his gyroscope. "Um... tell me about the project, Larry!"

"I showed it to you last week!" Larry snapped. "It's a simulated navigation system for airplanes."

Luther did in fact recall seeing a sneak preview of the apparatus Larry had made from a piece of board, a gyroscope, and two flashlights. At the time, he had a limited understanding of how it all worked, and since Larry never got to demonstrate it at the science fair, it remained a puzzle thereafter. Luther knew he just needed to be patient; after all, Jack Oliver had insured that the car accident wouldn't take place, and that the safe return of the gyroscope was now imminent. "Yes, you showed it to me," was all Luther could find to say.

"You'll see it for real tonight," Larry said, a bit irritated.

"Maybe you should be getting home, Luther," Doris interjected, knowing that Darrel would likely be looking for him soon.

Luther really wanted to stay, but did as he was asked. "See you tonight Larry," he said as he rose from the table to leave.

"Hey, wait a second!" Larry spouted, holding out three fingers.

Luther did the same as the boys repeated their ritual: "Nyuk, nyuk, nyuk!"

Doris rolled her eyes and sighed.

Larry stuffed his mouth with more vanilla wafers.

Luther left and giggled all the way home.

His house was quiet when he stepped through the front door. His mother was on the sofa, curled up in a fetal position. She lifted her head just enough that he could see her facial bruises.

"Quiet, Luther," she half-whispered. "Darrel's asleep at the kitchen table."

"Are you okay, Mom?" he asked in a hushed tone of his own.

Maxine just gazed at him with an expression that belied her words. "Yeah, I'm okay." Of course she wasn't, and though someone else might have reacted to Luther's clueless query with more candor, she couldn't. She was his mother, and she knew it was a miracle that Luther could ask the question at all. Her protective maternal instincts also came into play as she urged him to a safer location: "Why don't you just stay in your room tonight? I'll bring you something to eat a little later."

"Okay," he answered quietly, and immediately headed upstairs. Unfortunately his feet weren't as quiet as his voice had been: Luther was a big boy, and the steps pounded as he made his ascent. The noise apparently woke Darrel, for Luther heard voices through the floor of his room. In response to the unintelligible grumbling of a male voice he heard his mother say:

"Yes, he's home. He went to his room."

Grumble grumble...

"Yes, I'll start dinner soon."

Even when Maxine's answer was *yes*, Darrel remained abusive. His fist landed loudly on the kitchen table in response to her compliance.

Luther was still exhausted, so he lay on his bed. It was much more comfortable than it had been the night before in the little apartment: he was seven years smaller so there was a lot more room to stretch out. The mattress was also seven years softer, and that, combined with a belly full of chocolate milk and cookies, made for a sweet nap. Luther drifted off, dreaming of gyroscopes.

He awoke a bit later to an unusually quiet house. By this hour Darrel would normally have been watching television and the sounds of cookery would have come from the kitchen. But none of that was happening, and despite his instructions to stay in his room, Luther went back downstairs. All the lights were off, and he groped a bit to find a switch. "Mom?" he called out.

There was no reply.

He turned on a trail of lights as he made his way to the kitchen. The small table was littered with nine or ten empty Piels beer cans, each one exhibiting Darrel's trademark: an intact pull tab flanked by two triangular piercings. The resident alcoholic preferred to open his cans the old fashioned way.

Luther instinctively spun around, spying a hastily-written note stuck to the refrigerator door with a plain round magnet.

Luther-- gone with Darrel was all it said.

That meant they'd headed off to some local bar so that Darrel could get even drunker and exploit his enabler. Luther remembered days like this very well: a few times he had been made to come along. When Darrel drank, Maxine became little more than a decoration on his arm. She followed him, attended to him, agreed with everything he said, and treated him with undeserved respect. She was terrified of him.

"They'll probably be back late," Luther said out loud, looking at the kitchen clock: it was 6:12. He had a golden opportunity to get out of the house and over to the school in plenty of time for the science fair at seven; get his gyroscope back and return home before he'd be missed! And he didn't even have to move Boy to the back yard.

Luther headed out the front door, not even thinking to put on a jacket. He marched down Tenbrook Street toward the school, reviewing the day's events in his mind. It seemed like the accident had been forestalled without his intervention, and he believed even more strongly that his only task now was to retrieve that gyroscope. But as he slogged along through the rain puddles in the darkness, another thought entered his mind. *Wait... if the car can't be driven, how are they going to get to school?*

Suddenly Luther saw his own shadow cast on the trees ahead of him by a pair of headlights behind him. He moved to the left to let the car pass, but instead it slowed down and idled next to him. It was a two-door white sedan, and Luther was a little apprehensive of its purpose until he saw Larry's face through the rolled-down rear window.

"Luther! Wanna ride to school?" he yelled.

"I guess," Luther said a bit suspiciously. "Sure, why not?"

A woman he didn't recognize was driving, and she opened her door to allow Luther to slide into the back seat next to Larry. It was cold outside, but the car was warm.

"Thanks for the ride," Luther said politely, still wondering exactly what was going on.

"You're welcome," Jack Oliver replied, turning to show Luther whose car he'd just gotten into.

Their eyes met, and for a second it all seemed to make sense. Wow, Jack Oliver had really taken care of everything, including the ride to school! Luther also remembered the key in his pocket, but mentioning it in front of everyone would raise many questions. So instead of speaking to Jack Oliver, he quickly shifted his attention to Larry: "I guess everything's ready for tonight?"

"Oh, it's ready!" Larry said. "The question is, are *you* ready to see... the 'All-Mechanical Inertial Navigation Operating System'?"

"So, you went with the A.M.I.N.O. system," Luther remarked. "Pretty big name!"

Jack Oliver faced forward and looked out the window.

"Well, it needs a big name to distract from just how simple it really is!" Larry replied jokingly. "It's not like I had lasers lying around in the basement, so I kinda had to fake it! Besides, I'm just using models to explain the basic theory."

"By the way, you better be careful with that gyroscope," Luther said. "My dad gave me that."

"It will be returned unharmed," Larry said, sounding annoyed.

Jack Oliver spun around in his seat once more and glared at the cousins questioningly.

Luther spoke impetuously: "Larry, was something wrong with your car?" He felt like he was sharing a wonderful secret with Jack Oliver.

"Yeah, there were two flats!" Larry replied.

Jack Oliver rolled his eyes and shook his head as he turned away for the last time.

Luther was puzzled by the reaction, but had little time to think it through before the woman who was driving stopped the car.

"I'll drop you boys off at the main door, okay?" she asked.

"Thanks, Mrs. Oliver," Larry said, as he slipped out of the back seat.

"Yeah, thanks," said Luther. *Mrs. Oliver?* he thought. *Is "Oliver" Jack Oliver's last name? And is that his mother? And why isn't he coming inside?* Luther slid across the back seat and exited from the same door as Larry, wondering how much he knew about this mysterious boy from the gray cocoon. But any questions would have to wait. The school building greeted the cousins with bright lights from within.

The science fair was bustling with students and their parents, and once Uncle Lou and Aunt Doris arrived, Larry got to demonstrate the A.M.I.N.O. system, which didn't work properly until Luther attached a string to the gyroscope to hold it upright for the sake of the presentation. One flashlight was fixed on the gyroscope and another was attached to a small piece of plywood that tilted back and forth underneath it. The result was a very crude representation of a steering system where the two light beams could indicate an airplane's orientation to the surface of the Earth. The name was the most complicated thing about the apparatus, but the concept was pretty heady for the seventh grade, so Larry got accolades.

By 8:30 the event was over, and the Bergers and Luther packed themselves into Uncle Lou's tiny little Rambler for the short trip home. Luther confiscated his gyroscope and held on to it proudly, knowing it would somehow help the only girl who had ever kissed him. He felt giddy and peaceful, having accomplished his mission.

CHAPTER EIGHTEEN

L UTHER HAD never seen a dead person before. When he was seven his father died, but the casket was closed by the time Luther was brought into the parlor. Then when he was fourteen Larry died, and like before, there was no open casket. So Luther was fourteen again before he finally saw a dead person, and in fact, two.

It was a pair of pictures that would remain vivid in his mind, and in his dreams, for the rest of his life. In a scene lit only by the waxing crescent moon and the streetlamps that lined Tenbrook, Luther recorded the indelible images of his best friend and his mother as they were snuffed out and literally dropped into his lap. Larry was first: whipping violently into Luther's right side as the metal frame of Uncle Lou's Rambler crumpled around him. Luther felt his lower arm snap in two as his favorite cousin became a virtual projectile fired from just inches away. But fate wasn't finished yet. The second shot came from the other car as Maxine's body was thrown headfirst through the frame of her shattered windshield and partially into the backseat where Luther was a passenger.

At first he didn't know it was her. In that instant when time changed, he only recognized the top of a person's head with wet, tousled hair ramming through the window on Larry's side, as the two locked-together cars slid to a stop. The half-second of ensuing silence was broken almost as violently as the windows when Aunt Doris let out a short scream from the front seat. Uncle Lou just sat there in a daze. It wasn't until Luther recognized Darrel through the shattered glass that he finally realized the identity of the second person who lay across his lap. It was several minutes before help arrived, and by the time the emergency crew sorted everything out, Luther was in an ambulance on the way to the hospital, and he had finally seen a dead person. And in fact, two.

As he lay there listening to the wailing of the siren during the short trip, many thoughts ran through his mind. It wasn't supposed to happen this way, and damn, his arm hurt! And was the thing he was lying on called a gurney or a stretcher? And the color of the fireman's hat was almost the same shade as the giraffe Pez dispenser from Murphy's Mart. And why was that bastard Darrel up and walking at the scene? As the police systematically took down information in the midst of the chaos, the uninjured drunk driver nonchalantly swished back and forth in a failed attempt to look sober. All Luther heard him say was, "I tole 'er not to... she pull'd m'arm..."

And now Luther rode to the hospital thinking not about his dead mother and cousin, but about the difference between a gurney and a stretcher; and about Pez. He knew he probably ought to be feeling something else, but it just wasn't there. Maybe he was in shock. He tried to think about gyroscopes instead, to take his mind off the pain in his arm.

Darrell was taken away and charged with two counts of vehicular manslaughter. Lou and Doris Berger were treated for minor injuries and released to plan two funerals. Luther was kept in the hospital overnight to make sure his compound fracture didn't become infected.

After that, the house on Tenbrook Street sat empty, Darrel went to prison, his dog went to the pound, and Luther went to live with his Aunt and Uncle.

And so it began.

CR♦♦ED

Luther looked around his new room. Well, it was really Larry's old room. The Bergers were sensitive to the possibility that Luther might find it unsettling to sleep in his dead cousin's bed, and offered to set up a bedroom area for him some other place in the house. They were more than a little surprised when he said it didn't bother him at all. Doris and Lou were both haunted by what had happened on the corner of Tenbrook and Lark Lane; the scene of the collision was visible from their front porch, and the memory of that night slapped them in the face every time they walked out the door. They agreed that if their sensibilities didn't improve soon, they'd put the house up for sale.

Meanwhile, Luther finally had furniture that wasn't little-boy-sized, and a few pieces of new clothing, since the things from his old house were mostly too small. He also brought his microscope with him, and of course his gyroscope, which was salvaged from the wreck of the Rambler along with Doris' purse, an umbrella, and the contents of the glove box. Luther's twin treasures, both gifts from his dad, now sat atop Larry's chest of drawers. More than once he found himself automatically reaching for one of them with his right arm, stopping abruptly when he felt the pain from his bruises and saw the thick white cast that he constantly forgot was there. *I broke my right radius and my right ulna*, he'd think to himself, recalling the diagrams of human bones he'd looked up in Larry's Junior Encyclopedia. It was the kind of resource he never had as a child, and even as a twenty-one-year-old college student he would have been fascinated to have a book set like that right in his own house. In fact, there were a lot of things about living with the Bergers that Luther found he liked. In addition to the array of books and educational materials that had been a normal part of Larry's life, there was always good food in the house. There didn't seem to be too much concern over money. And though Uncle Lou seemed a bit aloof, Aunt Doris was able to spend quality time with Luther every day; something Maxine couldn't manage with Darrel around, and had no incentive to do once he was gone. In contrast, Luther and his aunt talked about a lot of different things, and he found it strangely comfortable to share his thoughts with her without worrying that she might find them odd. It was a different kind of conversation than he'd ever been able to have with his mom; Doris shared lots of facts about the world and challenged Luther with interesting questions that he couldn't always answer right away. And she was always jubilant when he came back later with an answer, even if it was a wrong one.

But despite the perks of living with the Bergers, Luther didn't want to grow too accustomed to a circumstance that was only temporary. He'd retrieved his gyroscope and knew it was just a matter of time until he went back to 1977 to help Brooke. Of course the more lasting outcome of the time journey wasn't what he expected; Larry still died and his mother did as well. Yet he made an odd peace with that result: Larry's fate was the same, and his mom had been spared years of suffering. She herself had said she didn't really *live*, she just *existed*, and to Luther her abrupt demise was a terrible but logical solution to her problem.

The two deaths also had less of an effect on Luther than on those around him. He didn't miss deceased family in the same way as everyone else. He politely tolerated two wakes and two funerals, watching people weep and shake their heads in disbelief at the unfairness of it all. And everyone that came wanted to console Luther; yet from his perspective it was *they* who were in need of solace. He must have said "…it's okay. You're okay…" a hundred times to various relatives and friends as they hugged his stiff frame and told him to "be strong," and offered advice that was really of no consequence to a person like him. Because death wasn't an ending: it was just a shift of consciousness. It was the light moving from the inside of that person's head to the inside of Luther's. Ever since his dad died, Luther could still feel the man's presence. Of course he wasn't still "there" in the sense that one could have a normal conversation with him; but he was still very much "there." And now so was Larry, and so was Maxine. And they were all a part of who Luther was.

Each passing day left Luther more restless. Each night he'd dream of waking up in his old lumpy bed that was too small, but in the morning he'd open his bleary eyes only to find he was still in Larry's bed. And as much as he appreciated the house and the food and the talks with his aunt, the situation made him uneasy, like perhaps things were going to stay this way. How could he help Brooke if he was stuck in the past? And even if he were to go back, Luther wrestled with the ominous scenario of what life in 1977 might be like with his mother gone. He knew that hypothetically her death would have to reshape the future, but he couldn't come to terms with the reality of such a change. So he tried to ignore the questions that were too big to answer, until the day Jack Oliver showed up again. Then those questions became too big not to answer.

CR✦✦ED

It had been two-and-a-half weeks since the accident, and Luther had yet to return to school. He assumed there was no point because he'd be leaving anyway; but now he wasn't so sure. The house on Lark Lane had been put up for sale and the Bergers were preparing to move to another part of town with their nephew. The sky was overcast and Luther sat on the front step without a jacket. He found it difficult to wear long sleeves over his cast.

Aunt Doris was there too, and gently placed a hand on his tow-headed crown as she urged him back to school. "You'll feel a lot better once everything's back to normal," she said.

Luther worried that if he did return it might somehow jinx things and seal his fate: like he was accepting this new life in place of the old. Of course he couldn't explain something like that to Aunt Doris; his eyes leaked little tears of frustration as he looked at the ground and said "I don't think I should go."

She sighed and went back indoors saying, "Maybe tomorrow." After what her nephew had been through, it was best not to push.

"Luther?" said a voice from the sidewalk.

Startled, Luther looked up and saw Jack Oliver, clad in a mustard-colored long-sleeved shirt and brown corduroy pants. "It's *you!*" Luther snapped. Maybe Jack Oliver had finally come to help him get back to 1977!

"Is this where you live now?" Jack Oliver asked.

Luther rose and strode halfway down the Bergers' walk. "Yeah, so?" It was a surprisingly uninformed question to be coming from the enlightened soul in the gray cocoon.

Jack Oliver went on. "Listen, I heard about Larry, but I didn't know about your mom until today. I just wanted you to know I'm sorry."

Now Luther was even more perplexed. How could Jack Oliver not have known about Maxine when he was behind the whole plan? Luther wrinkled his brow and took a few more short steps toward the smaller boy. "Well maybe you *should* be sorry! I saw you messing with my aunt's car." Maybe he could at least get an explanation of Jack Oliver's intent. "Why did you do that?"

But Jack Oliver's response didn't make any sense. "Listen, I know what it's like to lose people you love. Especially all of a sudden..."

That was the same sort of comment Luther had heard over and again at the wakes and funerals. Maybe Jack Oliver wasn't all he seemed to be. "You don't know *anything*!" Luther said with surprise.

"It's not your fault." Jack Oliver uttered.

Of course it's not my fault, Luther thought. *My idea would have worked!* He replied: "Then it's *your* fault!"

"Luther, don't try to find fault in this, find a solution instead."

Wait... was that a challenge? Was this a test of some sort? Luther offered a logical answer: "A solution! Okay, go back in time and don't mess with the car!"

"How do you know that would make any difference?" Jack Oliver responded.

How could Jack Oliver not be understanding this? "You changed the car!" Luther reiterated. "It wouldn't have happened that way if you didn't change the car."

"I guess that's possible," Jack Oliver said, "but nothing ever happens all by itself. Everything is in relation to everything else!"

"But *you* didn't belong anywhere in relation to that car!" Luther clung to the hope that there might still be a way to fix things. If he could just make Jack Oliver see that, perhaps the night of November 5 could be readjusted for a more favorable outcome. He continued: "Larry was my best friend! If you didn't mess with those tires he'd still be alive!"

"But you don't *know* that!" Jack Oliver said.

Now Luther fought back angry tears, "...and then maybe only the *other* car with the *drunk* driver... would've..." he suddenly realized the futility of his position.

"I'm sorry," Jack Oliver interjected. "I know you can't see it, but I was just trying to do the right thing..."

"You don't know what's right! What's gonna *happen* to me now?"

Luther didn't see his Aunt Doris step into view through the glass door behind him as Jack Oliver replied, "Luther, once or twice in your life, fate taps you on the shoulder. If you turn around and look, he'll show you the direction you're supposed to go."

The frustration was too much, and Luther burst into tears. "Well this is for fate!" he said, punching Jack Oliver in the stomach with his good arm, and knocking the wind out of him. The bulky cast on his other arm caused Luther to spin around, and he found himself looking through the glass, right into Doris' eyes.

Their visual connection was brief; Doris ran outside past Luther, toward the boy who was now lying in a heap on the front walk. "Are you alright?" she said, turning him over enough to see his face. "Jack! Is that you?" she cried out. Then she looked up to scold Luther: "Young man, I will *not* allow this kind of bullying! Just wait until Uncle Lou gets home!"

Stunned and confused as to how he'd gotten there, young Jack caught his breath and managed to sit up. He rose to his feet, dusted off his corduroys and turned to go.

But Doris wouldn't let it be over just yet. This was a good opportunity to establish herself as the new parent. "Do you have anything to say to Jack?" she demanded of her nephew.

Red-eyed and confounded, Luther addressed Jack, "So what do I do with the gyroscope now?"

"What gyroscope?" Jack replied, equally perplexed.

What gyroscope? Luther thought. *Jack Oliver doesn't even remember about the gyroscope?* He suddenly felt like he had no blood.

"*Apologize*, Luther! Say you're sorry!" Doris prompted impatiently.

"I'm sorry," Luther said quietly, and began to cry uncontrollably, silently.

Now embarrassed as well as perplexed, Jack quickly turned and walked around the hedge in the direction of Tenbrook Street.

Doris couldn't bear to see the scene of the car accident just then, so she gave Luther a half-spin and gently marched him toward the house.

"I'll go to school tomorrow," he said with resignation, his voice shaking.

Once inside the door, Doris turned to her whimpering nephew and embraced him, as her own tears began to flow. Luther's usual stiffness was gone, and for the first time in her memory, he hugged her back. They stood there crying together for a long while.

CR♦♦ℬ

"Pass the peas."

Doris wordlessly slid the bowl across the table to Lou, who scooped a couple of small spoonfuls onto his plate.

Luther looked back and forth at his aunt and uncle, who both seemed to be struggling with the circumstances.

"So Luther," Doris finally said, "do you like the turkey and stuffing?"

"Um, yeah. Yes, thanks," he replied, sensing the heaviness in the air.

Lou set his fork down. "It's only been three weeks, Doris. You shouldn't have done all this. It's too soon."

"I wanted to celebrate Thanksgiving. It's a time for families. What's wrong with that?"

"Because this isn't our fam--" Lou stopped short, shocked by his own bluntness. He looked at his nephew for the first time during the meal. "I'm sorry, Luther. I didn't mean it that way."

"It's okay, you're okay," Luther replied, not understanding why an apology was necessary. He looked at the serving bowl that was right beside his plate. "Can I have more mashed potatoes?"

Doris sighed and mustered up a smile. "Of course you can, sweetie. You don't need to ask."

Luther dolloped a large serving of potatoes onto his plate. "Gravy too?"

Doris raised her red eyebrows and looked at her husband, who met her gaze with mild chagrin.

"I guess I forgot it's only been three weeks for Luther too," Lou said. "Have a lot of gravy, Luther. It makes everything even more delicious."

Doris became a little misty-eyed.

"Thanks for this meal, dear. Everything tastes wonderful," Lou said, now misty-eyed himself.

"Happy Thanksgiving," said Luther with a mouthful of potatoes and extra gravy.

CHAPTER NINETEEN

THE BIG unlabeled truck backed into the driveway at 510 Webster Place. It was a local move, so the Bergers didn't have to hire a long distance company like Allied or Mayflower; they found a mom 'n' pop mover that was a lot more affordable. After all, this wasn't something they'd prepared for. If it had been a change of job or a financial windfall they would have been able to give it more thought. But this was a hasty relocation to get them away from an awful remembrance. They finally sold their old place and quickly picked out a new one, the only real stipulation being that it had to be close to Lou's job. They had asked Luther if he was concerned about attending the same middle school, but with Larry gone it didn't really matter to him. So the Bergers packed their things and moved across town to a new neighborhood where everyone could start fresh.

Luther walked through the empty house with its worn wood floors, into the room that was to become his. It was a small space, but quite adequate for sleeping and being alone. Luther's new bedroom window looked out on a rather spacious backyard, a feature he liked. He wanted to see the area first hand, so he went out to explore while the movers carried in the first load of boxes. Within the chain-link borders of the yard there were four bare trees, a small sheet metal storage shed with sliding doors, and not much else. The cool January breeze blew lightly, and Luther looked up at the sky sort of expecting to see a huge face with pursed lips as the source of it. But there were only clouds. He chuckled at his own silliness.

"New next-- next-door neighbor I suppose?" said a voice from behind him.

"Yeah," Luther answered, slowly turning around.

"I'm a-- a new neighbor too, then." It was a teenage boy standing just on the other side of the fence. He seemed overly bundled-up for the weather, with a heavy hooded winter coat, big puffy mittens and a muffler that covered most of his face.

"You're new?" Luther asked, trying to get some sense of what this person looked like under all the layers. "Did you just move in too?"

"No, but-- but if you don't know me yet then I'm new."

An odd idea, but it made perfect sense to Luther. "I guess that's true!" He already liked this boy.

"But I-- I don't know how long we stay new. Maybe just-- just 'till we're not strangers."

"Well, when is that?"

"When we're-- we're old I think."

A few times in his life Luther had met someone who stuttered, and at first this boy seemed like one of them. But the more he listened, the more he realized that it wasn't exactly a stutter...

"But not-- not like an old man. It's when-- when time just gets old. Time, not-- not people."

The "stutter" was really just an odd way of repeating certain words in each sentence, and the sentences themselves were quite curious. Luther found the interaction odd but engaging. He'd never met someone like this outside of his head before. "So how long then, like fifteen minutes, maybe?"

"Before we're-- we're not strangers. Yeah, fifteen-- fifteen minutes." The boy pulled up his coat sleeve and pushed down his mitten revealing a watch: "It's two-- two twenty now," he said. "At two-- two thirty-five I can tell you my name."

"And then we won't be strangers," Luther said. "So I'll wait to tell you my name too!" He was loving the eccentricity. It reminded him of the "sacred pact" with Larry, but felt even more comfortable.

"You can-- can come in my yard. Yeah, come-- come over," the boy said.

Luther hopped the fence; something he was able to do again with his smaller body. "How old are you?" he asked as he landed.

"I'm thirteen-- thirteen," was the reply.

"I'm fourteen," Luther said. "Do we really have to wait fifteen minutes? I could just tell you my name now..."

But before Luther could finish, the other boy clapped his mittened hands over his hood-covered ears and held them there. "No-- no!!" he shouted. "Fifteen minutes-- minutes!"

"Okay, I'll wait!" Luther said abruptly.

Just then a tall woman came from inside the house, approaching the boys with friendly caution.

Luther was in a position to see her face, and for a moment struggled to recognize her. Quickly he figured it out: this was the chirping-shoed plaid purse lady from Murphy's Mart! She looked a lot younger, but it was unmistakably his old friend. "Hello, ma'am," Luther said.

"Well hello," the smiling woman responded. "Are you our new neighbor?"

"Don't ask-- ask his name, Mom! Not for-- for fourteen minutes," the coat-clad boy demanded, looking at his watch again.

"Well why not --" she began.

The boy cut her off, almost shouting. "And don't-- don't say mine! For fourteen-- fourteen minutes! At two-- two thirty-five!"

Luther shrugged and looked into the familiar face of the woman who of course didn't recognize him. "It's okay, you're okay," he said.

She looked at him curiously, and simply replied, "You're okay too."

Suddenly a girl's voice sounded from the back door. "Mom! How do you 'fold in' semi-sweet morsels?"

"I'll be right in to show you, sweetie..." the woman semi-shouted. Then she returned her attention to the boys.

Luther wondered how she'd handle this absurdly delicate 'name' situation, and was pleased by her solution. "Well, neighbor, why don't you come into the kitchen at two thirty-five? My daughter and I are baking cookies! You two boys can play in the mean time."

"Yeah-- yeah," said Luther's new friend.

"Mom, the batter's ready *now*! Come inside," said the girl in the kitchen as she popped her head out the back door.

Luther gasped as he found himself staring into the most beautiful green eyes he'd ever seen. This wasn't the first time he'd seen them, and he now had to wait out the longest fourteen minutes of his life...

໖♦♦৪৩

"McCloskey," Brooke said. "It's Irish!"

Luther grinned from ear to ear as he politely munched the warm chocolate-chip cookie his angel had baked for him. Not wanting to talk with his mouth full, he just listened.

"And Philip and I are twins," she winked, "right little brother?"

"I'm only-- only three minutes younger," Philip said, eating his cookie with less elegance.

Luther could finally get a good look at Philip's face: beneath the smears of semi-sweet chocolate was a waxen complexion and a perpetual smile. *So this is what an autistic person is like*, he thought. *And he's a genius like Einstein!* Luther was already familiar with the other two faces: Brooke, though a bit gangly and much younger here, had lived in his dreams for weeks, and Mrs. McCloskey was his friend from Murphy's Mart, though she didn't know it yet.

What she did know was that her oddball son had made fast friends with the new neighbor boy, and that was something to celebrate with cookies.

"So where do you go to school?" Luther asked Brooke.

"Kennedy," she replied, "and Philip goes to a special school."

"Special? Like for geniuses?" Luther asked naïvely.

For a moment both ladies looked strangely at Luther, presuming he was mocking Philip. Mrs. McCloskey gestured to her daughter, and Brooke quickly reacted: "Philip, I need to show you something upstairs!" The skinny siblings scrambled from the kitchen.

Luther was confused by the sudden exodus, and Mrs. McCloskey spoke quite frankly. "Luther, please don't make fun of Philip. He can't help the way he is. He's mentally retarded."

"But he doesn't have those Mongoloid features, does he?" Luther asked.

She wasn't sure how to respond to that, so she just added a word of advice. "Look, if you're going to befriend him, then befriend him. But don't tease him. He gets enough of that."

Luther had no idea what she meant or what to say back to her. So he just said *something*: "I don't know what to say, ma'am. Philip has autism. He's like, a genius."

Mrs. McCloskey was speechless. She just stood there open-mouthed while Luther blundered on:

"Like when he put the coupling and the golf ball together to make a heart valve…"

"What kind of gibberish is this?" she said apprehensively. "I think it might be best for you to go!"

"Oh, I'm sorry…" Luther replied.

"I'm sorry too," she said.

Wondering what he had done that was so offensive, Luther left and went back to his new house just as the movers were bringing in the first pieces of furniture. Doris was circulating throughout the rooms, directing the placement of the cargo. Lou had gone back to the old house to do some fixing-up for the new owners.

"Where have you been, Luther?" Doris asked.

"At the McCloskeys' house," he answered. "They're our new neighbors but Mrs. McCloskey doesn't like me."

"Doesn't like you?"

"Yeah, she told me to leave."

Doris sensed the need for some diplomacy. "Which house is it?"

"Right next door. Brooke lives there. And Philip."

"Stay put, Luther. I'll be back in a few minutes."

Luther anxiously paced the floors, splaying his fingers as the movers looked at him curiously. He hoped he hadn't already ruined his chance to love Brooke. When he wandered into the front bedroom and peered through the window, he spied Aunt Doris and Mrs. McCloskey standing on the front porch next door. Doris was talking and gesturing, arms out, palms up, appearing very conciliatory. As she listened, Mrs. McCloskey's cautious expression gradually melted away, and Luther could tell she was saying "Oh...!" just before placing both hands over her mouth. Then she began sharing some things of her own, occasionally motioning toward her house. After a few minutes, the two women headed for the Bergers' house, still chatting.

"Luther!" Doris called out. "Someone wants to see you!"

He emerged from the bedroom, wondering if he was going to get a scolding.

"Luther, I'm sorry I told you to leave. You're welcome in our house any time," Mrs. McCloskey said, smiling kindly. "Philip needs a friend like you."

Luther was pleasantly surprised. "It's okay, you're okay... um, thank you," he replied politely, looking down at her shoes.

The two ladies smiled at each other.

"I'm inviting you over for another cookie if you'd like one, Luther," Mrs. McCloskey said.

"You mean now?" he replied.

"Yes, right now," she said encouragingly.

And as they walked out of the house together, Doris could hear her nephew ask:

"Do those shoes squeak when you go to the grocery store?"

"Well if they do, I never paid attention," was the lighthearted reply.

ଔ✦✦ଵ

In the coming months Luther found himself in an unexpected place. The life he'd once been anxious to leave behind now seemed ideal. The fact that his dream girl lived right next door was only part of it; he'd also made a true-blue friend in Philip, and in his new junior high school he was considered a very bright, even gifted student. And rightfully so: with his extra six-and-a-half years of education he had a distinct edge over the other seventh-graders. The Kennedy school administrators would just scratch their heads looking at his previous school transcripts, wondering if perhaps Twin Springs had sent over the file of some other Luther Howell. His precocity soon became the talk of the teachers' lounge, and it wasn't long before Lou and Doris began to receive letters recommending that Luther transfer into the most advanced sections. And though he didn't really understand the significance of the change, Luther took on the more sophisticated course work with ease. And happily so: Brooke was also an outstanding student, and by the spring semester she and Luther ended up in many of the same classes.

CR♦♦ℰℭ

An object at rest tends to _____
a. start moving
b. stay at rest
c. create a force equal to any surrounding movement

Luther chuckled to himself as he filled in letter "b" and put his pencil down on his desk. He finished the exam before anyone else, even Brooke, and felt rather accomplished.

The vigilant teacher, Mr. Mason, took note and confiscated the paper, reading Luther's answers as he strolled silently around the room checking for cheaters.

Brooke finished next, taking a quick look sideways to confirm that it was in fact Luther who had finished first. "Aw, man!!" she said under her breath.

"No talking, Miss McCloskey," Mr. Mason scolded.

Brooke shrunk back in her seat.

Luther felt proud. He was getting used to the idea of being the smart one. He also found it fitting that it was in another similar physics class where he and Brooke had first met. He sat quietly with his hands folded on the desk in front of him.

"Time's up," Mr. Mason said. "Pencils down, papers turned over. I will collect them."

A collective groan echoed through the room: close to half the students hadn't finished the pop quiz.

The short, spectacled instructor began his post-quiz lecture as he moved through the room gathering papers. "So, we left off yesterday talking about common illustrations of Newton's Laws of

Motion. I asked you all to think of examples; did anyone come up with any?"

A few hands went up, and Mr. Mason chose a girl in the front row. "Yes, Liz?"

"The baseball bat hits the baseball and… um, changes its direction," she said.

"Okay, good start. And what does that illustrate?"

Liz thought for a moment. "Um… Newton's… third law?"

The teacher tried to provoke a broader response: "*Just* the third law? Anyone?"

Brooke's hand shot up.

"Yes, Brooke?"

"All three laws!" she practically spit out the words, anxious to give a correct answer before Luther. She was a competitor at heart.

"Okay," said Mr. Mason. "Let's go through them one by one and see if that's true. What's the first law?"

Brooke was unhesitating. "Objects in motion will stay in motion until an outside force is applied."

He responded: "So in other words a thrown baseball will just keep going forever if it doesn't run into something?"

"Um… well not exactly…"

"Why not?"

She began to rethink her answer. "Gravity, I guess…"

"Good! Now we're getting somewhere," Mr. Mason said. "Anything else?"

"Air molecules," Luther chimed in.

"Yes! Both of those. Remember that only in a gravity-free *vacuum* will things keep moving… that's how the planets can keep orbiting our sun in space where there's no air.

"So," Brooke asked, "does that mean the first law doesn't apply after all?"

"Sure it does," Luther said, "'cause when the baseball is thrown, it's passing through molecules of air and dust that have mass, and that will slow the motion down. Then when it touches the ground it'll finally just stop."

Mr. Mason was beaming. This was the kind of moment teachers lived for. "And why is that?" he asked a hypothetical question only to answer it himself: "It's because of the other half of the first law: an object at *rest* tends to stay at rest unless an outside force is applied. So either way, why do both objects eventually end up at rest? Why doesn't the Earth move instead?"

Luther answered: "The mass of the Earth is way more than the mass of the baseball."

With his lesson rolling along quite nicely, Mr. Mason continued: "...which brings us to Newton's Second Law: The greater the mass of an object, the greater the amount of force needed to accelerate it. And as Mr. Howell has already explained to us, that's why the ball stops instead of the Earth moving."

The first girl, Liz, shook her head as she listened to the classroom exchange. "But my example was the ball changing direction-- not stopping," she said. "So wouldn't that be Newton's Third Law?"

"For each action, there is an equal and opposite reaction," the teacher answered. "Yes, I've been saving that one. Of course that's demonstrated when we hit a baseball, but let's look at the *whole* picture. Somebody tell me *why* the ball changes direction."

Several hands went up. Mr. Mason chose Maurice, one of the few black students in this newly-integrating school.

"The bat is bigger and heavier, and is going the opposite direction." Maurice said.

"Okay, good. More mass and more acceleration. But if you're the one swinging that bat, how do you know you've hit the ball?"

"You can see it going away from you!" Maurice clowned.

The class laughed.

"All right then," the teacher regrouped. "Let's pretend you're blindfolded. *Then* how would you know?"

"You can feel it," Maurice said.

"So even though the mass of the bat is greater, the mass of the ball creates enough resistance that the person holding the bat can actually *feel* it?"

"Yeah..." Maurice answered cautiously, not sure where Mr. Mason was heading with this.

And the teacher just kept teaching... "And where does the force come from to swing the bat in the first place?"

"The player's arms move the bat!" Maurice said.

"Just his arms?"

"Well… he's got to swing his body around too…"

"…which also uses his legs then, right?"

Maurice's thought process was obvious, as was that of much of the class.

The teacher went on: "…and the legs that support the player are resting on what?"

"The ground!" several students answered; "The Earth!" said a few others, in a simultaneous "a-ha" moment.

Now Mr. Mason's lesson rounded third base: "So is the object *at rest* ultimately what makes the baseball change direction-- just because it has so much more mass? Does that seem reasonable?"

Luther jumped back in: "Well, there's things at rest *and* in motion causing the baseball to react." His mental wheels whirled. He imagined a catcher's mitt softly dissipating the force of the baseball; a sharp contrast to the hard swinging bat.

"Okay, that's kind of a trick question," the teacher went on, "because even the Earth is in constant motion in space. It just seems to be at rest to us because we are so small comparatively. We can't see the whole picture…"

Luther's fervor began to show as he interrupted with a verbatim memory from Ms. Fuller's class: "…because we are finite beings in an infinite universe. There's way too much out there for any of us to keep track of; yet it's still human nature for us to try and explain everything. Chaos theory suggests that not only is it impossible to make predictions with perfect accuracy; it's also impossible to explain known outcomes with perfect accuracy."

Mr. Mason politely tried to redirect: "Um, we won't be discussing chaos theory per-se in this class; but you raise an interesting point, Luther! Anyway, getting back to… "

But Luther couldn't help himself: he just wasn't finished. "…like suppose you're watching a football game. The quarterback is fading back to pass just when you look away, and when you turn back around the *defense* has just scored! Was it an interception or a fumble? It's got to be one of the two if the ball was on the defense's thirty yard line…"

The teacher became less polite as he tried to reclaim his class. "Luther! Enough! Back to the laws of motion, everyone."

Luther splayed his fingers and raised a tensely-stretched arm.

"Luther! For heaven's sake! What??"

"Could I just ask a question?"

A heavy sigh. "Yes. One question."

"Does the flap of a butterfly's wings in Brazil set off a tornado in Texas?"

Exasperated, Mr. Mason walked up beside Luther's desk and placed a hand on his shoulder. He understood that an enhanced intellect was often accompanied by enhanced eccentricity, but a line had been crossed. "Luther, I think you need to calm down. Why don't you go see the nurse."

Brooke jumped into the fray. "No, he'll be okay." She looked across at her friend, "It's okay, you're okay."

As Luther returned her glance, the young girl's lovely green eyes had an immediate soothing effect. "It's okay," he said. The tenseness in his shoulders and arms diffused.

Mr. Mason wasn't exactly sure what had just happened, but the result seemed to be a positive one, so he decided to let things go. And as he began to try and restore the momentum of the interrupted lesson, he found his own thoughts suddenly interrupted by the seeming wisdom of what Luther had just verbalized. "Wait, Luther: what did you just ask a moment ago?"

Assuming he was still in the soup, Luther floundered: "Oh, I'm sorry…"

Brooke intervened again: "It's okay, Luther. What was that you said about a butterfly?"

"Does the flap of a butterfly's wings in Brazil--" Luther didn't get to finish his sentence. It was cut short by the collective gasp of the class as their attention shifted to the windows, and what was happening outdoors.

Mr. Mason turned and saw it too: butterflies! There were hundreds, maybe thousands of them, all different colors and sizes, suddenly swarming right outside, as if trying to get the attention of his class.

Most students rose from their seats and ran wide-eyed to watch through the glass, as the mélange of brightly painted wings fluttered in a silent concert, illuminated by the warm spring sunlight. The orange and purple and blue and green-hued insects darted about like little paper fans surfing the wind, occasionally brushing up against the window panes, to the delight of their audience.

Mr. Mason remarked curiously to himself: "Butterflies don't swarm in Maryland! And different species don't mix like this..." his verbal thoughts trailed off, engulfed by seventh-grade laughter. He smiled a dumbfounded smile as he watched the show.

Luther just remained in his seat, not looking at the butterflies but instead listening to the instructions they had brought to him from their side of creation.

As the rest of the class unknowingly got a glimpse of the light in Luther's head, the swirling funnel-cloud of color moved away from the building, dissipating as quickly as it had first arrived. A wonderful hush came over the room.

"...set off a tornado in Texas?" Luther blurted, completing his thought from before.

The hush became a profound silence as the students returned to their seats.

Before sitting down, Brooke stopped next to Luther's desk.

He gazed up into her eyes, finding them far more beautiful than all those butterflies would have been, had he looked at them.

Brooke stared back at Luther, unable to understand the kinship she was suddenly feeling.

Luther briefly assimilated the message he'd just been given, and said, "I'm going to take care of you, Brooke."

She just smiled and returned to her desk.

CHAPTER TWENTY

T HE STRANGE and splendid storm of butterflies was the talk of Kennedy Junior High for the next few days, but it was gradually overtaken by more pertinent subjects of-the-season such as baseball and the spring dance, and by mid-June of 1971, school was out for the summer. The rock group Alice Cooper wouldn't release their similarly-named hit song until 1972, nor would Mr. Lorenz present his paper about butterflies and tornadoes until that year. So, Luther's Lorenz-inspired quotation seemed quite brilliant, and in Mr. Mason's judgment, such genius was to be recognized. Eighth grade was set to be a banner year.

Meanwhile, Luther had accepted, and in fact embraced his life with his aunt and uncle, and because of his tight friendship with Philip, he received V.I.P. treatment from the McCloskey family. But the brief moment he and Brooke shared in class hadn't been mentioned again. Just as well; Luther wouldn't have known what to say about it anyway. His grasp of the whole incident was different than that of everyone else there: for him, the butterflies weren't so much to be seen as heard. And hear them he did: receiving lasting guidance from an otherwise ephemeral moment. His interaction with Brooke was just a part of the whole. Now he just had to wait for the right time.

☙✦❧

"I like the way the top of it kind of goes in a slow circle and then gets faster!" Brooke said, watching the toy gyroscope spin on her living room floor.

"That's 'precession,'" Luther replied. "The top of it circles faster as the wheel spins slower. Then the whole gyroscope finally falls over when it gets too slow."

"I remember that from physics, Luther. You don't have to tell me!" Her competitiveness had carried over into summer.

"I want-- want to get my top," Philip said. "It spins-- spins the same way."

"A top doesn't have the same kind of framing as a gyroscope," Luther said. "It's different."

"I'm gonna-- gonna go get it. From my-- my room." And he was off.

Once her brother was out of earshot, Brooke said to Luther: "Just let him do it his way. We think if he gets enough encouragement he might come out of it."

"Come out of what?" Luther asked obliviously.

"You know, his condition."

"His autism?"

"Well, maybe. Yes. Autism."

"'Cause he's like, a genius you know."

A dampened din came from upstairs as Philip rummaged through the toy box he'd had most of his life.

Brooke picked up the gyroscope which had finally toppled, and set it in motion again, running the rubber-coated part of its spin axis along the edge of the coffee table. She placed it on the table top and spoke as she watched it defy gravity. "You know, Luther, we always thought Philip was mentally retarded. But you mentioned 'autism' back when you first moved in, and it made my parents think. A retarded person wouldn't be as smart as Philip. My mom even bought a book about autism where a doctor says it's psychological."

"*The Empty Fortress*," Luther said brightly, "by Bettelheim. 'Bettel,' like in 'nettle' or 'kettle.'"

"Jeeps!!" Brooke spat out; half-impressed and half-disgusted. "Is there *anything* you don't know?"

Luther had only read the first thirty-one pages of Bettelheim, and that had largely been a vocabulary lesson. Nevertheless, a few significant morsels had managed to make their way into his memory banks from other sources. "Bettelheim says that your mom didn't take care of Philip, and that's why he's autistic."

Brooke found that notion to be quite offensive; and yet right in line with what her mom had told her about the book. Bettelheim's version of autism was indeed quite an indictment of the mother. Brooke settled for a semi-response: "Well, we know he's not retarded anyways."

"'Cause he doesn't have those Mongoloid features." Luther parroted once again.

"The 'Mongoloid' features aren't a part of being mentally retarded, Luther. That's a different thing called Down syndrome. Philip doesn't have that."

"Down syndrome…" Luther repeated, feeling the shape of the words on his tongue. "Down syndrome. You know a lot of things too, Brooke!"

A mollifying response. Brooke was a bit nonplussed by his total *lack* of competitiveness.

"I found-- found it!" Philip blurted, awkwardly negotiating the sharp turn around the bottom of the staircase into the living room. "And even-- even the string, too." He locked his elbows and held out a wooden top in one hand and a long, frayed string in the other.

The toy looked as if it might have been painted red at some point, but it was so worn that Luther couldn't be sure. "Make it go, Philip!" he encouraged politely.

Philip was already carefully, feverishly wrapping the string around the little cone, and before anyone could say anything else, it was in motion, skittering across the floor.

"Ha!" Luther cried out, surprised by the top's somewhat imposing personality. "It just goes wherever it wants!" He grabbed the gyroscope and set it in motion once more on the table. The rigidly-framed apparatus stayed right where Luther put it; spinning obediently, while the top continued its circular self-tour of the floor.

"It does seem to have a mind of its own, doesn't it?" Brooke added.

After demonstrating its own brand of precession, Philip's top finally spun out and stopped. He began to rewrap the string, readying it for another ride. "Put the-- the gyroscope on the floor this time," he said to Luther.

They each set their devices in motion (Philip's with much less accuracy) and sat back to watch. Again, the gyroscope held its position while the wooden top traced a seemingly random pattern of spirals that gradually decreased in size. All three pairs of eyes watched with interest as the top inched closer and closer to the gyroscope.

Finally Brooke remarked, "Kinda looks like a little tornado, doesn't it?"

"A funnel-- funnel cloud," Philip added.

Abruptly, Luther's thoughts turned back to Mr. Mason's class. *A funnel cloud of butterflies.* He jerked his head around to look at Brooke, just as the two spinning objects were about to bump. But instead of the clacking collision he was expecting to hear, there was a sudden silence followed by a gentle voice:

"You want to take care of her?"

Luther replied, "I want to love her." And he realized he was back in the cocoon with Jack Oliver.

"Then now's the time," the other boy said, and as before, the communication transcended physical speech.

"I'll go home and get it," Luther said. "But what if she doesn't like it?"

"Don't worry about that. Just take care of her," Jack Oliver replied. "It's okay, you're okay."

Luther liked that response. "I'm okay," he said. Then he thought of something: "Hey, Jack Oliver, I'm sorry I punched you..."

Instead of a reply, Luther heard the *clack* from the contact of the toys, and was jolted back into the reality of the room. Brooke and Philip both laughed as the two gadgets knocked each other over. Luther just stood up and faced the door.

"Going somewhere?" Brooke asked.

"I'll be right back, Brooke!" And he practically bolted out of the McCloskeys' house, leaving their front door wide open. Hurrying next door into his bedroom, he found a large shoebox on Larry's old dresser, pre-packed and waiting. Luther grabbed it and headed back, arriving just as a very irked Brooke was about to close the door.

"Shut the door when you go in and out, Luther!" she snapped. "You'll let all the bugs in and all the air conditioning out!"

"Well, I'm sorry," he said slowly, holding out the shoebox. "Brooke, I brought you something."

"Me?" she said with curiosity. "What is it?"

"My dad gave it to me when I was seven," he said.

"What's in-- in it?" Philip wondered aloud.

Brooke placed the box on the coffee table next to the motionless gyroscope and removed the lid. "This is a microscope..." she said perplexedly.

Philip slid in beside his sister on the couch and craned his neck to see the contents. "A microscope-- microscope and some slides! Some slides-- slides!" he said excitedly.

Brooke seemed uncomfortable. "I don't understand, Luther. You said you're giving this to me?"

"Yes."

"Why? Why are you giving me a microscope? *Your* microscope, from your dad?"

"You're supposed to have it now."

"Why?" She was touched and befuddled.

Luther blinked nervously. "You need to look at the butterflies."

The response only added to Brooke's confusion. Recalling certain bits of etiquette taught to her by her mom, Brooke answered rather automatically: "Thank you, but I can't accept this, Luther. It was from your dad..."

Luther began to feel anxious. Brooke *needed* this microscope, or at least *he* needed her to have it. His eyes began to tear up as he splayed his fingers. "My dad..." and his next words were not his own, "...my dad would have loved you and wanted you to have it."

Brooke had just been socked between the eyes. Now she began to fight tears as well. "Well... golly Luther. I don't know what to say..."

Philip just grinned and said, "You should-- should take it, Brooke. Take it-- it and say 'thank you' to Luther."

Brooke didn't know exactly what she was feeling or why it was so important to Luther that she have this gift. But she also recalled another of her mom's lessons about receiving things graciously, be they compliments or presents. She looked Luther in the eye and said, "Thank you. Thank you very much. I know this must mean a lot to you."

Luther replied, his words again coming from beyond himself: "Look closely at the butterflies, Brooke."

Philip just giggled and began to sort through the slides.

⚬୧♦♦୨⚬

The weeks of summer passed slowly for Luther as he awaited eighth grade and whatever Kennedy Junior High School might have in store for him. Since being sent back from 1977 he'd completed two important tasks: retrieving his gyroscope and passing his microscope along to Brooke. He didn't know why either of those things needed to be, but he did them as instructed. Now all he could do was wait and wonder. Obviously this trip back in time wasn't going to be some quick fix for his life in 1977. And as he finally began to contemplate more seriously what his old life might actually be like with his mother gone, he realized it was impossible for things to return to the way they once were.

He'd also begun to have strange dreams in which he returned to the cocoon with Jack Oliver, recalling bits and pieces of what had been said there.

You learn new things every day, and after a while, all that knowledge adds up. If you just figure out how to organize it, you can do great things with it!

Jack Oliver's words were haunting, and a bit intimidating. It wasn't in Luther's nature to pursue greatness, but he certainly liked to learn new things. And keeping his ideas organized was indeed a challenge. But even with his aunt, his school teachers and Brooke in the picture, Luther had no greater protagonist than Philip: the first person he'd ever known who reminded him of himself. Well, except maybe for Jack Oliver in the cocoon. So as summer unfolded that year, Luther continued to interact and learn; to teach and be taught, and to not be intimidated by strange new ideas and concepts…

CR♦♦ℰↄ

"So how-- how do you know heat rises? Maybe cold-- cold falls instead." Philip scratched his nose as he spoke, looking fixedly at some invisible thing out in the McCloskeys' back yard. He crouched on the grass, rocking gently.

"Everybody knows heat rises!" Luther said defiantly. "Heat is energy, and energy is when atoms move faster, and when they move faster they need more space to move around so they expand…" he stopped abruptly as if he knew Philip would interrupt…

…which he did, right on cue: "That's just-- just relative density you know. Because who-- who decided what's up and what's down?"

Luther followed the odd non sequitur with ease. In fact, he'd once wondered the same thing. "Yeah; like when you look at a map, who decided that north was supposed to be 'up'? And maybe when God looks at the Earth, he sees the axis going horizontally instead--"

"…instead of-- of vertically. Yeah-- yeah," Philip completed the thought.

By now Luther had grown very accustomed to Philip's odd speech pattern. The repeated words were a comforting confirmation that Philip was indeed Philip, and that Luther had a complement somewhere in the world. Though their conversation had abruptly seemed to switch subjects, it made perfect sense to them both. Luther took the next turn: "And when a rocket takes off from the Earth, isn't it really going 'up' if it takes off from the North Pole and 'down' if it takes off from the South Pole?"

"Yeah 'cause-- 'cause south is supposed to be down, you know."

"The map said so!" Luther added.

Then in a rare moment of physical connectedness, they looked each other in the eye and burst into laughter. Though they both knew what was so funny, it was Philip who articulated it:

"Maps can't-- can't talk!"

Luther fell gently onto the grass and began to laugh harder. His giddiness was not so much from the shared joke, but from something he was experiencing for the first time in his life: an effortless friendship!

"Careful, your-- your head!" Philip said, as he looked out into the yard again.

"What? Why?" Luther responded, freezing in position as if he were atop a landmine.

Philip scrambled a few feet to the spot, never leaving his crouching position. He looked a bit like a spider, or a spider monkey. He stared intently at a specific spot in the grass, finally touching it with the palm of his hand, like he was petting a dog. "Wanna see-- see something?"

"Okay…" Luther said apprehensively.

Philip gently, carefully grabbed the grass and pulled up a perfectly round plug, about nine inches across. He set it to one side with care, and reached into the shallow hole he'd uncovered, extracting a round cookie tin swathed in plastic wrap. He began to peel off the layers.

"What's in it?" Luther asked.

Philip carefully, methodically pried the lid off of the can and set it aside. He reached in and brought out a pack of Wrigley's Spearmint Gum and a tube of Gleem toothpaste. "They taste-- taste the same. But one's-- one's spearmint and one's an *ex*periment." He laughed.

Luther glanced into the cookie can and saw that it held more packs of gum and tubes of Gleem. "What's the experiment?" he asked.

"Making gravity-- gravity," Philip said, unscrewing the toothpaste cap. Then he held up the tube with the opening facing down and squeezed ever-so-gently. "Falling from-- from the sky," he said, as a small bead of toothpaste dropped onto the grass.

"Gravity. So what?" said Luther.

Philip turned the tube upright and squeezed again, harder this time. The little blob of paste pushed its way out of the opening and settled on the outside of the tube. "Floating up-- up from the bottom of the ocean," he said.

"So," Luther ventured, "you're making gravity by squeezing the tube?"

"No it's-- it's relative density, not squeezing. The toothpaste-- toothpaste is one density; and the sky is less dense and the ocean is more dense. The sky-- sky forces things down and the ocean forces them up. So the-- the toothpaste floats to the top of the water and falls to the bottom of the sky. And so-- so do people."

Luther scratched his head. "People and toothpaste don't have the same density, Philip! And people only float 'cause they're full of air."

Philip closed his eyes. "Toothpaste floats-- floats 'cause it's full of air too."

"You're talking about *buoyancy*, not gravity, Philip."

"All the-- the same thing."

"No! Gravity attracts, buoyancy repels!"

"Buoyancy is-- is upside-down gravity." Philip said gleefully.

Luther was getting a bit frustrated. "We stick to the Earth because gravity pulls us down!"

Philip just pulled his knees up under his chin and rocked like some wise old man in a rocking chair. "Maybe the-- the Earth pulls us down. Or maybe-- maybe the sky pushes us down. Like heat-- heat rises or does cold fall instead?"

A little spark of understanding took form as Luther spoke. "'Cause who decided what's up and what's down?" he completed Philip's train of thought, which had now come full circle. And though he couldn't really explain it, the disjointed ideas strangely seemed to go together. Maybe 'gravity' was simply all the molecules that were moving more quickly-- repelling the slower ones! There was undoubtedly more to it than that, wasn't there? Luther had learned that gravity was a force of attraction between objects, but also that nobody could completely explain it. Philip's simplified version seemed to make more sense than anything Luther had encountered previously.

"Philip! Is *that* what happened to all our toothpaste?" It was Brooke, standing behind the boys, a few feet from the doorway of the house.

Startled, Luther glanced back quickly, noticing above all else that Brooke's green eyes didn't look quite right against her pink short set. He wondered how long she'd been there. "Hi, Brooke!" he said.

She didn't answer, but looked curiously at the scene as her brother and his comrade investigated their newly-unearthed treasure.

"Don't tell-- tell Mom," Philip said.

"Why not?" his sister shot back.

"She'll take-- take them away. I can't-- can't have toothpastes."

"Well, you hoard them! What do you need all that toothpaste for anyway?"

"It's my-- my gravity experiments."

Brooke rolled her eyes and moved closer, peering into the cookie tin. "Hey!! Is that my gum? You took my *gum*, Philip!"

Philip rocked again, hitting his forehead with the ball of his hand with each forward movement. "I shouldn'a-- shouldn'a stole your gum, Brooke. It just-- just goes with the toothpaste!"

The young girl reached into the can, rescuing the abducted gum packs. "I've been looking for these! All I had left of my candy stash was cherry cough drops!"

That triggered something in Luther's memory: "I thought you didn't like cherries," he said.

"I love cherries," Brooke replied. "Why would you think that?"

"Well, one time you said..." Luther stopped himself, remembering that actually she *hadn't* said. That was in the old version of the future. He self-corrected: "Never mind. I made a mistake."

Brooke ignored Luther's clumsy response, choosing instead to lightly scold her brother. "Don't take my stuff, Philip! This is *my* gum!"

Still seated on the ground, Philip began to rock more intensely. "I'm sorry-- sorry, Brooke. That's called-- called stealing!" Philip began to sob awkwardly and rock more slowly.

Luther watched his future love interest as she thoughtfully surveyed the pitiful scene. Brooke's expression went from annoyance to resignation, and finally tenderness. She shrugged and sighed, saying: "I won't tell Mom about the toothpaste, okay? I'm just taking my gum back."

"Okay-- okay..." Philip said, his knees muffling his voice. "You're a-- a good sister."

Brooke affectionately patted the top of her brother's head, said, "See ya' Luther," and went back inside.

"Bye, Brooke!" Luther answered.

Philip scrambled to replace the toothpaste tubes, re-wrap the cookie tin and return it to its secret burial place.

"Is that to keep your mom from finding it?" Luther asked.

"Keep her-- her from finding it!" Philip replied, completing his camouflage by setting the grass plug back in place. He inspected it carefully, running his fingers around the edges.

Luther's brain was engorged with new ideas; he felt the need to go home and think. Or maybe keep from thinking. "I have to go Philip. Wanna talk more later? Or tomorrow?"

"Or tomorrow-- tomorrow," Philip parroted.

Luther wordlessly hiked back into to his own house, plopping down on the sofa. He stared at the turned-off television set for several minutes, until Aunt Doris came in from the kitchen and noticed him there.

"Luther, are you all right?" she asked.

"M-hm," he replied mundanely. He was overwhelmed with thoughts about gravity and buoyancy and Brooke. And what was up and what was down; and whether heat rises or cold falls. Why did it have to be one way or the other? Couldn't it be both? Couldn't they just adjust to each other? And Brooke was so pretty. And so nice.

"Maybe you should take a little nap, sweetie. You look tired," Doris said, her voice interrupting the tidal wave of ideas.

"Yeah, maybe," Luther replied, now heading down the hall toward his room. He looked out his bedroom window into the back yard next door. Philip was gone for the time being; it must have been dinner time at the McCloskeys'. Luther drifted to sleep almost immediately when his body hit the mattress. He had funny dreams about toothpaste tubes floating and flying, and about Brooke offering him a cherry cough drop, saying: "Here, I don't like cherries!" while sucking on one herself.

He was awakened by a whoop from outside. He'd apparently been asleep for a while: when he looked out the window Philip had returned to the yard and was re-examining the contents of his cookie can. He took out some items, stood up and literally jumped for joy, making wonderful nonsense noises that matched feelings Luther had sometimes experienced but could never articulate. Looking more closely, he saw that Philip was holding three packs of gum and grinning ear to ear. But his verbalizations were almost other-worldly. It was like the 'communicating without speaking' that Luther had experienced in the cocoon with Jack Oliver. And as Philip celebrated the gum that had mysteriously reappeared in his secret hiding place, Luther's gaze drifted upward to a figure in Brooke's bedroom window. Her face was beaming, and Luther knew that if he could see her eyes more closely they'd undoubtedly be twinkling. And he also thought she might be rocking back and forth just a little bit.

CHAPTER TWENTY-ONE

S UMMER SETTLED into September. Eighth grade came and went, and Luther learned a lot. In fact, he never seemed to lose anything that went into his head. It was all stored there in the layers of lessons, ready to be retrieved on cue. In addition to the traditional schooling received at Kennedy, he also enjoyed his aunt's custom tutelage and the frequent challenges that emerged from Philip's quirky intellect. Sometimes, as in the case of "gravity toothpaste," the lessons seemed silly; yet there was usually an underlying hint of genius in them. Luther's maturing intuition told him that there were important things to be gleaned from Philip's folly, if he could only figure out how to separate the seed from the chaff.

The half-way point in Brooke's eighth grade year was a time of transformation, and when spring came in and winter's layers came off, it was evident she'd blossomed along with the vernal flora. Schoolboys now hung back in the hallways to watch Brooke go by, wondering why they hadn't noticed her before. But Luther didn't see any change; those familiar green eyes were the same as they'd always been. And her competitiveness toward Luther was steadily quelled by her appreciation of his sweet spirit: she saw him as a teammate rather than an opponent, though it was unclear exactly what game they were playing. Brooke simply felt about Luther the way she felt about Philip: questions were unnecessary and it was okay just for him to be.

The ninth grade year that began in the fall of 1972 occurred during a time of demographic adjustment in parts of Maryland. Suddenly it seemed there were too many students for the existing high school buildings, and some creative decisions had to be made: for a time the junior high schools would need to absorb high school freshmen. And though this meant that sophomores were now the lowly newbies in the high schools, it also meant ninth-graders like

Luther and Brooke got to be the big wheels for an extra year. More importantly it meant that Luther didn't have to change environments just yet, as he had grown used to Kennedy Junior High and its teachers, and had in essence 'learned how to learn' there.

The memories of his future grew less important to Luther as he relived his teenage years, shaping a new existence in an obviously positive way. Every so often he tried to pretend that *his* life was the only one being changed in an otherwise static world. But quickly he'd remember his dead mother and the fantasy would evaporate. In truth, everything happened in relation to everything else, and for each action there was an equal and opposite reaction. And as Luther had seen, in something as complicated as a human network, one couldn't choose where or how those reactions would occur. In a vain attempt to save his cousin he'd lost his mother; all the while seeing his own life improve.

But there was one particular thing from the old future that haunted Luther. It was something Brooke had said on the night he met her, amid the flickering fluorescent displays of the pastry and Dr. Pepper machines:

… you're just like Philip… he was my brother. He passed away four years ago.

The stark, scary statement ran through Luther's mind frequently: this being the fall of 1972, "four years ago" now meant 'sometime next spring.'

Luther had once read Dickens' *A Christmas Carol* for an English class. Though the language was archaic enough to be confusing, he made it through the book with much help from Doris. He felt a particular connection with the character of Scrooge when confronted by the Ghost of Christmas Yet to Come. Luther had even memorized a short section, which he recalled often:

> *"Before I draw nearer to that stone to which you point," said Scrooge, "answer me one question. Are these the shadows of the things that Will be, or are they shadows of things that May be, only?"*
>
> *Still the Ghost pointed downward to the grave by which it stood.*

"Men's courses will foreshadow certain ends, to which, if persevered in, they must lead," said Scrooge. "But if the courses be departed from, the ends will change. Say it is thus with what you show me!"

"Say it is thus!" Luther would sometimes utter to nobody, sitting cross-legged on his bed, rocking anxiously. Aunt Doris' paraphrasing of the elevated text had made the meaning crystal clear. He knew that if Philip's life was to be saved, Philip's course must be somehow changed. But he had no idea how that might work: Brooke hadn't elaborated on the circumstances of her brother's death. Would it be an accident like Larry, or mysterious complications from rubella like Luther's father? Would it be cancer, which would have taken Maxine had it not been for Luther departing from his own course? And when was this event designated to occur? Brooke had said "four years ago" in May of 1977, but that was very vague. The one thing Luther did know was that he needed Philip, and so did Brooke. Strange as he was, the autistic teen was the glue that held the other two friends together. It was through him that they were able to interact. Luther feared that if Philip wasn't there, not only would he lose his best friend, but he and Brooke would drift apart, and his chance to take care of her-- to love her, would go away.

By April of 1973, the ninth grade was inching toward the goal line, and the students at Kennedy anxiously awaited the beginning of another summer vacation. Brooke looked forward to dating. Throughout ninth grade her parents had told her she needed to wait "until she was in high school," and despite her protests that technically she was, they were unyielding. It was a convenient way for concerned parents to shield a blossoming daughter for a little more time.

Luther was less excited by the promise of summer than by the subsequent school year; though he was apprehensive about the change of environment. Even more so, he was afraid of the imminent, mysterious fate that awaited Philip. It was April, and nothing had happened yet, and each passing day made his concern more pressing. So as the boys convened for one of their frequent afternoon think tanks in the McCloskeys' back yard, Luther found himself secretly watching Philip's back; always trying to second-guess the moment and method of that death-specter's arrival...

CR♦♦ℬ

"Okay, this-- this one's gonna stay on," Philip said, holding a beat-up Chevy Malibu over an orange length of Hot Wheels track.

His legs dangled from the tree limb where he sat, and Luther was concerned that he might fall. Despite his own size, Luther offered to climb the tree instead, but Philip would have no part of it.

The boys had carefully constructed a test track using the flexible plastic pieces, and though Brooke told them they were both too old to be playing with little cars, they looked on it as a scientific experiment rather than a play session.

"Careful up there, Philip!" Luther said nervously.

"I won't-- won't fall," he replied. "This is-- is the one that will work. You'll see-- see, Luther!" And he released the tiny automobile, which began its steep descent from the low-lying limb to the surface of a picnic table about five feet below, before wiping out on the abrupt curve that came next. "Oops, I-- I was wrong," Philip said.

"I told you, it's gaining too much momentum on the way down," Luther responded. "We have to start it a little lower."

"Not lower-- lower, Luther. It could-- could just go *slower* and it would make the curve," Philip offered.

"How are we gonna make that happen?" Luther asked. "There's no driver and no brakes! It's gonna go however fast gravity makes it go based on how we set it up."

"Mass and-- and velocity make momentum," Philip said, "and gravity-- gravity is just relative density."

"I don't know about that," Luther replied. He was suspicious of Philip's assertion that gravity was a force of repulsion rather than attraction; but only because it was easy to assume that Sir Isaac Newton was smarter than Philip. If nobody could completely explain gravity, how could one theory really be any better than another? He flipped back to the first subject: "But velocity is speed *and direction*, so when a car with this mass tries to change direction going around the sharp curve, it flies off the track. We need to get rid of the curve."

"No, watch-- watch," Philip said, pulling a lighter-weight plastic car out of his shirt pocket. Before Luther could react, the little car was zooming down the track and navigating the curve with ease. "It has-- has less mass!" Philip grinned.

"Well yeah," Luther offered, "but we're trying to get the *metal* car to stay on the track."

"It has-- has more mass so we have to slow it down," said Philip. "It's easy-- easy you know."

"You're being stupid. There's no brakes."

"No, lift-- lift the track back up right there," he pointed to the picnic table. "Prop it-- it up on something so the speed gets slower and then it can change direction."

Luther was a little embarrassed by the simplicity of Philip's solution. "Oh yeah," he said, "we just need to get it going uphill again." He'd been trying to figure out how to modify the car rather than the environment. He looked around for a prop.

"A brick-- brick is good," Philip shouted from his perch. "There's some-- some under the porch."

Rather than have Philip risk a fall, Luther shouted "Stay put!" and scurried over to the McCloskeys' back porch where he found a small pile of loose bricks beneath the wooden steps. He grabbed three and carefully stacked them on the picnic table under the section of track with the sharp curve. Then he retrieved both of the toy cars and carefully handed them up to Philip.

"Watch this-- this one!" Philip said, as he released the metal Malibu. Now it followed the track perfectly, rounding the curve as just like its plastic counterpart had done.

"The velocity decreases when it goes back up the ramp," Luther said. "Now try the plastic one!"

Philip already was. The cheaper, lightweight car whizzed down toward the picnic table like before, but came to a quick sliding stop on the curve just after ascending the steep little ramp.

"Now it has too *little* mass!" Luther mused.

"Its density-- density is closer to the air so it slows down sooner," said Philip. "It's 'cause-- 'cause of relative density."

"Well maybe, but it's definitely too light-weight," Luther said. "How can we fix the track so both cars make it all the way through?"

"You have-- have to take the bricks back out for the plastic one," Philip said.

"There oughtta be a way to have it happen automatically," Luther countered, "but the track would have to know the weight of the different cars, and also how fast they're going."

"And then-- then maybe a blast of air to slow down a faster or a heavier car."

And in one of their frequent semi-sequitur moments, Luther steered the conversation in a curious direction. "You know I was in a car accident once."

Philip didn't miss a beat. "I know-- know 'cause my mom told me. Your aunt-- aunt told her."

Luther's intention was not to get sympathy, but to invite Philip into a discussion he'd thus far only had with himself. "I wish there was a blast of air that could slow down a real car like that!" he said.

"Then your-- your mom wouldn't've got killed. Through the-- the windshield."

Luther didn't blink. "Yeah, right into my lap," he added unabashedly. There was no suitable place in this friendship for offense to reside, so it simply didn't. Every statement was taken at face value.

"I think-- think even a blast of air wouldn't have helped those cars. They were-- were coming from two different directions."

"And they were real cars, not Hot Wheels," Luther said. "The momentum is way too great for a blast of air to make any difference."

"Maybe a-- a tornado would do it," Philip began...

Very suddenly, and for only a second, Luther was in the cocoon and Jack Oliver imparted a thought: "Listen carefully, then jump!"

...Philip continued: "Or maybe-- maybe the air should'a come from *inside* the car to move the people out of the way." He leaned back as he spoke, as if he were being blown rearward by a gust of wind.

And as instructed, Luther jumped just as Philip seemed to lose his balance. He'd "fallen" from that branch lots of times with nary a bruise, and now giggled as Luther hit the ground with an audible *oof*, successfully cushioning Philip's landing.

"Ow!!" Luther shouted from amid the pile of human limbs. "Hey!! Ow!!"

"I didn't-- didn't mean to hurt you, Luther," Philip said.

"It's not you! Ow! I'm stung!"

Philip rolled off of his friend as Luther jumped up to examine his arm. A red spot was beginning to raise up, and the area began to smart. "Ow!" he reiterated.

"Go home-- home and get a Band Aid," Philip said with matter-of-fact concern.

"Yeah, I'd better," Luther replied. "Ow! I landed right on that bee!" And he quickly left through the gate in search of Aunt Doris.

Philip crouched alone on the ground, examining the stingerless bee that now sputtered around in little circles before finally falling dead. It reminded him of his tornado-shaped wooden top coming to rest when it no longer had the momentum to keep spinning.

CHAPTER TWENTY-TWO

"O DEATH, where is thy sting?" Luther said, unearthing the familiar words that were buried somewhere in the strata of his memory.

"No stingers in here," said Jack Oliver.

"Hmph!" said Luther. "I expected there to be some pain."

"Nah. Life has pain, death doesn't. Other than that they're pretty much the same."

Looking slowly around at the inside of the cocoon, and at the mysterious bubble of a boy he'd come to know as Jack Oliver, Luther asked: "If you know so much about death, does that mean *you're* dead?"

Jack Oliver laughed. "Is *anybody*?"

Luther laughed too. He'd spent fifty-five years sharing the inside of his head with so-called "dead" people. Now he was standing there in his oversized, middle-aged body, facing his own finality. Compared to the heart attack a moment earlier, he found this experience less dramatic than he'd expected. Jack Oliver was right: life and death were really pretty much the same. "So, do I even get to see my life pass before my eyes?" Luther asked.

"Why?" Jack Oliver replied. "You remember it all anyway. I mean, we could touch on some key points, like the full scholarship to MIT and the graduate degrees from Caltech. Or how about inventing the HAL System? That was a good one!"

Luther sighed. Those weren't the things he wanted to be remembered for. In fact, when he was invited to the White House to accept the National Medal of Technology and Innovation, he politely declined. He just wasn't interested. His life-goals were aimed elsewhere. "Jack Oliver, remember a long time ago when you told me I'd love lots of people?"

"I remember it like it was today! Sure, I said you'd take care of us all. And that you should focus on the gyroscope instead of the microscope."

"Yes, and I guess I did all of that. But you know I mostly wanted to take care of Brooke, and never *did* do that. I mean, after high school we went off to separate colleges. We kept in touch through letters, and eventually email; but I wanted to make a *difference* in her life."

"O death where is thy sting?" Jack Oliver intoned mischievously. "You obviously don't know everything."

"I don't understand," Luther said.

Jack Oliver began to look less like a bubble and more like a person as he spoke. "Isn't Philip still alive?"

"Of course he is," Luther said, "he and I have kept in touch too."

"And do you know *why* he's alive?"

Luther nodded, "Because somewhere along the way, his course was changed, just like mine."

Jack Oliver became more energized as he shared the surprise: "Well, remember a long time ago when Philip fell out of that tree? That's where his course changed."

Luther still recalled the moment vividly. "What? He didn't even fall that hard!"

"It wasn't the fall, Luther. It was the bee. You literally saved him from the 'sting of death.'"

"He had a bee allergy?"

"He still does! For that matter, so did your dad."

"What?"

"It's easy for a little red stinger mark to get lost in the rash of rubella."

"Are you kidding me? My father died from a *bee sting*?"

"Yes. But Philip *didn't*, and your precious friend Brooke was able to live her life right beside her twin brother. You took better care of her than you ever knew. And then she was able to take better care of Philip than anyone else."

Luther beamed. "I loved her. I loved them both."

"And you took care of them both." By now, Jack Oliver's appearance had become clear enough that Luther could finally make out his complete image. This was not a little boy; it was a tall young man, maybe twenty-one years old. His eyes were blue, not green.

"You look different," Luther said, a little puzzled.

"Different than what?" Jack Oliver teased.

Luther examined the tiny brown spots on his own hands. "And how come I look like *this* but you only aged a little?"

"Actually, I didn't age at all."

"But you took me back to 1970, and you were like, twelve," Luther said. "Now it's 2012 and you're only few years older!"

"You re-lived all those years, Luther. I only visited you for a few brief moments."

"No... you were there for at least a few weeks! I remember seeing you in the halls at school until we moved in January."

"That wasn't me."

"What do you mean, 'not you'?"

"I guess I never formally introduced myself." He reached out his right hand, which Luther grasped and shook. "I'm Jack Oliver Junior. They call me JJ. Pleased to know you!"

For a moment Luther was puzzled, and simply stood in place, continuing to shake JJ's hand. Then he began to giggle, and suddenly an uncontrollable feeling of mirth gushed through his body. He'd never known anything like it before, and he finally fell backwards, rolling with laughter. "That explains quite a bit," he chortled.

The cocoon dissolved, the ambient silence subsided, and now Luther and JJ were back in the presence of everyone who was normally "inside" Luther's head. He could sense every soul that had ever been a part of either of their lives.

JJ smiled as he spoke: "Everyone in your life is here by design, Luther. And you're in everyone else's by design. Including mine."

It took a moment, but Luther managed to regain his composure. "So the other Jack Oliver was your dad!" He frowned playfully. "Boy do I have some questions for him."

"I'm sure you do," JJ said. "But he's not quite ready to meet you yet; that's why I'm here. You and I are more alike."

"Alike?"

"Of course. We're like visitors in a country where we don't speak the language of the locals, so we communicate with them through cues and gestures and do our best to try and fit into their culture."

Luther briefly assessed the statement. "I think I know what you mean; our brains work differently, don't they?"

Now JJ laughed. "A brain is nothing but a filter through which a soul experiences earthly life. Once the filters are out of the way, everybody can communicate like we do. But right now my dad's brain is still in the way!"

Luther understood exactly. And somewhere, so did Philip.

All of Luther's life he'd very been aware of the presence of all the others, but the inside of his head was an undefined environment. Now with the cocoon gone and JJ's physical image revealed, Luther began to see, rather than just sense. There was the bright whiteness all around him. There were the endless rows and columns of souls, each one distinct yet part of the whole, and each one a part of who Luther was, and would become. He could especially feel the pervasive presence of his father saying: "Nice job with the gyroscope, Luther!" Both men smiled.

Then, from the midst of the whiteness, emerged a being also clad in diaphanous white. Like her gown, her red hair flowed behind her as she floated toward Luther, and he instantly recognized his mother. She was beautiful, peaceful, and completely healed. No words were spoken as she landed silently and embraced her child so warmly that he thought her arms must really be angel wings. And at that moment Luther began not only to sense and to see, but to fully feel.

"O death, where is thy sting?" he wept joyfully.

"We don't sting," Maxine whispered, "we just take care of one another."

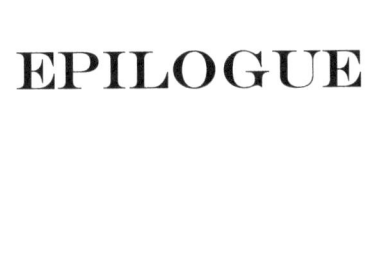

EPILOGUE

You can't connect the dots looking forward;
you can only connect them looking backwards.

--Steve Jobs

2028

"A CHRONIC infection of the small intestine," Marcus said, shaking his head. "I still find that mind-boggling."

His wife of forty years sat in a chair with her back to him, looking out the window. "They haven't stopped for hours. And it's not just the Monarchs-- there are all different kinds and different colors!"

"You seem more interested in those butterflies than in your presentation," he remarked.

She shook her graying head. "My presentation is the product of sixteen long years' work, and honestly, I'm pretty tired of it. But a butterfly migration like this is extraordinary! The sky has been *filled* with them all day."

Marcus seemed amused. "You found a biological cause and cure for autism, and *you're* paying attention to butterflies."

"Well, they seem connected somehow. Haven't you ever had a feeling that you couldn't explain?"

"Yes, dear. The first time I looked at you."

She turned around in her chair and smiled at her husband.

He continued, "And those are still the most gorgeous green eyes I've ever seen."

"That's a nice thing to say to a gray old lady."

"Oh stop. You'll always be my girl, Brooke."

"And that means more to me than all the medical papers in the world," she replied contentedly, before turning back to the window. "You know, I saw butterflies mixing like this once before. I was a youngster, and Luther Howell was there."

"God rest his soul. He was quite a pivotal person for you."

"It was certainly a seminal moment when he gave me my first microscope. But then years later when he left me his money and his patents, I could pick up where O'Connor and Sydney were forced to leave off in their research. There was suddenly funding for a dedicated laboratory and employees, and full-scale double-blind studies! And even at sixty-something, we saw a difference in Philip's behaviors when we figured out how to target and treat that infection."

Marcus chuckled. "Practicing tomorrow's speech on me? I was there, remember?"

"I always practice on you. That's why I married you," Brooke teased. "Well, and you used to be handsome, too."

He laughed out loud. "If you hadn't become a microbiologist, you might have had a career as a stand-up comedian."

Brooke was now concentrating intently on the brilliant blanket of butterflies as it headed south. "Nothing but color, all the way to the horizon," she said. "And maybe this is crazy, but it's almost as if I can feel what they're feeling... if butterflies even *have* feelings."

Marcus moved closer to the window to share his wife's view. He gasped when he looked outside. "Wow! I had no idea what you were seeing... this really *is* spectacular."

"Every one of them has its own little life," Brooke reflected, "but they move together like they're all sharing the same one."

Marcus kissed his soul mate on the top of her head. "They're a little like us, aren't they Brooke?"

"They're a *lot* like us," she replied, with a single tear rolling down her cheek.

And the setting sun gradually went from orange to auburn, softly illuminating all the butterflies as they passed from one side of heaven to the other, like silent little angels.

www.ingramcontent.com/pod-product-compliance
Lightning Source LLC
Chambersburg PA
CBHW062138170626
46813CB00002B/746